"In an act of historical imagination, Heather Hammer has captured crofters' lives in the nineteenth-century Shetland Islands. She has also captured the essence of their Methodist spirituality and daily religious practice that made God real to them. Anyone who wants to understand how religion actually works to make life better will find this story encouraging."

—RANDI J. WALKER, Pacific School of Religion, emerita

"Heather Hammer is an amazing storyteller. Having known her and her parents, it is fascinating to read this family, fictionalized story that her father, Robert C. Leslie, a renown Methodist scholar and theologian, had told her. I was completely drawn into the story and highly recommend *Shetland Mist* to anyone interested in stories of family, faith, migration, and change."

—KAH-JIN JEFFREY KUAN, Claremont School of Theology

"*Shetland Mist* reveals the inner, spiritual prayer life of Ann Leslie who slogs through the sloughs as well as highlands of faith, facing the struggles and tragedies of daily living. Ann's theological reflections about what she believes, especially about suffering, from her Methodist teaching, worship, and song, are thought-provoking and inspiring. I found the story to be haunting for days to come, wanting others to have read it so I could talk about it with them!"

—SALLY DYCK, bishop, United Methodist Church

"In this page-turning historical novel, Heather Leslie Hammer powerfully weaves her family history, the lives of early Methodists who sustained one another through communal faith, and a person's journey to and with God through questions and doubts while seeking answers to the unfathomable suffering and hardship that humans face. Although the book is fiction, it is a most accessible theology book for anyone searching for the meaning of life and ways for embodied faith without theological jargon."

—BOYUNG LEE, Iliff School of Theology

D0762470

"It is the dream of many Americans to be able to trace their ancestry directly to the places from which our ancestors came. Heather Leslie Hammer has done it! She tells the story of her forebears coming to America as a gifted storyteller, carefully laying out a plot focusing on personalities and sensitive to the nuances of the places 'over there' in 'the auld country,' and on this side as well. This is a story of an American family well worth the telling!"

—TED A. CAMPBELL, Perkins School of
Theology, Southern Methodist University

Shetland Mist

Shetland Mist

A Shetland Family in the Methodist Movement

HEATHER LESLIE HAMMER

RESOURCE *Publications* · Eugene, Oregon

SHETLAND MIST
A Shetland Family in the Methodist Movement

Resource Publications
An Imprint of Wipf and Stock Publishers
199 W. 8th Ave., Suite 3
Eugene, OR 97401

www.wipfandstock.com

PAPERBACK ISBN: 978-1-6667-5185-7
HARDCOVER ISBN: 978-1-6667-5186-4
EBOOK ISBN: 978-1-6667-5187-1

10/21/22

In memory of my father, Robert Leslie, who told me this story

Contents

Acknowledgments

THIS BOOK HAS BEEN in my thoughts since my father took our family to Shetland when I was eleven. My dad, Robert Campbell Leslie, was the grandson of young Robert Leslie who came to America. I am grateful to my Shetland relatives for their warm welcome on a return trip in 2018, especially Betty Burgess, Gladys Eunson, Edith Leask, John Sinclair, and Alice Walker. Thanks also to the delightful people I met at the Shetland Family History Society, the Shetland Museum, the Crofthouse Museum, and the Adam Clarke Memorial Methodist Church in Lerwick. Although I have researched the settings of Lerwick and Exnaboe on the island called Mainland from the years 1829 to 1873, I have only scratched the surface of what life must have been like. I have used the actual names, birth and death dates, and causes of death of my great-great-grandparents, Ann and Robert Leslie, and their nine children. However, this is a work of fiction, and I have changed some details, such as the birthplaces of Ann and Robert, to develop the theme of migration and change. All historical and cultural mistakes are my own.

For a scholarly testament to the resilience of Shetland women, see *Myth and Materiality in a Woman's World: Shetland 1800–2000* by Lynn Abrams. I invite you to use the glossary for help with Shetland words and, if you possibly can, plan a visit to the Shetland Islands.

Many thanks to all who have encouraged me to write this book: my writers' group—Claire Chow, Amy Pittel, Jill Snodgress, Ellen Turner, and Kristie Wang; the congregations I have served as pastor; dear friends; my wonderful husband, Jim; and our fabulous children, Sepp and Leslie.

1

Ann and Robert

SPRINGTIME 1829

ANN CLOSED THE DOOR of the schoolhouse and walked hastily through the town of Lerwick to the harbor. It was a windy spring day, and she felt her spirit rise as the mist cleared. At the sea the fishermen were selling their catch from boats tied to the dock. Rays of sun shimmered on the bay like a host of azure damselflies. Gentle ripples rocked the boats, and the men called out to shoppers on the landing. Ann stepped carefully onto the rocks of the adjacent breakwater and scanned the harbor to see whether a particular fisherman had come into shore. Yes! At the far end of the pier Robert Leslie stood in a yoal, tossing a rope to pull his craft to berth. He was tall but with a slight build. His movements were youthful and confident. Ann sucked in her breath and approached him, stepping from the rocks onto the wooden dock and along its planks. Curls of sandy hair jutted out from his cap and moved with the wind that had chafed his sunburned cheeks. He saw her coming and kept his eyes fixed on her figure as she advanced the length of the pier. The wind filled her skirt, and its color drew Robert's gaze to her matching, soft-green eyes. Blushing, she looked away and then back to find his face still turned toward hers. He smiled as she approached him, took off his woolen cap, and nodded his head in greeting, "Hello, Ann. Are you here for fish or to see me?"

The feeling of deep color rose in her cheeks, and she cast her eyes down shyly. The breeze caught her hair and whipped an auburn strand across her face. Tucking the wisp behind her ear, she looked back while Robert eyed her steadily. "I'm here for fish. Do you have a fresh cod?"

"Yes, indeed. For you I have whatever you ask." He took a fish from the shot room at the bottom of the boat, gutted it for her, and expertly scaled it with his knife. Then he wrapped it in a piece of cloth, leapt adeptly from the boat onto the dock, and handed her the fish with a smile. "For you, a gift."

"Oh, no, Robert," she protested and handed him a copper penny.

But he stuffed his hands in his pockets. "Will you meet me at the loch tomorrow?" he asked.

The sun glistened in her eyes, and she replied, "Yes. After I dismiss my class, I'll see you there."

Ann began the walk home, pleased with her meeting with Robert. Her legs felt light and free. She quickened her steps, and childlike pleasure broke out across her face. If someone were watching, the observer would imagine her to be not a teacher but a schoolgirl on the last day of the term. Clinging to the codfish, she hurried up the cobblestoned street from the harbor over the Hillhead to her family home on the outskirts of town.

Ann's younger sister Mary sat by the fire in the common room, struggling to focus on her lessons. The inkwell stood at attention between the Holy Bible and *The Collected Poems of Robert Burns*, open to Mary's poem of the day. Ann sat down beside her and began to read, but her thoughts drifted away like the waves that pulled out to sea from their island coast.

> When o'er the hill the eastern star
> Tells bughtin time is near, my jo,
> And owsen frae the furrow'd field
> Return sae dowf and weary O;
> Down by the burn, where birken buds
> Wi' dew are hangin clear, my jo,
> I'll meet thee on the lea-rig,
> My ain kind Dearie O.[1]

"Annie, what is this word?" Mary underlined the word with her finger.

---

1. Burns, *Complete Poetical Works*, 474.

"'Tis 'bughtin.' You could have sounded it out by your own mastery of letters, little Mary. *B* like in 'beauty,' that's what you are, a beauty and a bonnie lassie, if I ever knew one. 'Tis the *gh* that stumped you, surely. We just leap over those letters when they land together in a word." She hopped her finger over the word on the page. "Just skip a stone across the water from the vowel *u* over the *gh* and pay them no mind." Then she laughed as she thought, at least one can skip over those letters most of the time, though not in a word like "laugh." How strangely we spell the words we speak so readily in Scots or English, she pondered. 'Tis no wonder one must practice the rules yet be daring when attacking the mystery of reading. Would it not be a marvel to read the classics in a place like Edinburgh, where young men study? Perhaps women would be admitted someday. But would she have the courage to travel beyond the island? Could she face the challenges of leaving home and parting from all that was familiar? She returned to the poem. "Say the word now, Mary."

"Bughtin. But what does it mean?"

"Well, 'tis the important question, true. It must be something we make time to do, ending as it does with *in*, short for *ing*. Shall we read for a clue?"

"Very well. The next part talks about the oxen coming home weary from the field."

"Excellent."

"I read ahead while you were gazing out the window dreaming of your 'Dearie O.'"

"Mary! Not at all! I was just thinking it be time to wash the windows, now that 'tis springtime with longer daylight, and we might actually see something through the glass besides the dark sky." She peered through the windowpane, soiled by sand and birds. "So, if you already read ahead, what do you suppose the word 'bughtin' means?" She paused. "What does Father do at the end of the day when he comes home for tea?"

"He puts the sheep into the croo for the night."

"So, he does. There you have it. Bughtin means folding the sheep for their bedtime. You know about that, do you not, Mary?"

She sighed, "Ah, yes, I must help Father every day with the ewes and their peerie lambs that wander off." She looked up at her sister. "But I want to be a teacher like you, Annie."

"Well, we shall see. Just keep reading and exercising that bright mind God gave you." Ann stood up. "Now 'tis time for me to chop the onions and taaties for the chowder. We all have our tasks in order that the family can eat. You can be grateful we have food to cook and animals to tend, and I suppose it humbles us to chop and milk." Ann gave a tug on her little sister's braid and poured water from a crockery jug into a porcelain basin to go about washing the dirt from the garden vegetables.

At the tea table, Ann's mother ladled the soup and passed the bowls to her husband, Ann, Mary, and Ann's two younger brothers, before she served herself. She complimented Ann on the tasty fish chowder and asked, "So you had time today to go to the dock and buy cod?"

"She wanted to see her 'Dearie O,'" teased Mary.

Their mother looked at Ann and smiled. "Oh, you have a favorite fisherman?" she asked directly, sensing that Ann would want to tell the family. "Just so he is no papist. Father would never abide one of them in the family." She glanced at her husband across the table. "So, what is the lad's name, Ann?"

"'Tis Robert Leslie, and his people are Methodists, not Catholics, so don't worry, Mam. They are good people, I am told. And, anyway, he's not exactly 'in the family' yet."

"So, you know this fellow?" Ann's mother was always one to speak frankly.

"Not well. I've only conversed with him a time or two."

"Or three or four," said Mary. "She's always watching for him at the pier."

"Now, Mary. You needn't speak about everything you see," Ann scolded her sister with a feigned scowl.

"Well, Ann, you are eighteen," said her mother. "'Tis time to be finding a husband, and a fisherman is not a bad catch. Cod is bringing in a good price, I hear. We should like to meet the fellow before you get too serious."

❧   ❧

Ann left the schoolhouse and walked quickly out onto the moor, heading, as she did every day now, over the hill to the loch where she would meet Robert. As summer approached, the days had lengthened, and golden afternoon light bathed the hill ground and the sky. Ann checked the position of the sun and figured she still had time before her family would expect tea. The wind blew her hair from its twist, and as she ran her fingers through it, she smiled, recalling how Robert pulled her to him, the feel of his hands in her hair and his soft beard on her face. With Robert, she felt alive in a way she hardly understood. It was like new grass breaking forth from the soil. Her heart pulsed in her chest as she crested the rise and gazed down at the sunlit loch, shimmering as a thousand stars in a dark winter sky. There, fishing at the bank was Robert, her Robert, perched easily on a rock, eager to hook a trout to augment his catch from the past night in the open ocean. Ann quickened her pace as she carved a path downhill through the heather. Just then Robert turned from the shore, and when his eyes met hers, he quickly set down his rod and secured it with a stone. She rushed to him, and they embraced by the water's edge.

The sky, the rocks, and the loch shaped a quiet sanctuary just for them and the black-headed gulls that hovered close by. The wind blew an insistent chill off the water, and Robert lifted a blanket from his pack and laid it on the heather. He pulled her to the ground gently, covered her with his wool sweater, and drew her to him in the quiet beauty of the afternoon. They lost themselves in the vastness of the land and sky. The salt air and the fragrant hill ground aroused Ann's senses, as Robert held her close. His caresses transposed her to a strange place. She discovered in his embrace a sentiment completely new to her and yet somehow old and true, like the ancient broch standing in the center of the loch that linked them to earlier times. He touched her tenderly at first and then with urgent desire. His kisses drew her from all measured thoughts, like the tide, a force of nature itself. His breathing quickened, and she responded to his growing need. But then, something shifted her internal pendulum from passion to reason. In an instant, her mind marched back to morals, and she pulled away in retreat. "We mustn't, Robbie."

"Then marry me, Annie."

She paused and gazed tenderly into his youthful face. "But, Robbie, you are only sixteen."

"I wish I were older, if you would love me more."

"How could I love you more?"

"Then marry me. We'll never be rich, but we won't go hungry either, so long as you'll eat my fish." He chuckled as he kissed her lightly and then lifted his head onto his bent arm and looked down into her eyes earnestly. His words were deliberate, as if he had been planning to share them just this way on this day. "There's a small croft for lease in Dunrossness, at Exnaboe, near the southern tip of the island. My father heard about it. 'Tis nothing fancy, but we could work the land, and 'twould be close to Virkie for me to catch a sixareen. If we saved money, I could buy my own boat, and then I'd be both fisherman and crofter. And you could be my helper and my wife."

Ann had stopped breathing when she heard Robert's proposal unfold. Her eyes opened in surprise to note the eagerness that lit up his face. She quickly grasped the sureness in his voice. It was a bold notion, and yet he made the plan seem simple. She breathed again. "Oh, Robbie! I should like that very much. But what about my teaching? There is no school there."

"Well, you could teach our children—the peerie ones we'll be having."

"Robbie," she searched his eyes, "I want to be with you. Every day I think of you, and every night. But . . ." She looked away, and then back into his ardent expression. "I see how hard life is. Some years my parents haven't even enough grain for the animals. Will we be able to afford to live on our own so soon? We are so young!"

Robert ignored her remark about age and continued laying out his plan. "There's plenty of peat on the land for fuel. And the stones can be removed for a garden. Perhaps we'll get a cow and some sheep. It will be hard work, but we will be together, and, God willing, we will have a good life."

They kissed and held each other until the air turned cool as the sun slipped behind a cloud. Robert's loving hold reassured her. Not only his arms but also his confidence in their future together shielded her from doubt. Finally, they parted with promises to speak to their parents. The sun dropped behind the western hill, and Ann climbed back the homeward path in haste. She stepped lightly and imagined a wedding in August when the white heather would be in bloom. As the wind blew over the rise from the ocean, she pulled her shawl tightly to her chest.

⟡ ⟡

Alone before bed, Ann prayed . . .

> O God, I need to speak to you, but I know not how. Am I a fool to think of marriage? Is this your plan for me? 'Tisn't what I had imagined just yet for my life. I had always longed to study, as men do, at university, should women only be admitted someday. Was that just selfish thinking, a childish dream? How could I have ever paid the fees, and how could I have left Mother and Father and the children? You planted me in a family that needs me, and yet you gifted me with a mind eager to learn. And now, you have given me Robert, and I love him.

'Tis hard for me to believe this peculiar state in which I find myself! Is it truly love? Yes, so it must be! I do love him. I am sure of it, even though he is so young! Anyone would say he seems older than his years, and so brave. He has no fears. He can fish for hours in the lonely night, tossing the nets and hauling in the catch, and come home still ready to go out again another day. He hasn't a worry in his sweet head. From where does he get his courage? In him must dwell a core of childlike goodness, which you have planted, and therein grows, it seems, a spirit of great hope.

Where is my faith, O God? Why do I lack confidence to go forward with marriage and family? Is this the right path for me? Is it your will? Give me assurance, O God, that you will be there when Robert goes out to sea, and I am alone in the cottage. Will you stay by my side when the pains come, and we have our first child? And how will we fare when the bairns come one after the other? What if there be not enough food to eat? Robert says we shall always have fish. Can we live on fish?

I think I am asking for faith, nothing less—faith in the future. I cannot live without it. Keep me in your company, dear God, and make me worthy of your love. Amen.

SUMMER 1829

The days grew long, and the summer solstice came and went. School was out for Shetland families' usual summer toil. Ann and her sisters worked in the garden until their backs stiffened. Her father and the boys tended the crops and the animals. After tea the women and girls tried their best to stay awake to spin wool and knit shawls while the sunlight lasted. But finally each evening their eyelids dropped, and one by one they lay down for bed. Only Ann read her books into the night by the light of the midnight sun, without need to burn the oil the family used sparingly through the dark winter months. Oh, to read and imagine the lives of characters in former times and distant places! Ann traveled far from her Shetland home: she was Penelope on another rugged coastline waiting for Odysseus to return from war. The heroine's longing for her husband brought Ann back to Robert and to becoming his wife. She smiled as she drew a smooth wool blanket over her body, rested her head on her feather-down pillow, and laid the book aside to sleep. She drifted off, content in the quiet of the night and in the promise of another summer day.

Each dawn brought Ann closer to her wedding day. Robert's father, James, was known as one of the best fiddlers on the island of Shetland they called Mainland. Robert and Ann asked him to lead the wedding party and to play as they processed from his crofthouse east of Scalloway to the Mail family cottage in Lerwick.

❧ ❧

Rain poured in torrents on the afternoon appointed for the wedding. Robert had announced that the family would follow James on the footpath through the peat fields to the beat of his favorite Shetland airs. Ann feared that the fiddle's old wooden body would drip with moisture, ruining the instrument for good. She sent Mary to look out the window of the Mails' cottage to watch for them and tell her when the procession arrived.

"Look! They are coming!" called Mary to Ann in the bedroom from the window in the day room. "Mr. Leslie is leading the march, but not with his fiddle. I can see its leather case under his arm. They are singing together as they walk along. But, my, how they are all drenched!" Mother went to the window to see, and then busied herself making room by the door for the coats and boots and with a rack on which the stockings could dry.

As Ann dressed in her parents' bedroom, she chuckled, imagining Robert's boots filled with rainwater, as the men had trudged along the country path. They were Methodists, so without the fiddle, they probably sang the Wesleyan hymns that they knew by heart and paced in time to the music. Ann cracked open the bedroom door to see as the minister, family, and friends arrived, and she watched as they shed their soggy coats, boots, and socks. Ann's mother welcomed the clan cordially and gathered them informally around the peat fire in the center of the residence to warm their hands and feet.

Mary approached Ann in the bedroom to see if she was ready. The bride's neck and cheeks flushed rosy-red above her white neckline, as she inspected herself in the glass. Her dress was just the color of white Shetland sheep. She combed her soft brown hair loose, as she knew Robert favored it. Curls fell onto her shoulders. The ringlets bounced as Ann paced about nervously, her heart beating as feet would soon pound on the dance floor. She was in high spirits and yet still anxious about the weight of the day.

Mary served the guests hot tea. And when they had warmed themselves by the hearth, they sat on benches and chairs on the sides of the main room, sharing the excitement of the day. Merry laughter punctuated the muffled voices. Then a hush fell over the assembly as the wedding party stationed themselves in the middle of the room. The time had come.

Ann threw one last look to the mirror to check that the folds of her long wool dress fell gracefully, and that the bits of white heather she had tucked into her rich brown hair were still in place. She opened the bedroom door, and as she stepped forward into the common room, her eyes swept across the people until they met Robert's gaze and locked. The moment she had been waiting for had finally arrived. Heat rose in her cheeks as she looked straight at Robert and advanced toward him. He stood tall and proud with his dark-blond, wavy hair combed back and his shirt buttoned to the neck. His beard was trimmed, and his cheeks were as red as the sunset on a hazy day at dusk. He smiled, and his eyes twinkled in his handsome face. Ann glanced about the room. Her parents had positioned themselves beside Robert's, and her sister Mary and Robert's older brother Stewart stood by as witnesses. Their other siblings, dressed in their finest clothes, waited on both sides. All eyes alighted on the bride as she smiled modestly and took her place beside Robert facing the minister of the Lerwick Kirk.

Ann paid attention as the preacher delivered the solemn liturgy of matrimony. He invoked the spirit of Christ to dwell upon the couple and admonished them always to do God's will. Robert and Ann beheld each other's eyes and exchanged the traditional spoken vows, earnestly promising to remain faithful solely to the other in holy marriage until only death itself would make them part.

Ann fixed her eyes upon her beloved as he recited the sacred words: "I Robert take thee Ann to my wedded wife, to have and to hold, from this day forward, for better for worse, for richer for poorer, in sickness and in health, to love and to cherish, till death us do part, according to God's holy ordinance; and thereto I plight thee my troth."

And then it was her turn to repeat the words: "I Ann take thee Robert to my wedded husband, to have and to hold, from this day forward, for better for worse, for richer for poorer, in sickness and in health, to love, cherish, and to obey, till death us do part, according to God's holy ordinance; and thereto I plight thee my troth."[2]

2. "Matrimony," in *Book of Common Prayer*, 187. The 1794 prayer book of the Church of Scotland was printed in Gaelic, but the 1800 prayer book of the Church of

Robert's parents stood silently with closed eyes. Ann imagined that they prayed for the young couple, trusting God that love would prevail through the trials ahead. Her parents, she knew, were skeptical because Robert was such a young lad, yet they were nonetheless convinced of their daughter's devotion to him. They also closed their eyes in prayer, surely for their daughter's happiness and, for the couple, a long and God-fearing life. Back when they married, they too had been young.

The minister's words went on, yet Ann heard them as if muted by the ocean's drumroll. She floated on the waves of a daydream, surging in and out of awareness of this profound moment in time. Then, she sensed the strength of Robert's arm to which she had been clinging, as the minister ended with the proclamation and the blessing: "Those whom God hath joined together, let no man put asunder. . . . I pronounce that they be Man and Wife together, In the Name of the Father, and of the Son, and of the Holy Ghost. Amen. God the Father, God the Son, God the Holy Ghost, bless, preserve, and keep you; the Lord mercifully with his favour look upon you and so fill you with all spiritual benediction and grace, that ye may so live together in this life, that in the world to come ye may have life everlasting. Amen."[3]

Then after kisses and cheers, the drinking and dancing began. The Methodists, especially Robert's mother, Ross, and her family, took no drink. Nor were they keen on dancing and merrymaking. But Robert's father, James, had made an exception for the wedding of their second son, the first wedding in their family. As James played his fiddle, the older kin watched, and the younger ones danced reels and strathspeys into the evening.

In the late-night gloaming, the sun began to sink, and with one last Shetland waltz the revelry tapered to a finish. The guests lit lamps and departed while they could still find their way home, humming the last lilting waltz tune played. Ann's parents gave the newly wedded couple their bedroom and settled themselves and their younger children in the common room for the night.

Lying in bed the next day, Ann prayed . . .

England contained similar phrasing in English, used here for the benefit of modern readers and because Shetlanders spoke Scots, not Gaelic.

3. "Matrimony," in *Book of Common Prayer*, 187–88.

Dear God, 'tis morning! Can it be that I lie here next to my husband? He slumbers so peacefully. Though I am tired, I can sleep no longer. 'Tis too early to rise, but 'tis light already, and my mind races with memories of yesterday. Oh, thank you, God, for our wedding day! I smile even now, as I recall Robert's eyes when I came out of the bedroom in my new dress. Oh, how I love him! He wore the look of love; I know that now. I will always remember the touch of his hand as we recited our vows and the way his eyes penetrated mine when he said, "till death us do part." I do trust him completely. And, God, I trust you to keep our love strong. You have blessed our union, and I do believe that your blessing will bind us forever. May it be so.

I give you thanks for our parents' blessing also, and for the happiness of our wedding day . . . and for our time alone in bed after it all. Help me to be a loving wife from this day forward. Amen.

AUTUMN 1829

The crofthouse at Exnaboe was to be the couple's new home. Robert packed his few belongings into a horse-drawn cart owned by a Scalloway neighbor of the Leslie family. The neighbor, his father, and Robert followed the same path the wedding procession had traveled the month before to the Mail cottage. There they collected Ann and the wedding gifts the couple had received. They filled the cart with housewares, linens, tools, clothing, and provisions. Ann's mother saw to giving her daughter sufficient staples to begin her married life, as well as fresh vegetables, bread, and cheese for the immediate days of settling in. Mary had sewn an apron for her sister, and Ann had packed her books and an oil lamp to read by. She assessed all the varied aspects of her life as they came together in the cart. Each item was a material symbol of something: learning, nurture, or labor. Her life would build on her past, and yet she would now be on her own. Oh, she would miss her mother, especially being the oldest child. How many times she had worked in the garden, made supper for the family, and helped with the laundry and cleaning. Now she would be the head of her own hearth, and she would be the one responsible for making a good life—not a daughter but a wife. A heady thought.

Ann's father tied the bed, table, and chairs, as well as the trunks of dishes and blankets, securely to the sides of the cart. Her parents and siblings embraced the young couple and bid them farewell as they boarded the cart and sat facing out the back. James and his neighbor steered the horse from the front, and they pulled out. Ann's mother wiped her eyes with the sleeve of her blouse. When she let her hands drop to her sides, she planted her body erect at the doorstep like a standing stone, and then she vanished as the cart rounded the first bend.

The couple began their journey toward the southern tip of the island, along a mere footpath, where ponies carrying peats and an occasional horse-drawn cart traveled. Tears welled in Ann's eyes. She felt young and unprepared for the jolts and turns she would encounter. After just uttering goodbye, a wave of homesickness engulfed her, frostier than the ocean mist along the coast. Ann had never slept a night away from home before this day. How brave she would need to be as she ventured off alone with her new husband, he only sixteen and she only eighteen. As if he read her mind, Robert took her hand tenderly. She turned to him. Although, surely, he also must have felt the weight of their new life together, she could read no anxiety in his face. Then she remembered his proposal and promise that she would be his helper and his wife. She squeezed his hand and found in his grip the security to know that she could feel safe, like a young seabird protected in its nest but ready to fly off from the windy ocean cliff.

They watched the rise around Lerwick grow small and then disappear as the open hill ground consumed their view. The weather was fair, and the couple sat calmly enjoying the rugged moor and the distant coastline with its windswept, crashing surf. The scents of dry brush and salt air aroused Ann to look about. The sea crept up close to them in the narrow voes that cut from the coast through the land. Sheep dotted the fields. They munched on grass, without a care for the passersby, and in their oblivion the travelers sat back and rested. The journey took nearly five hours, time to reflect in silence on the major leap they were taking. Ann realized that she had left another world behind. Images drifted across her mind. She found herself in the classroom of her schoolhouse leaning over a desk to help a student. The children had needed her. She blinked away tears as she comprehended that she would no longer be able to guide her pupils in reading and writing, nor her sister Mary with her lessons, nor even assist her mother with cooking and gardening. She already experienced loss. The children were growing up, of course, and they would manage without her, and she too would learn to cobble together a new life. This is how children became adults, after all. Robert put his arm around her, and she leaned on his shoulder as they bumped around the clumps of heather.

When the cart mounted a rise in the path, Robert drew her to him and declared, "Look ahead. We are almost there!" Ann twisted around in her seat and looked beyond the horse and drivers to scour the horizon for the crofthouse she would glimpse for the first time. There it was, set apart on a gray-green field facing a peaceful cove. The small house stood alone like an island surrounded by waves of grass. When the cart finally came to a stop in front of the cottage, Ann beheld their new home with unexpected pride. It was a traditional crofthouse, built perhaps a full century before, of gray Shetland sandstone and mortar, with a snug roof of thatch. Nothing fancy, but it looked solid and tidy. As they hopped from the cart, Ann gazed over the inlet to the open ocean. The horizon was distant, and like the future, hazy and only dimly visible. Dark clouds congregated in the sky directly above them, and they hurried to unload the cart before showers soaked their belongings.

Once their possessions were safely carried into the cottage, Ann opened the basket of oatcakes and kirn-milk that her mother had prepared. James and his neighbor sat at the table in the two chairs James had fashioned as a wedding gift, while Ann and Robert stood by. Ann smiled as she poured cool tea for each to drink. These were her first guests, and how thankful she was that they had taken the day to bring the couple all the way to their new home. Though the path had been rough, traveling by cart accomplished the move far more easily than had they traveled by boat with more than one trip needed to fit everything in. When they had eaten, and the horse had rested, James's neighbor stood up restlessly, aware of the need to be back on their way to Scalloway before dark. Reluctantly, James spoke the words that caught in his throat, "It now be time to depart."

Robert spoke up, "Thank you both kindly for bringing us here. We are grateful."

Ann gave them the shortbread her mother had baked for them to eat on the way back. She embraced her father-in-law, and for the first time spoke as his new daughter, "Goodbye, Father."

"Blessings, Ann." And to his son he admonished, "Be good to her, Robert. We shall pray for you both. Remember, God be your companion."

They waved them off and then began the task of unpacking and arranging their cottage. Ann had made muslin curtains for the two small sealskin windows of the crofthouse. She hung the cloth and smoothed her hands over the stiff, new fabric. It was clean, and the windows looked fresh and neat when she had finished. She smiled inwardly. With earnings from teaching, she had purchased bed linens and towels in Lerwick before the wedding. That too was a good feeling, to have something to contribute to her marriage. Robert whistled as they busied themselves to make their house a home. In the but end, the center of croft life, Ann swept the packed-earth floor clean and wiped away the spiderwebs from the stone hearth. Later she would bring fresh sand to separate the hearth from the earthen floor. Robert carried a basket of peats into the house and set it by the fireplace. With a good deal of dry driftwood as kindling, he lit a fragrant blaze. Soon the cottage was warm despite the wet autumn wind. Ann made the box bed in the ben end with the new linens and the heavy wool blanket friends from church had woven.

Tired, the young couple sat down in the two chairs Robert's father had made for them. They drew close to the fire, side by side, nearly touching, on their first night in their new home. The couple yawned from fatigue but looked into each other's glowing faces with expectation. They had no words, for both were stunned to have come this far. Here they were, alone. Their life together began this night, in their own home, for better or for worse. Ann felt as if she were sitting in someone else's body, in someone else's chair, in someone else's house. She noted again, as she had mused on the long ride that day, that she was very far from home—was it twenty miles? The distance from Lerwick to Exnaboe was like a wide, wide ocean. Cut off from her family and her life as a teacher, she might as well have moved to America. Now she was a married woman in her own cottage with little idea of what would become of her. True, the life that lay before her was certainly of her own choosing, and yet what exactly had she chosen? She feared she had embarked on a long sea journey with no idea of the destination and no hope of return.

Robert looked at Ann, and in their silence, he stood up and stepped behind her chair. He set his hands gently on her shoulders. Tenderly he rubbed her tired muscles until her head and shoulders relaxed in his hands. He unpinned her hair and let it fall onto her shoulders and breasts. Then he came around to face her and raised her up by the waist until she stood before him and gazed into his eyes. She laid her head on his chest as his arms enfolded her to him. Ann breathed deeply and knew then why she had come this far. Eagerly they moved from the hearth to the bed.

In the morning there was much work to do. Together they dug a garden plot out of the wild hill ground behind their cottage. Robert broke up the earth with a shovel, and each time he hit upon a stone, Ann carried it to the edge of the house, where they started to build a wall to break the wind and create a sheltered yard. Ann collected pieces of dry heather and grasses in a straw basket and brought the tinder into the crofthouse to ignite the peat that would burn each evening. She inhaled the heady aroma of the plants parched from the warmest days of the year.

As Robert hoed the rocky earth, Ann noted his strength. They both had assisted at their families' homes, but laboring together, just the two of them, was a novel challenge. They were creating something new, not only in the garden but also in their future together.

The next day Robert got up before dawn to catch a fishing rig from the beach at the south end of the island. First, he poked the coals from the night before, added tinder and peat, and put the kettle on to boil. Then he dressed in his heavy knickers, sea coat, and cap. Still sleepy, Ann got up to cook oats for his breakfast and pack a lunch of kirn-milk and bannocks to eat in the boat. She poured leftover tea from the day before into a jug and packed it into his knapsack. At the door she kissed him goodbye. "So, 'tis how 'twill be," she said, holding onto his waist with his back to the wind. "You will leave me in the dark and not return until dusk?"

"Yes, lass. That be the life of a fisherman and his wife. We will have to live on kisses goodbye and then kisses hello again. Stay well, my love." And he turned and departed briskly.

"Stay safe, my husband," Ann called after him. She watched as he headed out toward the beach, taking long strides in the direction of the southern tip of the island, to Sumburgh Head, where a lighthouse stood on a high promontory and beyond that the open ocean. The wind whipped through the doorway, pushing its chill into the warm room. Ann closed the door and then lay down in the box bed in the ben end again and quickly dropped back to sleep.

She dreamed of stones. She was digging them out of the hard earth and carrying them into a barn out of the wind, back and forth, stones and more stones. In the barn there was a hayloft as in her Lerwick home. She climbed up the ladder and there picked up a book to read. She lay on the hay and turned the pages, her mind creating the text she would read in her dream. The sound of a gull stole her from reading and, at the same time, woke her from her dream. Too soon, the sun shone into the window from the east and shook her from her reverie. Wishing she could read in bed as in the dream, reluctantly she willed her body to rise.

Alone at the table, she ate her oatmeal and then dressed in an old skirt to work in the garden. She tied a woolen scarf about her hair to keep it from blowing in her face and making snarls that would take an effort to comb out. There was not much time. She would have to work quickly to get the winter vegetables planted and growing before the earth hardened with the first freeze.

Ann's mother had packed seed potatoes and cabbage seedlings. And there were delicate plants of land cress and lamb's lettuce that needed to be transplanted right away. Ann questioned whether the fragile greens would survive in the rocky, windy location where they were making their home, but she smiled, knowing her mother had wanted to give her something from her own garden.

In the back, behind the crofthouse, Ann lifted her long skirt and stooped low to the ground. She worked the cold soil with her hands and gently inserted the vegetables into the damp earth. She created neat rows and patted the ground around each tender plant. As she finished the plot, the sun rose high in the sky, peeking out from behind dark clouds. Ann surmised rain would soon fall. Pleased with her timing, she stopped to thank God for her work accomplished and for the raindrops that would water the garden and hopefully make the vegetables grow.

Ann stood to stretch and rubbed her hands to warm them. So, this would be her life. Robert had said it would be hard, but she must trust that it would also be good. It was a new beginning with much to learn. She liked new seasons, and she smiled and imagined that her life with Robert held promise. Though the ocean wind blew fiercely in her face, she stood on solid ground. The croft gave them land to till and a sturdy, stone house that no wind could blow down.

Ann washed her hands in the last of the water Robert had brought the day before from the burn behind the cottage, and then she retraced his boot prints on the grassy plain to bring back more water to the house for the next cooking and washing. Walking allowed her mind to escape beyond the duties of her hands. She gazed into the rain clouds on the horizon and remembered a poem by Goethe she had once committed to memory about the Erlking and a father's flight with his dying child in the night. As she walked, she recited the words aloud that she had learned from her minister who had taught her German. Stepping in time to the meter, she spoke aloud: "*Wer reitet so spät durch Nacht und Wind? Es ist der Vater mit seinem Kind . . .* "[4] Then she reflected to herself: how fearful is a mounting storm and how frightening the thought of losing a child! The urgency of the poem drew her into its story for a moment, as she recalled the compelling ballad with its lyrical lines. Its driving rhythm caused her to hurry as if she too needed to outrun the storm of impending death. Oh, to lose oneself in such dramatic verse! Could she ever locate her love of literature somehow on this windswept end of the island?

Before Robert returned that evening, Ann prayed . . .

> Dear God, 'tis raining hard, and I am sitting alone in the cottage. Sadness falls over me, and my tears nearly equal these showers from heaven. What am I to do? I am worried about Robert in the rig with the other fishermen. How far have they drifted out to sea in this storm? Will he be welcome as a new crewman? Stay with them and protect them, O God. Steer them from the rocks. Teach them prudence, that they might turn back to shore should the storm build. O God, my Robert has no fear! Lead him to use caution. He now has a wife and a home.
>
> I have no one to talk to but you. My mind wanders back to my other life. I can picture the schoolhouse, teaching poetry and history. I wonder how the children are faring this fall. Is Tommy completing his assignments? Will Jean be mastering her figures? Give their new teacher patience to help them. And give their parents enough wherewithal that the children need not be pulled from school.
>
> I imagine my family gathered in their common room, laughing and sharing stories of the day. Bless my parents, O God, and bring them bounty in the fall harvest.
>
> Water our new garden gently here in Exnaboe, dear God. Do not sweep it all away in a gale. Give the tender plants a chance to mature that we should have vegetables for the winter months.
>
> O God, help us Shetlanders. Give us courage to work this rugged land, and to fish these turbulent seas.
>
> Accompany me through this new loneliness. Bless Mother and Father and the children. And bless Robert's family too. Keep your light shining on us, O God, and help us prepare for the dark months. You are our hope and salvation. Amen.

4. "Erlkönig," in Goethe, *Gedichte*, 154, line 1.

2

Jamie

ANN GOT UP EARLY to see Robert off in the dark. Then, as the sun rose, she put on a warm shawl and went out back to milk the cow they had purchased that winter. Violet was lowing in her stall. "I guess 'tis just you and I, Violet." She patted the cow's side affectionately. "Such a pretty name you have." The cow mooed, and Ann washed her udder in cold water as she spoke, "Today I shall make time for the spring wildflowers, for they are just now pushing up through the earth. They will give our island some color, let's hope." Her mind drifted off, imagining the meadow and its lush fauna at this season. "I may already find marsh violets. Such a pretty flower, bonnie like you, but a deep blue, bluer than the sky. I am so tired of gray! Thank God, 'tis finally spring!" She set the milking stool beside Violet and positioned the bucket directly under the cow's udder. "Did you see the mayflowers in the meadow, Violet? Perhaps you will taste the fresh grass and bask in the warm sun there today, will you? But first, give me your warm milk to nourish this swollen body of mine, as well as my peerie one inside. Such a good lass you are, Violet." With skilled hands, Ann squeezed the milk into the pail, relieving Violet, who readily stood still to give up her milk.

The winter had been long, and Ann's belly grew with child until she could hardly imagine it any bigger. When she had first discovered she was carrying a bairn, she feared being alone, and some days she felt sick and weak. Fortunately, the first months had passed quickly, and now as she neared her term, Robert worked long days to ease Ann's toil around the croft. The couple had labored through the dark months of the year, both taking care of their chores, building their new life together as man and wife.

Fishing brought Robert decent wages from work on a sixareen rig, but it meant long hours away from Ann, often even overnight. With the earnings, Ann and Robert had been able to purchase the cow. After arduous shoveling and moving of stones, they beat the frost and cleared a field to plant oats to harvest in the spring. With the stones they removed from the soil, they extended the garden wall and built an enclosed byre onto the house for Violet. That way she no longer needed to be tethered in the but end of the crofthouse at the center of the couple's life.

With Violet, Ann had milk to drink each morning and again each evening. She made butter and cheese with whatever was left, and they were obliged to give a portion to the laird whose croft they leased. This first year, they had to buy oats for their porridge until the first crop came in. And Ann needed fabric for a larger dress to cover her extended belly and yarn for knitting clothes and blankets for the bairn.

With a peerie one growing inside her, Ann longed to be with her family. At Exnaboe she had only Violet to talk to, so she found herself in the cow's stall frequently between chores. "Oh, Violet, how can you always be so content? Do you not miss companionship as I do?" The closest crofting household was situated a mile away in Sumburgh. "I shall leave you next week and walk the distance to our neighbors if it be a fair day. From there I shall send a letter to my parents by way of Madge and Andrew, for they row the fourareen to the Lerwick market once a week." Once a month, Ann arranged to ride along. "So, Violet, when I am gone, Robert will have to do your evening milking." She sighed. "I need respite. 'Tis a solitary life." She patted the cow. "Do you understand, my bonnie one?" Ann looked forward to sitting with her parents in the warm home of her childhood, knitting and catching up on the family news. She peered into the cow's deep brown eyes. "You are a fine friend, Violet."

In Lerwick one early spring afternoon, Ann's mother said, "Annie, your bairn will be arriving soon." She searched Ann's face with motherly concern. "Should you not stay with us here in Lerwick, where we can fetch the doctor when your labor starts? I fear to think of you alone at the croft in Exnaboe with Robert gone to sea, should the child come before you expect it. One never knows when 'twill be."

"Yes, Mam," Ann replied, "we have spoken of the possibility of an early birth. But I do not wish to be far from Robert before the bairn is born. We have yet a month or more."

"Then both of you come and stay with us in the last weeks. Robert can fish from the harbor here and sell his catch at the pier as before."

"I would like that. I shall speak to Robert," Ann promised.

Her mother sent her home with jars of vegetables, which she had preserved, and a portion of the lamb stew she had prepared for the weekly Sabbath meal.

Her parents wished Ann and Robert would attend the kirk in town where they worshipped each Sunday and midweek too. But it was much too far, and besides, Robert's kin were Methodists, and he and Ann had begun to meet with a small group of like-minded believers at Sumburgh, close to their home, for midweek Bible and prayer meeting.

❧ ☙

The Methodists in the class meeting invited Robert and Ann to join them on the Sabbath, where several families met to worship. Perhaps a visiting minister or a lay preacher would preach. Robert took along the Bible that one of the first English missionaries to Shetland had given him at thirteen when he was confirmed. Ann wrapped her shawl tightly about her shoulders and around the baby in her belly as well. They walked hand in hand on a cool Sunday morning toward the croft at the south of Mainland, eager for worship and fellowship. Watching the seagulls fly and perch on rocks, they sucked in the good ocean air, nearly tasting its brine. Ann relished the time together with Robert close beside her instead of far out at sea. The headlands, alive with sea pinks, yielded a sweet floral scent. Ann breathed deeply and considered the future as they walked along.

"'Twon't be long now before the bairn comes," she started.

Robert's cheeks shone a rugged red in the sunlight. "What name shall we give the child, if it be a lad?"

She smiled at him. "Perhaps 'Robert' for you! Would you like that?"

"I suppose 'twould make me proud! And your father is also Robert. Of course, my father would love a namesake too."

"'James' for your father is a strong name. We surely do not want to name him after my grandfather. Imagine calling a peerie babe 'Hector'!" She smiled, hesitated, and then continued, "And if it be a lassie?"

"Why do you ask? Do you think 'tis a girl?"

Annie laughed, "Well, of course, it could be a lass!"

"If so, she could be Annie or perhaps Mary. What do you think?"

"Let's wait and meet her and then choose a name!"

"So, you want a lassie!"

Ann nodded, and they chuckled as they walked on. Then in a more serious tone, Ann broached the subject that had lodged itself squarely in her mind: "Robbie, Mother wants us to have the bairn in Lerwick where she can help and a doctor or midwife can be in attendance. What do you say to the idea of going there in a fortnight, in anticipation of my time, and staying through the birth and until the peerie one is strong enough to travel?"

Robert looked off to the horizon for a moment and then said, "'Tis kind of your parents to offer, but we have our own life here at the Boe. There is the cow to attend to now, and the garden. And the fishing is better for me when I join the sixareen from this southern location, and we row to catch the fish that swim in the sound between here and Orkney. I can earn better wages than by fishing by myself in a small craft from Lerwick, like before we were married. Besides, we do not own our own boat, and I would have to lease one, which surely we cannot afford. As you know, we must pay our tithe to the laird with the fish I catch and with a share of cheese and butter, as well."

Ann looked down at the gray moor as they walked along in silence. "But, Robert, you know I will be very busy with the peerie one, and I will not have much time for the garden. I suppose I shall be able to milk Violet. That must be done. But a mother's first job is to nurse her bairn. If we stayed with my mother and father, Mam and the others would do the cooking and washing for us. And besides, I would not fear being alone when the pains come. You do not know, but it can be awfully lonely all day at the crofthouse, even now. And the thought of enduring the labor pains alone frightens me."

"Yes, Annie. So you have told me. You have been pried away from your family and left stranded on this plot of land day after day when I go out to sea." He turned to her and added gently, "But soon you will have the bairn as your companion, and the days will pass quickly."

His tone had been cross, and she was not convinced that even the bairn could quell her loneliness. With mounting resentment, she replied, "You have no idea what 'tis like to be a woman and to have no one to talk to."

"You are right there. I have no idea what 'tis like to be a woman. But I know that you are a strong lass. You have your books and your thoughts to pass the hours."

She raised her voice, "If ever I had time to read! And, besides that, thoughts require expression. One cannot always grapple alone with ideas." She paused and then continued as tears filled her eyes, "By the time you come home at night we are both tired. We hardly talk." There; she had said it. She knew she was complaining, and so she stopped abruptly. Then after walking around another curve in the path, she changed the focus away from herself to him. "And you, do you have conversations with the other men on the rig?"

"Well, sometimes we speak of our families, and at night we tell the old stories that fishermen know. 'Tis true, the camaraderie passes the hours." He paused and then continued with an apparent effort to be encouraging, "Perhaps we'll find a lass who can keep you company and help when the bairn arrives." Robert seemed to indicate by the downward intonation of his voice at the end of the sentence that the subject was closed. Ann did not know of any girl nearby, so she sighed and silently resigned herself to be alone in the weeks to come.

Robert then made inventory of all the chores they needed to complete before the baby's birth. With eyes looking straight ahead in front of his feet as he walked, he listed them, not with worry but with serious intent: "We'll need to plant spring oats for us and barley for the cow. And, of course, we shall be obliged to give a portion of the crops to the laird. The winter garden soon will go to seed, and we shall want to plant new vegetables to harvest at the end of the summer. Naturally, 'twill be time to set out more taaties, as we've likely had our last frost." He paused. "I have the notion to build a cradle for the bairn, too." He lifted his eyes to meet Ann's. "Would you like that, Annie?"

"Yes, Robert, thank you for thinking of the child."

She looked down as his thoughts formed into words.

"I'll need to buy wood; this island has no trees. Or perhaps I can find driftwood. I intend to make a large one, so our bairn can sleep in it as he grows. We haven't much money now after the rent, but I should like to put away some earnings to buy sheep when we can. That way you will have wool for knitting—when you have time when the bairn is napping. And then perhaps you can sell shawls and jumpers for more income. There is plenty of shared grass for sheep grazing between crofts on the lea-rig. We Shetlanders are fortunate about that." He smiled and added, "If only we had a sheepdog like my father's."

Ann looked up when she thought of Robert's family.

She realized that, for Robert, life's problems were simply matters to deal with and fix. He had left his family home too but he harbored no worries. Simply with more labor, a solution was possible. He dismissed emotions as unimportant. Just so he accomplished his tasks, all would be well. Ann admitted to herself that his attitude was positive and practical. Yet she longed for him to understand her feelings. If only he would say he wanted her to be happy and not lonely. A wave of sadness cut Ann off from her husband, as if a rugged bluff emerged between them. They walked the last stretch in silence.

The path descended through a vale and then climbed up sand dunes by the sea. At the rise, Ann stopped to rest and catch her breath. She put her hands on her hips and bent forward to ease the ache in the small of her back. Robert laid his warm hand on her spine and put pressure there to ease her tiredness. He did know how to show his love with touch, Ann admitted. She reasoned for a moment and then reckoned he was doing the best he could as a husband. He was young, after all. He worked hard, and he never failed to show his affection for her in their lovemaking. She turned her head toward his face and smiled up at him. Lifting her cheek muscles alone brightened her spirit. Truly she should not complain.

They arrived at the cottage where the Methodists met on Sundays for worship. It was no chapel, but just a simple croft home that served as a meetinghouse for those who lived in the south of Mainland. Sheep grazed about the stone crofthouse. A middle-aged couple, Madge and Andrew, met Ann and Robert at the door and welcomed them into the but end. "You've come from the Boe! Come in!" Ann's eyes took in the wooden benches along the walls and open floor for the few chairs the family owned. More than a dozen adults had gathered, and Ann was pleased to see several children sitting comfortably on the earth floor.

A lay preacher began by leading the singing, lining each hymn for the little congregation to sing back and thereby learn the melody and the words by rote. Robert loved to sing the hymns, and he quickly learned the tunes and rhyming lines. The hymns were from Charles Wesley, who along with his brother John had led the Methodist movement in the previous

century. Ann learned that Charles had written thousands of hymn texts
and that they were popular throughout the British Isles and America. A
lay missionary by the name of John Nicolson had brought a hymnbook
to the people when he organized the Methodist society in Sumburgh a
few years back. The words expressed the ardent faith of the people called
Methodists, called so for their methodical practice of regular worship
and good deeds. Ann could sense the people's pride in singing. It seemed
as if the music lifted the people's spirits beyond the daily cares of earning
a livelihood. Everyone faced fears that loomed large in the simple fragility
of life, and yet here they found common strength in song.

At first Ann thought the Methodists peculiar. She was accustomed
to the Established Church, a church following the theology of John Calvin
and the Scottish reformer John Knox. She had been confirmed in the kirk
in Lerwick as a girl, and she had had no reason to question the beliefs of
the state church. Her family and neighbors were Scottish Presbyterians
and believed in predestination, with the notion that God preordained all
that happened. It was a simple and clear belief: that everything could be
attributed to a holy presence of the divine in one's life. Those who were
chosen by God would follow God's commandments and go to heaven
upon death. Of course, Ann and her family assumed they were among
God's chosen. They prayed that God would save them from the burning
fires of hell. If they confidently believed in the power of Father, Son, and
Holy Ghost, they would be among those saved.

Ann was learning from Robert in their talks as they walked to and
from worship on Sundays, and from the midweek class meeting they attended, that Methodists did not believe in predestination. Instead, they
believed that all people had free will to choose how they wished to live.
Humans were created in God's perfect image with power to make their
own decisions. Therefore, they could either do good or fail to do good.
It made perfect sense to Ann. She had often wondered what the point of
living was if everything in life had already been predetermined. Now she
felt, like the Methodists, that humans could choose to follow the teachings of Jesus if they wished to love God and serve their neighbor. Jesus's
teachings meant helping the poor, caring for those afflicted with illness,
and loving the individuals who were difficult or even just different in
some way.

Ann thought of the man who lived on the street where her parents' house stood and where she had grown up. He was shunned by the
neighborhood for living alone, never having been married, and being a

recluse. He was not invited to tea or to share in the harvest with those who had farms or gardens. Ann's father told Ann's brothers to stay away from him, although Ann wondered why. He seemed gentle and quiet, not in the least a threat to her or anyone she knew. Was he not just the kind of man Jesus would have spoken to and cared about? After meeting with her Methodist brothers and sisters, Ann was determined to look in on the man when she was next in Lerwick. Perhaps she could bring him some of their cheese and offer to show him her bairn after it was born.

When the hymn singing concluded, the preacher led the group in prayer and spoke intercession aloud for each person present: "For our brother Robert, we pray for safety at sea, and for his wife, Ann, health and a full-term confinement. We give you thanks for bringing the congregation through a nasty winter, and we ask for good weather for spring planting.

"Inspire us, your followers, to build a chapel here in Dunrossness, at Durigarth, to reach the people in Quendale who have yet to be touched by your love. May more people come to know your saving grace, we pray, for such would be your reign on earth.

"Loving God, we beseech you to grant each person the power to make wise choices, neither to indulge in drink nor gambling, nor to ignore the poor or those in prison. We humbly pray also for the world and for country leaders far from the Shetland Isles, that they might overcome their differences and make peaceful agreements to heal the world from war and greed.

"Help us understand that when we say the Lord's Prayer, we commit ourselves truly to strive for your kingdom on earth."

And then the group of believers recited aloud the prayer Jesus had taught his followers.

The words of all the people spoken together in this friendly cottage warmed Ann's heart. At that moment she trusted God and believed her own life to be saved. For the first time she understood the words "Thy kingdom come, thy will be done" in a way that made sense to her. The phrase summoned her to be more loving and to care more for the people around her. She prayed silently for God's guidance, as she and Robert were to become parents in the coming weeks. And she asked that her bairn would grow to be a caring person and even be part of making a better world.

In the silence that followed the Lord's Prayer, Ann thought of one more important thing: she asked God to help her accept her life as it was, she married to Robert, a fisherman, so often away at sea, but very much in love with her. With this important petition on her heart, she relaxed into a gentle peace of mind. Her tiredness lifted, and, in a peculiar way, the calm renewed her. Ann's bairn gave a kick, and she put Robert's hand on her belly to feel it bulge. The baby wanted to stretch.

The lay preacher gave a sermon about love, a person's most important behavior. Indeed, he made it sound like nothing else really mattered but to love deeply. Ann thought about her conversation with Robert on their way to the service. She confirmed that they did genuinely love each another. No matter what happened to them, she would remain convinced that they truly had experienced love. Indeed, love must have been what carried her parents from year to year. And her love for Robert had led her to leave her family and her teaching. She had chosen love over security or personal dreams. Life was not perfect, she admitted; there were hardships and disappointments, but if one could honestly say "I love you," surely a marriage could endure anything. Ann's mind wandered as the preacher finished his sermon. She was sleepy, and it felt good to rest closely next to Robert. She shifted her position to find a comfortable arrangement of her back and her belly and then returned her thoughts to the congregation, as the speaker concluded, "Each of you here abides in God's care." Ann pondered the comfort she found from that thought.

They stood to pray again, and this time, anyone who wished to speak offered a personal supplication to God. Madge asked for a blessing to be bestowed on her father, who was suffering from consumption, and on a neighbor, who was losing his croft for lack of payment to the laird. One woman asked for an awakening of faith and a true sense of God's presence in everyday life, for she had been feeling very low. Ann felt the woman was speaking her own thoughts, for she too hoped for a religious awakening; she also had lacked spiritual conviction. Robert gave thanks for the invitation to worship in a gathered community: "We are much obliged to be included in this house fellowship and for the welcome we have received this day."

After each prayerful intercession the people whispered, "Amen." Then they shared tea and bannocks before parting. The men chatted about their crops and the weather, while the women spoke of a peerie one who was soon to be weaned and of the older children who had left to work for the laird or would go out fishing to the haaf, or even on a whaling ship to Greenland. The young children played together, running about the crowded room. They did not wish to leave, though finally the time came to return to their homes on foot.

No one was to work on the Sabbath, so Ann had Robert with her all day, and she looked forward to the remaining hours of daylight. The sun came out from behind a cloud in salutation and beckoned to them on their homeward stroll. They walked along the sandy path, filled with serenity and a hopeful attitude about the coming days. Robert hummed a hymn tune that matched the rhythm of their steps. Then he sang the words as he recalled them from the morning:

> Be thou, O Rock of Ages, nigh;
> So shall each murmuring thought be gone,
> And grief and fear and care shall fly,
> As clouds before the mid-day sun.
>
> Speak to my warring passions, "Peace!"
> Say to my trembling heart, "Be still!"
> Thy power my strength and fortress is,
> And all things serve thy sovereign will.[1]

Ann smiled to hear Robert's resonant, baritone voice. She thought to herself, he truly believes what he sings: that God is with us to push away fear and grief. Can it be? Can God genuinely still a trembling heart?

Reflecting on the people they had met at the service, Ann asked, "Robert, did you hear Madge say that she has helped with the births of her grandchildren? Perhaps she could come and help when our bairn arrives."

"Who would care for her croft and sheep?"

"I am not sure, but Madge herself said 'twould be a neighborly deed to help us."

"'Twas certainly kind of her."

"Indeed, it gives me a feeling of relief to know that there are people to turn to on this part of Mainland." Madge's offer, in fact, brought her the kind of peace her husband had just sung about.

Robert looked into Ann's eyes, "You shall see. Things have a way of working out for the best."

Ann smiled at her husband, ever the optimist.

She remembered something else she wanted to speak to Robert about. The families in Exnaboe and Quendale had for some time wanted a Methodist chapel for themselves, and the preacher had mentioned it again that morning. "What about the Durigarth chapel, Robbie?" she asked as they walked along.

1. Charles Wesley, "Eternal Beam."

"Yes, this spring would be the time to build before the autumn rains. I've been thinking, when I plow the field behind the cottage, I should take the rocks to the site where the chapel shall be constructed. If everyone does the same, 'twill amount to a heap of stones."

Ann watched him stretch his arms out to the sides and then over his head, and she thought he must be picturing the drudgery of carrying stones by wheelbarrow nearly across the island.

"Who knows how to build a chapel, anyway, do you?" Ann asked. "Who do you suppose will draw up the plans?"

"Hmm, you're asking the very questions I have been mulling over in my head. 'Twill be one more thing to learn. And heavy labor." By now their croft was in sight, and Robert gauged its walls from base to thatch.

As they approached, Ann followed his gaze to the stones set snuggly according to their irregular shapes, nestled in the old cracking mortar that molded them together. They entered the cottage, and her eyes dropped to the earthen floor. She wondered if the villagers would find flagstones for the chapel floor and move them to the appointed site. Perhaps it would have to be a simple earth floor. Silence landed upon them as they shed their wraps and collapsed weary into chairs.

Robert's face fell. "One more thing to learn. Sometimes I do not know if I can handle one more thing." His cheerful spirit had hardened as the discussion of lifting stones so abruptly weighed him down. "Love, I am pure done in," Robert declared with a sigh.

She kept her eyes fixed on his face as she put away their things. "Robbie, darling, you'll be a help with the chapel, I know you will. But it needn't be exclusively your concern. Surely other men will step forward."

"I suppose." He stood again, impatient, with his hands on his hips facing Ann, as he continued, "But so often if you want something done, 'tis best to do it yourself." Ann understood, this was Robert's way: always doing for himself.

Her husband had worked so hard to make their lives possible, but he had never built a meetinghouse. Ann thought how fortunate they were to find a crofthouse already built when they were first married. However, they didn't own it, so they had to pay rent to the laird in the form of fish and wool, as well as money they earned from the sale of fish and knitwear. There was never enough left to buy what they needed from town. The life of a crofter was a constant struggle against the powers that prevailed over him: the landowning lairds, the rocky turf, and the turbulent sea. Survival depended on learning to make the most of one's resources, learning to tackle every new challenge, and learning to put one's life in God's hands; at least that was how Ann saw it: always more to learn.

Ann wished she hadn't brought up the chapel. Usually, Robert embraced each task in good spirit, but on this day his buoyant mood had fallen, and she could see that his duties had suddenly burdened him. They had enough challenges beyond their control. Surely Ann did not want to add to the weight he already carried.

Later when Ann went to bed, she shaped silent words of prayer . . .

> Dear God, what a day of mixed blessings this has been. I thank you for sending us to the Methodists. They are kind people. My body is tired from the walk and from the long day without a nap, but my heart is at peace. I thank you for Robbie, for his love and for his determination to be a good provider. Lift his worries, I ask. Help him learn that he needn't do everything by himself. He can rely on others, and he can lean on you. Teach me not to make demands of him. Help me show him encouragement, and always love.
>
> Remind me that love is patient and kind. As the preacher said today, "It beareth all things, believeth all things, hopeth all things, endureth all things."[2] Help me trust that love conquers fear. I pray this to you, O God, for I am convinced that you are the source of all love.
>
> Keep our bairn well until the time is right. Give me courage to face the birth and all the new responsibilities the child will bring. Hold our peerie family in your care, O God. Amen.

Later that month in the night, Ann's water broke. Warm liquid trickled down her legs and woke her. She got up to fetch a towel, and then she lay down again. In a few minutes she felt a dull cramp cross her belly. It passed. Then a little later the tug came again. It seemed to pull on her and then release. She turned to Robert and shook him gently by the shoulder, "Robbie, I think the bairn is coming."

Robert bolted into a sitting position in the box bed. "How soon? Are you in pain?"

2. First Corinthians 13:7.

"Soon, I think. You'd better go fetch Madge."

"Can you stay by yourself? What if the child comes before I return with Madge?"

"Then the bairn will be born without its daa. But do not fear, usually it takes some hours." She did not want to worry Robert, but she urged him to be off straight away.

Robert pulled off his nightshirt. "You said it takes some time. I hope you are right." He hopped into his britches, pulled on his wool jumper and cap as he hurried into the but end, lit a lamp, and ran off to Sumburgh to Madge's croft.

Ann got up and put on a clean nightdress and then climbed back into bed with an extra cloth under her. She had just washed the linens the day before, and they still smelled fresh like the wildflowers in the meadow. Ann assured herself that all was well, and she was ready. She breathed deeply. Truly, she need not fear. Robert had just finished the cradle, and she had lined it with a soft blanket, which she had knit in preparation for the birth. They still hadn't chosen names, but they would in time for the child to meet its grandparents. Another pain tightened over her lower body. "'Tis labor, all right," she spoke out loud to the silent crofthouse walls. God willing, she would soon have her bairn in her arms.

Ann tried to sleep but could not, so she got up, pulled on her boots, and went out to the shed to relieve herself. It was light out. She heard Violet stirring in her stall. Oh, dear! Of course, the cow wanted to be milked. Ann did not know how long it had been since Robert had left. Would he already be at Madge's house by now? How soon would they be back, and could Violet wait? Ann decided to try to milk the cow before she went back to bed, so she grabbed her shawl and hurried to the damp byre.

Mustering courage, she greeted the cow, "My sweet Violet, today is the day! Do be quick and cooperative with me. Let's see if we can get your milk into the bucket before I have another pain across my belly." Violet turned to face Ann. She blinked her wide brown eyes as if to say, "Well, I'm ready! Go right ahead!" Ann stooped beside the beast and bent to place the pail in its position. Then a pain crept across Ann's stomach, and she hunched over, nearly falling into the muddy straw beneath the cow. She groaned as this time the ache took over her body. The cramps were coming now closer together and insistently. When the pain passed, Ann sat down on the stool and began to milk. For a few moments the rhythmic motion eased her thoughts from the impending birth. But Violet had not filled the bucket before another pain squeezed Ann's womb. She breathed deeply and tried to relax, the way she remembered her mother doing when she gave birth to her little brothers. When calm returned, she reached for Violet's teats again. The cow seemed to sense something different this day. She let Ann know she didn't like the change and kicked up the straw under her feet. Ann patted her cow and reassured her, "Don't worry, now, Violet. You will be fine. Extra clover for you today if you just let me finish here." Finally, Violet's udder shrank, and the pail was full. Ann opened the gate and let her out into the pasture. She did not try to carry the milk into the house but left it in the stall and lifted just her own heavy body back into the cottage. How soon would the bairn come? She made it back inside, but just as she arranged her bed linens in the but by the hearth and climbed under the blanket, another cramp wrenched her as if from inside out. She cried aloud as Robert and Madge entered the cottage and rushed to her side.

Madge had come prepared with clean cloths. She directed Robert to fetch fresh spring water and stoke the fire. Madge helped Ann turn onto her side and pressed hard on Ann's lower back as another pain took hold. Wiping her sweat-drenched forehead dry, she spoke words of encouragement softly in her ear. After the uncomfortable tightening was over, Madge urged Ann to turn onto her back and lift her legs. "Let's have a look. How soon will this bairn make its appearance?" Madge asked.

"It cannot be too soon," Ann replied wearily.

After a gentle inspection, Madge said, "Any time now. Do you feel like pushing yet, Annie?"

"Yes, I do!"

"Then take a good breath and bear down with the next pain, and let's push this peerie one out, shall we?"

Robert returned with the water. He dropped a peat on the fire, washed his hands, and joined the women as he kneeled near Ann's face. With the next cramp, he supported her shoulders as she pushed, grunting until the baby's head crowned.

"That's it, good work, Annie. We are almost there. A couple more pains with pushing, and you will have your bairn in your arms."

Each contraction was stronger than the last, but now that Ann could push, at least the pains did not threaten to overtake her ability to remain in control. Finally, she heaved, bearing down as hard as she could, and the child's head emerged. Then out slid the shoulders, the torso, and the legs. "That's a good lass!" Madge reassured. "'Tis a boy!"

"Oh, Annie, you did it—a boy!" Robert exclaimed with tears streaming down his cheeks. Ann sighed from exhaustion but then smiled at her bonnie laddie now in full view. Madge wrapped the baby and put him to his mother's breast. Ann looked down at the bairn and then up at Robert. They needed no words; his gaze said it all. Following Madge's instructions, she expelled the afterbirth. Then Madge bathed the child and wound a bunting tightly around his sweet body and laid him beside his mother on the blanket. Robert leaned to touch his first child. He was such a little one, all pink with lots of hair, though Ann thought he hadn't felt small to push out. Robert's look told Ann he could not believe what had happened, this miracle they had just shared. Ann smiled up at her husband and then drifted in and out of sleep.

With both Ann and the baby content, Madge cleaned up the bedding, while Robert brought in the milk and poured some into a cauldron to heat with oats for their breakfast. Ann opened her eyes to behold the child. Holiness spread over the house. What could be more sacred than the gift of a healthy baby? Mother and child rested peacefully like the blessed Madonna and her babe long ago.

☙ ❧

Mother and child rested in the but end through the day and then settled in the couple's box bed in the ben for the night. The next morning, words came to her . . .

> Dear God, can it be that our peerie laddie is here in his cradle beside our box bed? He is perfect. A night and a morning ago I had not met him, and now he is part of the family. I am ashamed that I have not stopped to thank you. What a gift you have given us! Thank you too for Madge, an angel whom you sent us. Dear God, watch over our bairn. Keep him safe from harm and help me know how to care for him. I think we should name him James Robert, Jamie for short. I shall see if Robbie agrees. In your blessed name, I pray. Amen.

AUTUMN 1830

Robert's father, James, fell ill. His mother, Ross, traversed the rocky country path to Ann's parents' home in Lerwick to send the message to Ann and Robert that Robert should come home to Scalloway right away. Ross told Ann's mother, who asked Madge at the market in Lerwick to summon Robert when she returned to the south. Madge arrived home by boat and walked to Ann and Robert's croft with the troubling news. It was in the afternoon, and Ann was home alone with the bairn. Robert was finishing the chapel at Durigarth with the other Methodists who volunteered their time when not out at sea.

Ann paced the house waiting for him. In the early-autumn gloaming, he returned to the croft after a long day of labor. Annie met him at the door, while the bairn slept peacefully in his cradle by the hearth. "Robbie, dear, your father is not well."

"What is the matter?" he asked urgently.

"You must go to him. Madge came with the message today from your mother. My parents had relayed the word when she was in Lerwick at the market."

"What ails him?"

"'Tis the mortal pox, they say. Others have it in Scalloway. I'm afraid 'tis bad."

Robert's forehead creased with worry. He sat down and put his head in his hands. After a moment, he stared across the room and said, "I shall take a boat tomorrow from Virkie, around the head, north to Scalloway. It will be faster than traveling overland up the island by horse."

"Should we come, Jamie and I?"

"No need to put the bairn at risk of illness, nor a rough boat ride," Robbie dismissed her suggestion and continued to stare off toward a distant place with eyes wide with apprehension.

Ann agreed with his judgment, but she was sorry not to be able to go along. She could not shake the anxiety that had been looming in her thoughts all afternoon and evening. Life is so precarious, and what if Robert's father had not long to live? She wanted to give her husband reassurance, but truthfully the situation appeared bleak. A sudden thought surprised her, something positive to say: "Oh, Robbie, I am so glad we named our first child after your father."

He turned to her, "So am I. I only wish my father had spent time with our Jamie. Perhaps we can all go to visit my parents later in the summer if the weather permits."

Ann thought, *if James lives.* But she did not want to make her husband even more fearful than he already was. So instead, she tried to be supportive: "I shall pray for your father to recover." She went on, "If it not be the will of God, then, of course, we must accept whatever outcome God gives."

"Ann, I do not believe God wills my father to die at the age of forty-three!" Robert raised his voice. "Of course, we will pray for healing, but if he dies, I will not blame God."

Ann wished she had not said anything about God; she had only intended to comfort him. In her heart she had doubts about whether praying for healing worked anyway. She just thought it was what people did when they were troubled and felt helpless. She had thought Robert would be pleased to know that she would pray for his father. But after Robert's rebuff, she felt foolish and wanted to apologize. She was about to take back the part about God's will when Robert turned from her and walked with heavy steps to the ben end. Ann felt rejected at the very moment she most wanted to console her husband. She looked at Jamie asleep in the cradle by the hearth. The lad was Robert's father's namesake. Robert undressed and then lay down in the ben without even eating the supper Ann had left out for him. She peeked into the box bed. In minutes he was asleep, and Ann found herself alone with her unsettled thoughts. If only he would talk to her. She depended on Robert to be her companion in the isolation of their modest home far from her family. Without his communication, she admitted to herself that she felt alone, like a piece of wood from a damaged boat washed ashore.

There was still very little darkness that autumn night. Ann slipped quietly into the box bed where Robert breathed heavily. Later, when Jamie woke, she fed him sitting by the embers in the but end with a shawl wrapped around them both. She talked to him in a quiet voice, "Oh, Jamie. I fear your grandfather is very ill. If only he were strong and healthy, as you are." She rocked the bairn and sang to him as he sucked peacefully with eyes closed.

After Jamie was filled and content, Ann laid the child in his cradle, and she leaned back in the resting chair. There, in the but end, Ann drifted into a fitful slumber, dreaming of crashing waves and windswept graveyards. At some point in the early hours of the morning Robert must have got up quietly and left the house to find a boat that would take him north to Scalloway. Ann knew that the local laird had a craft, and for a fee Robert could sail the distance and likely arrive there by noon. Ann wished Robert had talked to her about his plans. She was not sure whether his father would still be living by the time he would arrive home. Ann wished she had not been asleep when he left. Naturally, he was preoccupied and apprehensive about his father's condition. After all, they said the pox was "mortal." Ann understood that he had no idea how long he would be gone, but she wanted him to talk to her about his intentions, and even about his fears. It was so like him to be silent when it came to emotions. She would have to wait at the mercy of the unknown. Patience, along with the duties of croft and child, would have to be her pastimes.

Ann got up with the bairn, nursed the happy child, and then laid him back in his cradle where he cooed happily. "There you go, Jamie. Oh, for life to be so simple—drinking and sleeping." She followed her morning routine, first milking the cow. "Violet, here I am with you again all alone; even Jamie is quiet in his cradle. And who knows when Robert shall return? You are my steady companion. I thank you for that." She gave Violet a love pat on her backside and sat down to milk her. "Bless you, you always listen! And you give us milk and rarely problems."

With Violet and Jamie both cared for, Ann turned to the hearth to make herself some oat porridge and a hot drink. She poured fresh milk onto her oats and into her tea and breathed in the good aromas. Then she sat down to enjoy the simple comfort of warm food. Her thoughts went to Robert and his sudden departure. The heat from her teacup warmed her hands and her face as she drank. Her body relaxed, and clarity quickly materialized out of the steamy air. She decided she had a choice, whether to resent Robbie's curt words and abrupt leave-taking or to make the best of the day before her. By the time she had posed the question in her mind, she had already decided: of course, she must make the best of her family's circumstances. After all, Robert could not help that his father had fallen ill. He was troubled, and understandably so. She too was worried about James. Should he die, how devastated Robert would be! And Ross would suffer from grief and economic struggle as well. Fortunately, Robert's brother Stewart was still at home, but he too would likely soon marry and then leave the homestead. Living at the far end of the island, she and Robert would not be able to help Ross with her crops and livestock. There was much about which to be concerned.

Then Ann remembered that she had promised to pray for James. As she sat at the table, she closed her eyes and breathed in deeply. She waited. Nothing came: no right words to utter and no sense of anyone listening either. She was distracted. In her mind, instead of communing with God, she argued with Robert: why wouldn't he talk to her? Why couldn't he express his fears and his hopes? Her muscles tensed, and she felt ashamed of her inability to quiet her mind. When she tried to pray, instead of feeling a connection to God, Ann felt separated, ill at ease and far away.

Her hands held the warm teacup still, but her mind raced with accusations . . .

> Where are you, God? How can I pray if I have no words and if my heart is so restless? What is the purpose of prayer at all? Even if I could find the words to ask, would you really answer? And if, in fact, you do not will a person to die, why does the person sometimes die, nevertheless? Why should I pray for James to recover if you may not even be able to make him well? What does it mean to believe in God if I cannot believe in prayer?

Ann opened her eyes and concluded that she simply could not pray at that moment. She released the teacup and raised her hands to her temples. Her head reeled with questions, and her stomach churned with conflicting sentiments. Doubts tumbled about in a troubling quandary, as if debris were flung into a surging hurricane, waiting for stillness at the eye of the storm. Perhaps later, outside, she would try again.

While Jamie was content in his cradle, Ann gave him a love pat and went out into the garden to pick a few summer vegetables. There would be no fish while Robert was gone, so taaties and turnips would have to do. She had only herself to feed, so the preparation would be swift. Perhaps she would walk on the moor and enjoy the purple heather still in bloom. Surely that would lift her spirit.

It was a fine autumn day. Ann took a shawl and tied Jamie onto her front, binding him inside the soft wool against her warm body. He gurgled with happiness as he rode along in this cozy wrap. Ann tipped her head to Jamie's face peeking out from the pack and kissed him on both of his ruddy cheeks. "Such a bonnie laddie, Jamie! Shall we walk on the hill ground along the voe, perhaps to the cliffs at the head? See the purple heather, and smell it too? Ah, we have a lovely day before us." Ann put one hand under the bairn to lift some of the weight off her shoulders. Her rhythmic steps, left and right, lulled Jamie quickly to sleep, as if he were rocking in his cradle by the fire. She thought for a moment that she needn't have brought the child along, for he could have slept in his own bed just as well. But they were together, and by then they had reached the sea where the sun and salt air would do them both good.

Ann climbed the hill to the lighthouse. Her gaze stretched to the rippling water on the distant bay below the rocky overhangs. The persistent crash of sea onto the base of the crags broke her thoughts of home and drew her into the mighty modulation of the ocean. In and out, relentlessly, the tide rocked waves onto the rocks. She sat down on a crag and cradled Jamie in her lap as he slept. The tireless sea swept away all thoughts of time and circumstance. Ann arrived at a state of calm, like a boat coming into its mooring when the wind has died down. Lost in the surge of nature all around her, nothing mattered any more but the rush and pull of the foamy water. Nature's force overpowered Ann's cares and hurled them out into the deep. Words formed in her mind to match the moment, and Ann found herself composing a hymn:

> God of quiet waters flowing,
> Send your breezes gently blowing
> From the sea to hilltops above.
> See your world in perfect splendor!
> In such beauty I surrender,
> Awed and humbled ever in your love.
>
> Darkened rain clouds filled with sorrows
> Turn to sunlight's sweet tomorrows.
> Seeds you sow and harvests you reap.
> God of every changing season,
> You, the mystery and the reason,
> Waken me from winter's bitter sleep.
>
> Ocean waves like cymbals crashing
> Send their drumroll rhythms splashing.
> Fill me with your music and might!
> Give me respite, restoration.
> Cast my cares into creation.
> Cleanse my soul and set my path to right.

She imagined sitting there at night and continued the flow of words:

> Gazing into darkest distance
> Stars resound my insignificance.
> God is great and I am small.
> Spirit present, power vast.
> Alpha first, Omega last,
> Majesty! O Maker all in all![3]

---

3. Hammer, "God of Quiet Waters Flowing."

She had composed a prayer, even one that could be sung as a hymn! Although it had been so hard to pray previously that morning, now sitting overlooking the ocean, Ann was filled with wonder. It was a sacred moment. For the first time in months, she wanted to write. The words had come to her so easily, now if only she could commit them to paper quickly before she forgot the images and the phrases.

Ann's heart lifted. In her hymn she had sung to God! She had found a divine presence in the surge of nature all around her as she sat on a rock, mesmerized by the open ocean. What lay beyond her vision? It was the unknown, and yet therein rested a mysterious strength and comfort. Perhaps this moment would define for Ann who God could be. Perhaps God could hover close and arrive in the form of a calm so gentle it could descend on her at any moment. Perhaps she could understand the divine, if she opened her mind as she did when she basked in the beauty of poetry. In that moment, Ann discovered a new insight: she could meet God where nature and verse crossed paths.

Ann returned home singing the words she had composed, aware that she had stayed at the head longer than she had intended. When she got back to the crofthouse, she changed Jamie and fed him. Then she quickly prepared her own tea, and after eating and washing up, she put Jamie down for the night and went to sleep as well. Sunburned and tired, but envigored by the ocean air, she slept soundly and woke in the morning with a secure feeling that all would be well.

As the sun came up, Ann prayed . . .

> Dear God, it seems I have turned a corner, and now I see my way clearly to accept the circumstance of this time in my life. If I can call upon you in the waves and the wind, then surely, I can know that you are always near. This morning I am grateful to be alive, and I entrust Robert and his father to your care. Come what may, you will be our rock and our light. I will listen for you in the wind, which is always with us on this island. With assurance of your love and with gratitude for your abiding presence, I pray. Amen.

Three days later, as Ann was nursing Jamie by the fire, Robert burst through the door with his hair matted down by the rain and his boots full of seawater.

"Oh, Annie. I hurried home."

Ann put the bairn into the cradle and rushed to her husband. She kissed him and helped him off with his wet clothes. The two embraced, and Robert clung to her as she asked him urgently, "How is your father, Robbie?"

Rain and tears dripping from his face, Robert buried his head in her hair and sobbed from the depth of his chest. Ann knew then, and she held him close. "He is gone, Ann. He died yesterday. The fever and the pox were too much—all over his body. 'Twas dreadful."

"Did he suffer terribly?" She searched his troubled face.

"When I got home, he was in pain and struggled to speak. With difficulty, he managed to say he loved us and gave us his blessing. Then yesterday he did not wake at all. Mother sat in the room with him and read from the Psalms." Ann nodded and looked deeply into Robert's face, where she saw a more furrowed brow than she had ever seen him wear before. Feeling his anguish as if it were her own, she shed silent tears, and Robert told more. "He never opened his eyes again. We were there—Mother, Stewart, and I—when he breathed his last." Sobs then racked Robert's shoulders, and his chest caved in. "The minister is telling Mam they should have been inoculated against the pox. We should be too, just in case."

Ann led him to the hearth where they sat together silently. A nagging premonition had accompanied her since the news of the illness first arrived. She had feared Robert's father would not recover. How would Robert take the loss? Breathing deeply, she relaxed back in her chair. How unexpected that she felt calm and without anxiety, ready to listen to her husband. Her time alone, after Robert had left, had steadied her, like a dory becalmed after a turbulent gale. So often people died when they contracted illness, and this one had been deadly. Her previous irritation at Robert's lack of communication had melted away, and she shared only the despair of her husband's loss. She yearned to comfort him, and, remarkably, she found the words she needed. "Oh, Robbie, I am so sorry. How sad I am for you, and especially for your mother."

Robert nodded and wept as Ann had never seen him. He caught his breath, dried his eyes, and then lifted Jamie into his arms. "Oh, Jamie, laddie, you shall not know your grandfather, nor he you." He rocked the bairn in his arms, and more tears fell onto the child's blanket. Raising his eyes from Jamie to Ann, he said, "Mother wants me to have Daa's fiddle. I never played it well, but I shall want to learn it now and then teach Jamie to play when he is older."

"Oh, Robbie, your father would be so pleased." Ann thought, how lovely it would be to have music in the house. Then her mind returned to the days ahead. "When will the burial be?"

"Sunday, on the Sabbath, just for the family, due to the epidemic going around. I shall return tomorrow or the next day. I just had to come tell you, and I wanted to hold you." Ann watched Robert's face as he spoke, "I need you, Annie. His death breaks my heart." He cried fresh tears and then regained his calm and gave Jamie back to his mother and embraced them both. "I feel like a part of me is gone, cut off. Daa was my strength. He taught me all I know: to fish and to farm. And he trained me to love God and to love my neighbors and, of course, my family."

Ann nodded as he released her, and she laid her free hand on his shoulder. She rubbed her fingers through his hair and down his cheek.

Robert looked into her eyes and whispered, "Before I met you, Father was my only strength."

"Now we have each other, Robbie."

He hugged her tightly. "Oh, Annie, never leave me!"

"Of course, I never will. I love you, Robbie. Nothing else matters now. We shall give each other courage. God will see that our love carries us over this sadness, and we shall face every challenge that comes our way, together."

That night after Robert had fallen asleep and was breathing steadily, Ann prayed . . .

> Dear God, keep Robert safe in Scalloway. Do not let him get the pox. Bless his family as they lay James to rest. May you hold them all in the palm of your hand. Amen.

3

Tragedy

SUMMER 1832

ANN WAS WATCHING FROM the open door as she prepared tea, so she saw Robert when he approached the croft from the beach. As he passed several sheep they had acquired, he called for Sheltie, the sheepdog, who ran to greet his master and licked his salty hands with delight. Robert entered the house with a sigh. "The laird is asking us to go out again tomorrow, Annie." Robert peeled off his wet fishing clothes and sank into the resting chair by the peat fire. Jamie ran on his little legs to greet his father with outstretched arms asking to be picked up.

Stirring the kettle of soup, Ann replied, "But, Robbie, you just spent three days on the sixareen. How can he ask that of you, and after the fishing disaster in the north last week?" She rinsed, then dried her hands, and went to him.

Robert's face dropped. "Well, yes, you might think a hundred men buried at sea would curb his greed for profit."

Ann kissed him on the forehead and then Jamie too. "Did you hear more about what happened?"

Robert's eyebrows tightened in a frown. "It seems the gale came up and the sixareens were too far out to make it back; that's what they are saying. At least seventeen boats are gone, and the remains have yet to wash up on the rocks somewhere."

41

"Oh, I grieve for the wives and mothers of those men!" She cast her eyes down into her apron.

"'Tis surely the worst disaster in Shetland ever."

"'Tisn't right, Robbie, such work!" She raised her voice as she spoke in anger. "They give you almost nothing to eat, just a peerie bit of oatcake, and you must tug on those long, heavy lines. And even when a gale comes up, you still must haul in the heavy catch. And what do you get? No sleep, no decent food, just a few cheap fish heads to bring home for soup and only measly pay." She shook her head. "You do all the work, and the laird gets all the profit."

"Well, that is because we are poor crofters. I must fish for our rent here, you know that." They sat quietly, resigned, knowing all too well their station in life.

"Come, you must be hungry." Ann ladled the soup into two bowls, and they ate their simple tea together. With Jamie on her lap, Ann offered him bits of cooled taatie and turnip from her bowl. Then she sang to him before laying him in his cradle by the fire. Jamie was a good sleeper; for that she was grateful.

She returned to sit with Robert as he asked, "How was your day, Annie?" Ann thought Robert kind to turn from his own worries and think of something pleasant to say.

"'Twas a fine day. Now Jamie takes one long nap. Sheltie likes to sit by him. He is very good about that. It gives me time to fetch water and do the wash. And today I worked in the garden until I was too tired to bend down." She looked him in the eye and confessed with a smile, "In the past few days I have even taken a nap myself."

Robert grinned at his wife. "So, you deserve to rest, my love." They led a hard life with always more work than could be accomplished in a day, yet they both managed to find moments of pleasure. He touched her cheek gently.

Annie's smile crept up her face until it shone in her eyes. "So, I have news for you, my Robbie dear."

"You do, do you?" He watched her eyebrows lift playfully.

"Jamie is to have a baby brother or sister."

"So! 'Tis true! I wondered, and I hoped!" He kissed her warmly. "Another bonnie bairn! How long have you known?"

"Just this week while you were away. I figured I must be carrying another." She turned up her nose. "I wish we could be together more here at the croft. 'Twas better when you fished for yourself and then sold the fish and paid the rent. Then you didn't have to sail out so far with the other men to the haaf." She raised her voice in irritation. "Surely the laird cannot expect you to turn around and go out again tomorrow. You deserve to rest."

"True, my sentiment also. But I shall sleep now and go out again in the morning because I have no other choice. 'Tis the heart of the season for long-lining cod and ling, and the other white fish that bring in a good price. Then when I return Saturday night, we can go together in the morning to the Sabbath prayer meeting and pray for the souls of those lost at sea. Church bells will toll in Lerwick all day, they say, and all of Shetland will mourn together." Sorrow fell upon them, like a rain cloud passing over the sun, and there was nothing more to say. Robert yawned, kissed Ann again, and went to wash and undress for bed.

Ann slipped into the box bed beside Robert and prayed silently . . .

> Dear God, thank you for bringing Robert home safely to Jamie and me. And thank you, for the peerie one I now carry.
>
> I mourn for the families of the deceased fishermen. God, help them! Grant the wives some comfort. And all the men, grant them your peace.
>
> Calm the seas tomorrow, and give us a chance for a good life, O God. 'Tis all in your hands. Amen.

Dawn on the Sabbath came early. Jamie had not slept well; Ann thought perhaps he had a cold. She had rocked him in the night in the but end, trying to keep him quiet so that Robert could get a good night's rest in the ben. After breakfast they dressed for church, but Jamie fell asleep before Ann could finish putting on his little britches. She spoke to Robert, "Jamie so needs his nap today. Shall we let him sleep in his cradle by the hearth while we go to the prayer meeting?"

"You know him. Will he stay asleep?"

Ann answered, "Yes. He is so tired today." So, they put him in his cradle and added peats to the fire to keep the house warm in their absence.

Robert patted Sheltie. "Watch over Jamie. We shall not be gone long."

The winds had calmed since the storms of the previous week. Silver beams broke through the gray clouds as Robert and Ann set out along the track. With Bible in one hand, Robert carried a basket in the other hand, which Ann had packed with shortbread and oatcakes. Ann threw her arms out, hands free! Oh, to feel the breeze and remember what it was like before, with no toddler to hold by the hand or carry as she walked over the hill ground.

All the Shetlanders in the south of Mainland had gathered in meetinghouses that day. The mood was somber. The men took off their hats and stood by, while the women sat in the few assembled chairs at Andrew's croft. Most of the families had their children stay home to spare them the sadness of the day. As they arrived, neighbors shared the facts they knew of the fishing disaster. Some had relatives who had lost a family member, and so after telling the stories that had passed to the southern tip of the island, one at a time they solemnly spoke the names they knew of the men who had died. Hushed silence followed each name. Then the lay preacher offered a prayer:

"God of the sea, grant the brave men who perished the tranquility of the next life that only you can give. Bestow upon them life everlasting, and may their souls rest in peace. O God of our islands, comfort the bereaved wives. Give them strength to go on living. Care for them with your faithful providence and strength." The leader choked up and had to pause before he finished his prayer: "Bless the children who have no fathers, and bless the wives whose husbands are no more. In the name of your Son, who knew suffering himself, we pray. Amen."

The prayer meeting ended with the singing of a favorite hymn:

> O God, our help in ages past, our hope for years to come,
> Our shelter from the stormy blast, and our eternal home.[1]

The singing seemed to bolster their faith. Ann left the food she had prepared for the others to enjoy, and embracing her friends, she bid them farewell with tears in her eyes. Then the couple went on their way, back up the path by which they had come, heads bowed. Ann supposed that silence could best honor the dead. Then suddenly the wind came up, and they hurried, for they saw that the sky had turned dark, threatening a storm any moment. Absorbed in thoughts, Annie considered how it could have easily been her Robbie lost at sea, and she pictured what it would be like now to be widowed with one child to care for and another

---

1. Isaac Watts, "O God, Our Help in Ages Past," #117 in *United Methodist Hymnal*.

on the way. She imagined the grief the fishermen's wives were feeling this day, as church bells tolled in town where there were proper churches. Shetlanders all shared the heaviness of their land's tragedy. The gloomy sky seemed to say that God grieved too.

Ann contemplated what it meant to sing the words of the hymn in worship that day:

> O God, our help in ages past, our hope for years to come,
> Our shelter from the stormy blast, and our eternal home.

Was God truly a "shelter from the stormy blast"? Not in the case of the fishermen who died! Yet certainly God was an "eternal home" for those brave men; that much she knew beyond doubt. They were now at peace, she believed. But how could she count on God as "hope for years to come," when tragedy had just washed away all hope for the families of the deceased? Robert put his arm around her, and his touch brought her back to the moment. Darkness descended upon their way as they quickly rounded the last bend before approaching their croft.

What sound was that they heard down the path? It wasn't the sheep. It was barking. But from where? It sounded like Sheltie. Was a sheep hurt? Robert dropped his arm from Ann's shoulder. They hurried along. Their sheep were huddling near the byre, anxious to get out of the rain. Sheltie came running toward them on the lane, woofing loudly. It was unlike him to leave the house and the sheep. And then Ann thought, Jamie! Was Jamie all right? "Jamie!" she called out, as she threw a worried glance at Robert and broke into a run.

Robert leapt ahead, running with long strides as he followed the sheepdog to the house. The door was open. Robert burst inside. Ann entered just behind him. A long howl sounded from where her husband knelt. She stared ahead onto the floor of the cottage. Jamie lay on the stone floor of the hearth, black with ashes, lifeless. Robert was lifting him up, as Sheltie barked frantically by the empty cradle.

Ann let out a shriek from the pit of her stomach, like the squeal of a wild grice. She stumbled forward and fell on Robert holding Jamie in his arms. The child's hair was gone, and his face was unrecognizable. His clothes were black, and he lay there like a charred piece of driftwood. Ann looked away and covered her face, bawling uncontrollably. Robert spoke to Sheltie in his disbelief, "What happened, laddie? Oh, Sheltie!" When his master cried, the dog stopped barking and began to lick the soot from Jamie's body. Robert put the child into the cradle and covered him with his blanket. Then he went to Ann and rocked her in his arms, as she moaned. Sheltie curled up in the corner of the room and whimpered softly, as thunder clapped and rumbled outside the cottage.

Time stopped. It must have been late afternoon, but the sky was as dark as on a starless winter night. Ann knelt by the cradle and rocked it gently. Her tears spilled onto the blanket that covered the little child's head. Could she bring him back? Could she rock him out of slumber, back to life?

Robert went out to milk Violet and let the sheep into the byre. He fetched water for the animals and poured it into a trough in the enclosure without thinking. These were the chores he did every Sunday afternoon. Ann reflected that it was good that Robert could function, because her heart ached and her limbs were frozen stiff. In shock, Ann remained on her knees with her head resting on her hands that rocked the cradle back and forth.

When Robert came in again, he swept the hearth of ashes and put on new kindling and peats. They would need to eat something and stay warm. He started a kettle of water for tea and found the remaining bannocks that Ann had made that morning. While the fire warmed the room and he waited for the teakettle to boil, Robert poured Ann a cup of fresh milk and handed it to her. "Annie, love, drink this. You must drink some milk."

Ann then remembered her unborn child and started to cry fresh tears. Her baby, Jamie, was gone! Her precious little laddie.

"Come, Annie, sit with me and drink this."

They sat side by side, at first looking into the fire as they usually did when warming themselves upon homecoming. But then as Ann stared at the gentle flames, the blaze before her turned into an inferno ferociously engulfing Jamie, and she turned away, screaming. "My poor bairn! My Jamie!" She gasped and covered her eyes to obscure the hideous vision and rocked in her chair until the terror died down. "We should never have left him." She sat limply, exhausted by grief.

Ann and Robert clung to each other in the night, crying off and on and breathing heavily between sobs. When they finally fell asleep, it was for a short time, only to wake and remember the tragedy they had just suffered, worse than any nightmare.

When Robert failed to report to the sixareen the next day, the laird sent his steward to inquire where the young man was. Robert received him at the door of the cottage with tired red eyes and a pale hue on his usually ruddy cheeks. "We've had a death in the family," he told the man.

"I'm sure the laird will send his condolences," said the servant. "Will you be needing a coffin?"

"No. Our son will be buried in his cradle. I made it for him, and my wife won't want to use it for the next bairn."

Word of Jamie's death spread around the tip of the island, and neighbors started dropping by with the best foods they could offer: mutton pie and fish broth, kirn-milk and summer vegetables. They tried to console Ann, but she could not bring herself to speak to anyone. Robert and his friends from the Methodist meeting went to dig a grave in the Dunrossness Parish Church burial ground, a few miles from their croft. The grave had to be big enough for the cradle, even though, inside, the body was shriveled and small. Fortunately, the soil was wet and soft to dig. Ann imagined the rain pelting upon the heads and shoulders of the men as they took turns thrusting the shovel into the stony earth. And she thought of her bairn, who would be buried deep down in the cold ground. Robert told her later, when they had finished digging the grave, that they piled the earth into a mound for a raised garden bed at the edge of the churchyard. Perhaps Ann would want to plant flowers there.

❧ ❧

Ann could barely remember the graveside service. She and Robert followed the coffin and led the people of the south in a procession through the mist along the path to the north. It felt as if Ann were going home again, toward Lerwick. Her life was backtracking. The Methodist minister was there to meet them in the churchyard, and he said some words; she couldn't remember what they were. Then the men lowered the sealed cradle into the lonely grave. Robert shoveled damp, rocky dirt onto the wood. It landed with a thud.

Ann's mother came from Lerwick and stayed when Robert went back out to fish. She brought books for Ann to read, hoping that her daughter would rekindle her love of literature and that reading would help her pass the time during her mourning while she waited for the next bairn. Although each week distanced Ann from Jamie's death and drew

her that much closer to the birth of her unborn child, she remained de-
spondent, trapped in the grip of grief.

Ann sat in her chair wrapped in blankets, looking down and feeling
hollow with despair.

"Ann, darling, I've brought you a very special book to read. 'Tis by
Sir Walter Scott, called *Waverley*." She waited for her daughter's response.
"Perhaps you have heard, Scott just passed away, and his books are all the
rage in Edinburgh. I was able to purchase a copy in Lerwick," she said as
she handed the book toward her daughter.

"Thank you, Mam," Ann said without looking up. Instead, she sat
bent over, void of any spark of life. Her mother slowly drew the book
back. Then Ann straightened her torso and turned her eyes toward her
mother as she tentatively reached out for the package. She unwrapped it,
and she felt the familiar weight of a book and the pleasant smooth surface
of the binding in her hands. "Is it poetry, Mother?"

"No, 'tis his first effort to write prose, what is being called a 'novel.'
It came out in 1814, and he has written others since." She sat down in the
chair beside Ann, smiling. "I shall look forward to reading it after you
finish. Then perhaps we can talk about it together."

"I doubt I have the spirit in me to read, Mam." She set the book
on the floor. "I can't seem to get up and do anything. 'Tis as if my soul
died with Jamie." She began to cry. Pulling the blanket up to her face, she
wiped her eyes.

"I know. There is nothing worse than losing a bairn, Annie." She
looked deeply into Ann's face, creased with sorrow.

Ann turned to her mother. "You lost bairns too, didn't you?"

"I lost two before they were born, after you. Then came Mary and
the boys." She smiled, but then the brightness dropped from her face
again. "But no child replaces another. Each is uniquely precious to its
mam, and I have always grieved for those two peerie ones."

"The neighbors keep telling me, 'You'll have another bairn soon,' but
that only makes me weep, thinking of when Jamie was born and how dear
he was to me." She stared off in the direction of the window, focusing on
nothing at all in the room. "My sweet laddie!" Ann dropped her head into
her hands and moaned.

After a few moments, her mother spoke softly, "Oh, lassie, I know.
He was such a sweetheart, my first grandchild. He will always be our
first." She reached her arm around Ann. "Carrying a bairn makes the
child part of you, and when you lose it, you lose that part of yourself."

Ann looked into her mother's eyes, glistening with tears.

"And Jamie had already come into his own. He had his own little personality. He could run after Sheltie exploring, and he loved to dig in the garden with me." Ann smiled as she remembered. But then fresh tears fell as she recalled what happened on the day that changed her life. "When I look at the hearth, I keep seeing the fire and Jamie's charred little body. I see it when I sit here, and I see it from the other room when I wake in bed in the middle of the night. This vision has taken over me. It possesses me. I cannot shake it." Again overcome, her sobbing flowed and stopped her from speaking more, like a tumbling rockslide that mercilessly dams a mountain stream. Ann reflected how her life was scattered, in ruins. A plummeting cascade of despair blocked all the pleasure she had known before.

A long silence fell between them before Ann's mother dared to go on. "Tell me, darling, what you saw when you came home and found him."

Ann breathed deeply, and though she feared the vision, it clung to her like a demon that she could not sever from her body, one that drew her to its horror with an eerie magnetism. "I ran to the house, after Robbie. We thought Sheltie was telling us something—something bad. There was a peculiar smell that hit me at the door, and Robert let out a grotesque howl. Sheltie was making a racket. My mind raced, trying to piece together what I feared was something horrid." Ann's mother nodded for her to tell more. After a moment she regained her strength to speak, and Ann looked toward the hearth and continued, "Then straight in front of me, my eyes fixed on the scene of Robert bent over the coals and Jamie's black body off to the side of the hearth between him and the cradle that was knocked over." As soon as she got these words out, she began to wail aloud as she revisited the frightening sight. "He didn't even look like Jamie," she gasped. Bending over in her chair with her handkerchief at her eyes, she wept on silently, overcome by the piercing memory.

Her mother let her cry. "Is this what you keep seeing then, Jamie's body?" she asked tenderly.

She nodded. "The black charred lump . . ." Her voice trailed off into sobs again.

"Oh, my darling. Oh, my love." They cried together until there were no more tears. Then her mother brought out a fresh handkerchief and Ann blew her nose, exhausted. They sat together without words. Summoning courage then, her mother went on, "Perhaps another day we can go to this image again and ask God to help you with it, so that it does not continue to haunt you. I know—I trust—that after some time you will be able to face what has happened, and you will learn to go on with your living, but only with God's help. And now 'tis too soon. You must rest." Ann stood up and walked to the ben end with the new book in hand.

❦

In the days when Robert was at sea, Ann's mother saw to the chores of milking the cow and caring for the sheep, gardening, cooking, and washing. Ann rested and read. *Waverley* told of a strong Scottish woman called Flora, whose devotion to Bonnie Prince Charlie and passion for her clan attracted great admiration. In contrast to Flora, another woman in the story, called Rose, followed reason and practicality as her accepted virtues and placidly went about her life in measured steps. Ann wanted to identify with Flora, the passionate one. Flora delighted in nature and the people around her, and she captivated Ann's imagination. Life was different in the Highlands than in the bleak Shetland Isles, yet Ann lost herself in the character of Flora, running through the heather with her tartan wrap flapping in the breeze. She admired Flora's love of country and dedication to family. Could she be such a woman? New thoughts stirred in her mind, and her heart felt stronger than it had in weeks.

As Ann's mother tended her daughter and the household, Ann rested. Robert worked hard and came home tired, but eager to be with his wife. He looked into her face with desire. "Annie, I know you are still grieving over our Jamie, but look at you, you are so beautiful." He pulled her gently into an embrace and covered her face with kisses. Ann broke out in tears, and that brought moisture to his eyes also. "I know you are still sad, darling, and so am I. And yet, you've become such a strong woman, and I love you so much for it."

As the days shortened, they began to talk about preparing for winter and the new bairn. Robert wanted to send Ann's mother home to Lerwick to her husband and her life. With Ann listening, he said, "I am confident that Ann can resume her chores. She is a strong woman—and bonnie, don't you agree?"

"Indeed," said her mother as she packed her things. Ann looked at Robert with pride. She was beginning to feel capable again. As her eyes swept across the room, the sound of the steaming teakettle and the smell of the warm soup beckoned her back to life. She stepped outside, and it was as if breathing came now more easily, and the soft colors of the sea and the pasture became comforts again.

After waving her mother off, Ann walked along the voe. She scanned the horizon and soaked up the beauty of her croft and coast, her home. Then in the quiet, she prayed aloud . . .

> Dear God, thank you for Mam. She has been so kind and such a help to me. May I be such a mother, O God. Keep her safe as she returns home. And thank you for our friends who have stood by us through this painful time. I see that we are not alone on this lonely tip of the island. We have people who care about us, and we have you to lean on.
>
> I have not been able to pray since Jamie died, but I need you, God. I want to be strong again. Stay with me through this dark fog and help me see the sunlight once more.
>
> Show me how to love my unborn bairn. 'Tis to be Jamie's brother or sister, and I want to love the child as I did him.
>
> God bless Robert. Keep him safe and help shoulder his own grief, O God. Show me that life will somehow soon be better. Help me to feel at home here once again. Amen.

4

Loss and Gain

SPRINGTIME 1833

THE FIRST ROOING OF the sheep produced baskets of soft fleece: mostly white but also some brown, gray, and black. Ann worried that the animals would freeze without their coats. The idea of losing another life was still more than she could bear, so she kept them in the byre until the spring grass grew tall. Through the lambing early that spring they'd lost a pair of twins, and Ann wanted their mam to stay healthy until next year, for another birth. A neighbor lent her a spinning wheel, and with the woman's help she spun the rooed wool into yarn. The work was tangible and some-how comforting. She felt no longer like a dead piece of furniture sitting in a lonely room; instead, she became a moving part, in fact, an integral element of life making something productive happen. It took her mind off her sorrow, and she began to feel like she was contributing to the house-hold again. Round and round, the days marched, one after the other in a cyclical rhythm that could not fail. Each evening as the sun went down, Ann sighed and thanked God that she had managed another day.

Rain poured down steadily one afternoon, and Ann stayed inside with Sheltie at her feet. She wound the yarn into balls as she talked to the dog. "'Tis a lonely time, Sheltie. But 'tis just the occasion for skeining this wool. I'll be using the yarn to knit warm blankets for our next bairn." She looked toward the hearth. "We'll keep the peerie one in the bedroom this time; I shan't put him here by the fire. So, we'll need plenty of warm night dresses and covers." Silent tears slipped from her eyes. "Oh, Sheltie, sometimes I cannot remember even what he looked like exactly, that is, until after he died." She touched the soft wool to the side of her face. "But this makes me think of holding him and kissing his soft, smooth cheeks." Sighing, she looked toward Sheltie as if he could bring her child back. "I want to remember how he looked before the burning—" Her voice broke off into silent weeping. Sheltie rubbed his head against her leg and looked up into her eyes. Ann returned his affection with a scratch behind the ear and then breathed deeply. "Perhaps I need to go home to Mam. I could weave and knit there while I wait for the bairn."

That night Ann approached Robert. "I am thinking I should spend some time at home with my parents before this one comes." She caught a quick scowl as it passed across his brow, but he held his words, allowing her an opening to tell more. "I can travel now, and I shan't be able to, once the bairn is born. You know I am still lonely since Jamie died."

"Yes, Annie, I know." He turned away with a sigh. Ann imagined that he wanted her to stay, do chores, and be there for tea each night when he came home from the boat. But when he turned back and looked at her deeply, he said, "I shall miss you, you know that. But if it will help you prepare for the next one, then go." He took her in his arms and the tension drained from her body onto his chest and strong shoulders. "'Twill mean I will not be able to go out overnight. I will not be earning the same wages as on the sixareen." She knew this would be a sacrifice. "I suppose I can put out a line to pull in some fish close to home, and we can hope that Madge and Andrew will take the catch to market in Lerwick when they go."

"And I shall ask to go by their boat to stay with my parents—only for a fortnight. We can make do on less income, don't you think?" She looked into his eyes hopefully. "I shall knit while I'm there and sell what I make at the shop where mother and Mary take their knitwear." Ann appraised his face for signs of displeasure but found none. She sighed with relief and got up to finish the dishes before bed. As Robert went out to check on the sheep and the cow, she noted his tired gait. He had been carrying the weight of most of the chores since Jamie died. How fortunate she was to have such a hardworking and considerate husband. Other young men they knew had taken to drink when the times got rough.

"Thank you, Robbie, for all you are doing. I do love you," Annie kissed her husband goodbye and set off with her traveling sack on foot to Madge's croft. At the bend in the path, she turned and waved to him standing outside their cottage with the morning sun shining from the east onto the wet grass at his feet. He waved back, and her spirit soared like the gulls taking flight over the voe.

Madge and Ann rode side by side knitting in the stern of the craft, while Andrew and their son rowed from the middle, each with an oar. "Is it too rough for you, lass?" Madge glanced down at Ann's swollen belly.

"No, surely not," Ann replied, though the thought had crossed her mind that the lurching boat could possibly cause an early birth. She reassured Madge, and also herself, when she added, "I still have a whole month to go." In the stillness that followed, she said a silent prayer for safety in her time away.

"I'll come again, you know, if you need me, that is, when the bairn arrives."

"Oh, thank you, Madge. What would we do without you?" She rubbed her belly gently.

"What would we do without neighbors and a loving God watching over us all?" Madge smiled at Ann, pleased to notice the glow of motherhood on her cheeks.

Ann lifted her eyes and swept the horizon. Could it be that she had not gazed at the sky since Jamie died? The clouds seemed to be in animated conversation: some white, billowing over the rolling coastline ahead, and some dark, hovering over the sea behind them. Moments passed, and a growing gleam of light charged across the sky. It vanquished the dark and shot golden beams, crowning the hills victorious before them. Ann relaxed.

"So, what do you say, will it be a boy or a girl this time?" Madge asked with a chuckle as she looked up from her knitting.

"Only God knows, but if I had to guess or dared to hope, I should say a lassie." Ann smiled shyly.

"'Twould be my wish for you, as well." The friends locked eyes for an instant.

"Madge, did you ever lose a child?"

"My mother did. A sister we had was stillborn. My mother never got over it. She was born on Christmas Eve, and Mother always cried at Christmas after that."

"Oh, dear. I wonder if I shall ever get over crying for Jamie."

"It gets better, Annie. Don't worry, time is the great healer—or perhaps 'tis God who is the healer over time."

"'Tis my prayer, that it gets better." Ann watched Madge put aside her knitting and bail seawater with the skill that comes from many years of practice. Madge was a woman she could admire. She was capable of every task on the croft, as well as on their boat, and at the market too. In comparison, Ann felt quite inadequate, and she admitted to herself that her heavy sadness kept her from functioning even as she used to.

"You'll see, 'twill indeed get better." They sat in silence, riding to the rhythm of the bouncing bow. After a few minutes, Madge began to sing in cadence:

> Will ye no' come back again?
> Will ye no' come back again?
> Better lo'ed ye canna be.
> Will ye no' come back again?[1]

The others joined in, and they sang the Scottish tune together. The wind tossed their hair over their faces, and the women laughed like young sisters playing in the meadow with a pet sheepdog. Ann tucked her knitting into the fold of her shawl and clasped her hands in her lap on her belly as they bounced along. She tried to hold the baby in her womb as still as she could. It pushed a limb against her taut skin, and Ann took Madge's hand from the bailing bucket and pressed it against the life she was carrying. The women smiled at each other, and Ann stirred with warmth, as if she and her peerie child-to-be already rested wrapped in a soft blanket out of the mist and sea spray.

Their singing turned to humming and then quiet, but for the rhythmic bobbing of the boat on the surf as they rowed along. Then Madge said, "You know you have a good man there, your Robbie."

"Indeed," said Andrew, and he turned and nodded toward Ann.

"I know as well," Ann responded. "Perhaps I take him too much for granted, though."

"You shouldn't, love," said Madge. "Not every lass has such a lad."

Ann remembered a bit of Shakespeare she had learned by heart, and pulled it up from her teaching days to recite to the rhythm of the oars in the waves:

---

1. Carolina Oliphant, "Bonnie Charlie," in Tomlyn, *Scottish Songs*, 88.

It was a lover and his lass,
With a hey, and a ho, and a hey nonino,
That o'er the green corn-field did pass,
In spring time, the only pretty ring time,
When birds do sing, hey ding a ding, ding:
Sweet lovers love the spring.[2]

That night Ann went to sleep in her childhood bed, tired yet exhilarated from the journey and then the hours of jovial camaraderie that reigned late into the night at the Mail cottage. Ann's mother had placed daffodils in her room. And she had draped over the bed a new shawl knit of fine white wool for Ann and a small blanket of the same wool for the new bairn that would soon be born.

In her familiar bedroom, Ann prayed . . .

> Dear God, here I am again, at home with Mother and Father, still a child in many ways. I remember when I was young, reading here in bed with no cares at all. And now, it seems, I carry heavy burdens. My weighty belly sinks into the mattress, reminding me of the last time I slept here with child, and I worry how I shall ever be a good mother and wife. Take the weight of my sadness from me, O God, and my guilt, as well. Forgive me for not taking better care of Jamie. Teach me to watch over my next child with more care.
>
> Thank you for Robert and his trust that I will be able to be the mother I want to be. I love him, O God; may he know that. And thank you for Madge and Andrew. May they take Robert's fish to market for a good price. Keep Robbie strong as he tends to Violet and the sheep—and Sheltie. God bless them all—and Jamie too. Keep him in your eternal care. And now help me to sleep and wake refreshed. Amen.

In the morning Ann slept in, but the sunlight shone into her bedroom window, and the smells of her mother's cooking wafted through the house and roused her from her bed. She found her mam alone in the

---

2. Shakespeare, *As You Like It*, 5.3.18–23.

kitchen baking bannocks for the midday meal. As their eyes met, Ann realized how much she had missed her.

"I'm pleased to see you have your appetite, Annie," she said as she served her daughter a second helping of porridge with dried rowanberries and sugar. "You are eating for two, lass. 'Tis a good sign."

"And 'tis good to be hungry again. I get tired of my own cooking, and I haven't had much interest in eating anyway."

Her mother stirred sugar and milk into her tea. "Tell me, darling, how are you feeling?"

"Better, some better, Mam." Tears formed in the corners of her eyes. "'Tis still lonely, though, and I fight with the memory."

"Is it still the picture of Jamie when he had burned?"

She nodded.

"Tell me again, and perhaps we can pray this image away. What is it that frightens you so?"

Ann let the tears flow. Her mother poured her a cup of tea and sat quietly across from her at the table by the hearth. She nodded with encouragement when her daughter looked up.

"'Tis always the same. When I look at the peat fire, or even when I think of it if I am outside or in bed at night, I see the black corpse." Ann wept as she put the memory into words. She held out her arms, as if holding the weight of a log. "'Tis charred like a piece of burned driftwood." She choked with a sob. "He was my bairn!"

"Oh, Annie, dear Annie," Ann's mother spoke tenderly. "Aye, he was your beautiful laddie. He was playful and so sweet." She paused, and Ann knew her mother would wait patiently. "How can we remember him another way?" They sat together in silence for some minutes. Ann drank her tea and leaned back in the chair to shift her weight and ease her posture. "What else is black like the log you see?" her mother asked. "What about a cloud of smoke? Could you change the picture to become a cloud of smoke?" She sketched a picture of the smoke with her fingers in front of her, the size of a log but wispy and dissipating. "And then, could you imagine that cloud lifting from the hearth into the sky?" She raised her hands as if the smoke drifted up and out the chimney. She hesitated until she saw that Ann seemed open to this image. "You know, clouds always move across the sky. They blow away, and if they come back, they are never the same."

Ann stood up and crossed the room to look out the window. She looked far off into the gray sky and watched the clouds move as they crossed over the farmland that bordered her parents' home. The picture out the window and above her in the sky kept moving. First gray, then gray and white, and then for a moment a patch of blue dared to appear, and then silver sliced the sky in two. Could she lift this persistent darkness and make it drift away?

Ann looked back at her mother who sat with hands folded. Her eyes were shut, and tears were streaming down her cheeks. Her mother's lips moved silently. Ann returned to her chair, and her mother took Ann's hand in hers and began to pray aloud: "Dear God, receive Annie's sadness and transform it. Take the picture of Jamie's charred body and change it with your healing power. Lift it into a puff of smoke and send it out into the heavens each time this image seizes Annie in grief. Let the vision not be fixed. Move it, O God, and distribute it as moving air in the sky. Though Jamie is dead, bring Annie back to life. We pray to you, for you are the one who can do all things." She sighed, and then when there was nothing more to say, she ended with "Amen." Quiet settled peacefully upon mother and daughter like warm air that blankets a crofter when coming in from the cold.

The women stood and embraced. Ann's enlarged stomach protruded between them, and they chuckled in unison. Her bairn decided just then to stretch, and both felt the clumsy push of an arm or a leg, and they laughed and kissed one another. "I think this one would do somersaults if it still had room to move about," Ann declared with a smile.

As her mother looked down at the low bulge of her baby, Ann wondered whether she had been wise to come to Lerwick so close to her time.

❧ ☙

Nearing the end of her stay with her parents, Ann was restless to see Robert again. She had woven a new blanket and knit several baby jumpers, some to sell and one to keep. On the last evening she went to bed early to get a good night's sleep before the ride home in Madge's boat.

Well into the night, Ann woke up with a pain gripping her middle. It passed, and another came, and then she knew the bairn was coming. She waited before calling for her mother, wishing not to worry her too soon. But after an hour, the contractions came rapidly one after the other, each one stronger than the previous. She got up and, in the darkness, felt her way down the hall and knocked on her parents' door. Ann's mother got up, sensing what might be happening. She quickly put on her shoes and coat, lit a lamp, and walked outside down the lane to fetch the neighborhood midwife. Ann went back to bed, arranging pillows to find a comfortable position. She tried to fall asleep, knowing that she would need every possible bit of rest before her labor began in earnest.

This time her water did not break for several hours. Daylight crept into Ann's bedroom to find Ann on her hands and knees with the midwife by her side assuring her through a hard contraction. At first the boys refused to leave for school knowing a niece or nephew would soon be born, but Ann's mother shooed them out the door. Reluctantly Mary too left for school, wishing she could witness the birth. Ann thought about Robert. If only he were here. Perhaps she should not have come to Lerwick after all. But the labor pains made Ann focus again on her breathing. The midwife massaged Ann's lower back and checked her readiness to push.

Ann's mother collected the blankets they had made for the bairn and brought clean sheets and a basin of hot water into the bedroom. She held Ann's arm as the women turned her onto her back and bent her knees. Wiping perspiration from her forehead, the midwife spoke words of encouragement, "'Twon't be long now, darling. You are doing just fine."

But the minutes turned to hours, and the baby did not enter the birth canal. The midwife whispered to Ann's mother something about turning the bairn, and Ann's mood plummeted. If only she could sink into weary oblivion, but the pains kept her mercilessly awake. Ann lost all track of time. Then the midwife spoke firmly, "We must push this peerie one into place," and she pressed on her belly with both hands. Ann let out a sudden scream as the baby moved at last into head-down position. The midwife had Ann then turn onto her elbows and knees. Finally, when she thought she could endure no more, she pushed with all her might, and a tiny little girl came into the world. The bairn was blue at first from the long labor, but after her first gulps of air she wailed and turned a healthy pink.

Just as the midwife and Ann's mother were wrapping the baby and handing her to her tired mother, Madge appeared at the bedroom door. She had delivered milk and vegetables, as well as Robert's fish, to the Lerwick market, and was stopping by the Mail cottage to take Annie home to Exnaboe by return boat. Surprised to see the baby already, Madge kissed Ann and smiled. "Well, I suppose you'll be staying a few days now. I'll tell

Robert he has a sweet little lassie. He'll be so proud." Before leaving for the dock, she added affectionately, "Blessings to you, Annie. Now you rest."

☙ ❧

Robert's mother Ross walked from Scalloway to Lerwick to see her new granddaughter when she heard the news. She had quickly knit her a new pink blanket. Ann wrapped the child in the soft wool with only her little round face peeking out. Both grandmothers fussed over the bairn as she slept beside her mother. They declared her to be tiny, like a rose bud, and Ross suggested, "You might call her Rose." It was close to Ross, and Ann and her mother exchanged smiles.

"But Robert hasn't even had a chance to meet his daughter yet," Ann said to her mother-in-law. "Surely her daa must agree on a name."

A day later Robert burst into Ann's room where she was sitting comfortably nursing the bairn. "Oh, Annie, I came as fast as I could!"

"Robbie, dear, how we've missed you!" Robert kissed her and touched the cheek of the tiny girl she held to her breast. Ann felt a surge of love travel through her body from her breast through her body as she gazed from father to daughter.

Robert drew a second chair close and put his arm around his wife. "Now I am outnumbered—two women to only one man." Both parents thought instantly of Jamie, and their eyes met, wide with awareness and punctuated with silent longing. A tear slipped from Ann's lashes, and Robert bent to kiss her moist cheek.

When the bairn had satisfied her hunger, Ann unwrapped her and gave her to her father to hold and admire. He touched her tiny toes and stroked her soft head. "She'll be a brunette like her bonnie mam."

"And perhaps with my green eyes, as well, what do you think?"

"'Tis the Viking in her! Oh, she'll be a feisty beauty. And so tiny!" He touched her little fingers and spoke softly to the bairn, "Such a peerie one, you couldn't wait a bit longer and grow bigger, now, could you?"

"No, she wanted to be a Lerwick lass, close to her grandmothers and her grandfather." She looked at Robert tenderly, as they both remembered the other family member gone, his father, missing out on the birth of his first granddaughter. She laid her hand on his leg as they both thought of James, and Robert's smile slipped away for just a moment.

"How Daa would like to be here now." He rocked his daughter side to side on his chest and hummed a melody Ann recognized as a fiddle tune his father had played.

"Your mother was here yesterday, and she begged us to come to Scalloway before we head back south. She's wanting us to have the bairn christened at the Methodist chapel there. What do you say? A real baptism would please my parents too." She looked at Robert to read his expression and hear his reply.

Robert gave the baby back to Ann who swaddled her snugly in her blanket and settled her on the bed to sleep. "Yes, baptism would be proper, and 'twould be good to have a blessing for this tiny one." Then he took Ann into his arms and kissed her face and neck. "Oh, Annie, I've been lonely without you." He held her body close to his. "I want to be home again with you—and the bairn."

Ann warmed in the embrace and then drew back to search his face. "While we are here, shall we then go to your mother's for a day or two? 'Twill make her happy, and if we have the peerie one baptized, my family will want to come too."

"Yes, I told the laird of the bairn's birth, so I can be gone a bit more from fishing. He's sending his steward to milk Violet and give Sheltie food. 'Tis generous of him." Robert looked out the window. "The sheep will fend for themselves now that the pasture is green and wet, and they can scavenge in the heather too."

"This summer we'll need the money you can make on the sixareen. I don't look forward to your being gone for days at a time again, yet we'll manage, this tiny one and I." She looked over at the infant sleeping peacefully. "What shall we call her, Robbie? Your mother wants 'Rose.'"

"How about Tina, tiny Tina?"

"Hmm. Tina, for Christina? or Valentina? or Clementina! . . . That's it!"

The doctor called on Ann that day at the Mail cottage to examine the mother and child. He declared them both in fine health and admonished Ann to get ample rest and drink plenty milk and spring water.

Robert joined Ann in her bed that night. They held each other tenderly and fell asleep in one another's arms.

In the early morning, Ann prayed . . .

> Dear God, what pleasure I feel this day! I have Robert on one
> side of me and Tina on the other. In the night I worried she
> would roll off the bed, so I didn't sleep soundly until I put her
> between us. There I knew she was safe and warm. Now she is fed
> and back on my left so that Robbie can sleep. Thank you, God,
> for giving us this precious bairn. I only ask that you keep her
> well all her years. Hold the three of us in the palm of your hand,
> I pray. Amen.

The neighbors in Scalloway brought their horse-drawn cart the next
day to carry the little family to Scalloway to stay with the Leslies. A
Methodist minister of the English missionary society was in town,
staying with a neighbor. The Leslies invited him to supper to discuss
baptism for little Tina.

"'Tisn't necessary to baptize an infant so early, you know," the
preacher said. "The Catholics are worried about the babe's soul, but we
Wesleyan Methodists believe she is already a child of God, born sweet
and pure. Baptism for us is a sign of God's grace and the gift of salvation
for all without merit."

Robert replied to the cleric, "I do so also believe. But we would ask
you to baptize the bairn now while we are here in Scalloway, where the
grandparents can come, and while you are here, an ordained minister, to
administer the sacrament." Robert looked at Ann for support.

"We have only lay preachers in Dunrossness, where we live to the
south," Ann clarified.

"Well, yes, I see. So, we shall baptize her tomorrow then after the
evening vesper service and hymn sing. Will that give you time to collect
the family?"

"Yes, thank you, Reverend."

Ross had sewn a christening dress and bonnet for Tina. She said
she would invite both families for a supper the next day before going to
chapel. She would serve fried haddock, eggs, cabbage, taaties, and oatcakes. Once agreed, she then set about assigning tasks to her children:
fishing, sweeping, shopping, and cooking. Ann and Robert would stay
in the Leslie cottage, and she would ask her neighbor to take in the Mail
family for the night, as it would be too late to go back to Lerwick after the

baptism. And besides, Ross said she would like to invite her guests back to the house for spice cake and tea at the end of the evening.

Ann was grateful for Ross's kindness in including her side of the family in the celebration. Indeed, she felt like she belonged now to Robert's kin. Though this was the first night she would sleep at the Leslie home, everyone treated her as if she were a sister. She smiled at the bairn in her arms and then at the family gathered around. How welcome little Clementina was! Ann could believe with confidence that God's blessings were showering down upon her, so naturally, as if a gentle spring rain were nourishing the fields.

The hymn sing ended with a lovely church song Ann had never heard before. It was one of Charles Wesley's with words that spoke to her of comfort. She listened to the gathered congregation sing in harmony the lilting tune:

> Thou hidden source of calm repose, thou all sufficient love divine,
> my help and refuge from my foes, secure I am if thou art mine;
> and lo! from sin and grief and shame I hide me, Jesus, in thy name.
>
> Jesus, my all in all thou art, my rest in toil, my ease in pain,
> the healing of my broken heart, in war my peace, in loss my gain,
> my smile beneath the tyrant's frown, in shame my glory and my crown.[3]

The minister then invited the Leslie and Mail families to the baptismal font at the front of the chapel. Most of the families with children left for home to put their little ones down for bed. A small remaining group moved forward to the vacant seats near the minister. Ann could tell that Robert recognized the neighbors and friends he and Stewart had grown up with because he smiled and nodded to them as they settled themselves. Ann looked tenderly at her husband and reflected on how comforting it was to be part of a community that cared about their newborn child. He put his arm around her as she held Tina in her christening gown, sleeping peacefully as the minister spoke the words of the Gospel according to Saint Mark:

> They brought young children to [Jesus], that he should touch them: and his disciples rebuked those that brought them. But when Jesus saw it, he was much displeased, and said unto them, "Suffer the little children to come unto me, and forbid them not:

3. Charles Wesley, "Thou Hidden Source of Calm Repose," #153, in *United Methodist Hymnal.*

for as such is the kingdom of God. Verily I say unto you, Who-
soever shall not receive the kingdom of God as a little child, he
shall not enter therein." And he took them up in his arms, put
his hand upon them, and blessed them.[4]

The minister took Tina from Ann, and she untied the bairn's bonnet
as he held her. Tina stirred, opened her eyes for a moment, and fell back
to sleep on the preacher's chest. He then said the words everyone was
waiting for:

"What name is given this child?"

Robert said, "Clementina Helen."

The minister continued, dipping his hand into the font and pouring
three handfuls of water onto her head, "Clementina Helen, I baptize thee,
in the name of the Father, and of the Son, and of the Holy Ghost, amen."
Ann smiled as Tina's head—all dripping wet—flopped to the minister's
shoulder and with her little mouth wide open let out a great howl to be
heard at the back of the chapel. The minister gently bounced the child and
continued over her cries: "Seeing now, dearly beloved brethren, that Clementina is grafted into the body of Christ's Church, let us give thanks unto
Almighty God for these benefits, and with one accord make our prayers
unto him, that she may lead the rest of her life according to this beginning."

Robert reached for Tina and suppressed a chuckle during the Lord's
Prayer, as Ann dried the baby's head with a handkerchief and then took
the child back into her arms. She exchanged looks with Robert, and
neither could refrain from smiling when they reflected on the minister's
words, "according to this beginning." It was perhaps not an auspicious
beginning, should Ann hope for a placid child. But she smiled with pride
that Tina had already found her own voice even at such a tender age. She
would be tiny, but strong in spirit and in conviction.

In the darkness in the bedroom at the Leslies', as she fed her bairn after
the service, Ann prayed . . .

Dear God, how filled with love I am tonight. Thank you for Tina
and her baptism. Bless our families and the Scalloway neighbors. Keep Tina safe all her days. Amen.

4. Mark 10:13–16.

Even after praying, Ann's mind raced, such that she could not sleep although the day had passed exactly as she had wished, and Tina now slept peacefully between her and Robert. Though all was well, the room was unfamiliar. The bed was hard. In the dark she thought about Jamie. He had never been baptized. Was she at fault for not bringing him to Lerwick for baptism by a clergyman? She did feel comfort from the hymn they sang at the chapel: indeed, Jesus was "a source of calm repose," and she wanted to remember that. Exactly what that meant, though, she wondered. Who was Jesus anyway; that is, who was he now in her life? Was there a difference between saying that Jesus was a comfort and God was a comfort? She tucked this question away to ask Madge sometime when they were alone together. And then, checking that Tina was not too crowded in the middle of the bed, she finally drifted off to sleep.

On their way along the homeward path to Exnaboe the next day, Ann held Tina in the back of the Leslies' cart while Robert and his brother Stewart drove the old family horse. Ann could hear the men sing island airs as they jolted over the bumps on the way. Stewart seemed especially happy, and Ann wondered if perhaps he had a lassie. Being near a newborn bairn might make him think of starting a family of his own. Ann only wished he lived closer to them, so that the brothers could sing together more often, and that there might be cousins close in age. It would be pleasing to be home again in their crofthouse at the Boe, and perhaps Stewart would spend the night before returning north. As she nursed her daughter, Ann detected in herself a new awareness of peace and contentment, more profound than she had known since she was married. When she peered out the covered cart, she noted the bright sun high in the sky and concluded that indeed life was good. Though the sun would set beyond the horizon and night would fall as they arrived home, without a doubt, the sun would rise again to usher in the light of a new day. The simple recognition of the rhythm of day and night elicited a sense of calm and assurance. Life ebbed and flowed with the constancy of the tide, and despite storms, the goodness of nature prevailed: the sky, the sea, and the land. The cart bounced along, and when Tina fell asleep, Ann easily drifted off into a gentle slumber also.

That evening after they had unpacked and seen to their evening chores of fetching water and feeding the animals, Ann tucked Tina into the box bed she and Robert shared in the ben end, and Robert built a peat fire in the but. Ann made tea: just soda bread from Scalloway, cold salt fish, and kirn-milk. The food satisfied their hunger after a long traveling day. Robert pushed back from the table after supper and sat with his arm around Ann sitting next to him. Stewart stretched out on the floor by the fire. Ann was pleased that he seemed to appreciate their cozy cottage where he could witness their contentment as a couple.

Robert stood up from the table and cleared away the plates. "Annie, I have a surprise for you. While you were in Lerwick and before I knew Tina was being born, I picked up Father's fiddle. I found I had remembered more than I thought." He took the violin out of its case and tightened the bow. Holding the fiddle with his chin, he played the open strings and tuned them as best he could by ear. "Listen." Then, with Ann and Stewart watching closely, he commenced a tune the brothers remembered their father playing. He stopped and started once or twice but then caught the beat and played through the reel as smoothly as if a set of dancers were giving "four hands round and back again." After he played the tune several times through, he finished with a final long note, and Stewart and Ann clapped as he tucked the fiddle under his arm and bowed with a laugh. "I had forgotten what fun 'tis to play!"

Next, he began a waltz that his father had played at their wedding. "Oh Robbie, how lovely!" Annie exclaimed. And recalling how she and Robert had danced as bride and groom, she asked her brother-in-law, "Stewart, do you have a lassie?"

Stewart blushed and said, "Yes, Ann, I do indeed. And, after I propose, if she says yes, I hope Robert will play at my wedding."

☙ ❧

Ann and Robert settled into a pattern, Ann at the croft and Robert usually on the water. At bedtime, Ann knelt beside her tiny girl asleep in her box bed and prayed . . .

> Dear God, 'tis hard to believe, but I am actually smiling. I had thought the web of my life had ripped apart when Jamie died here in our cottage. In fact, it had. It was torn to bits, and I was hurting. But now you have me weaving a new web, like a busy spider at work. You have helped me begin again, dear God. You are the Maker, and out of tragedy and loss you are making my life complete once more. You have given us Tina, and we have

our families, and now, of all things, there is music in the croft-house! Thank you! With these blessings, I feel new strength. 'Tis the power of love that mends the broken heart. You and Robert have helped me find the resilience I never dreamed I had. Thank you, and continue to bless us all, dear God. Amen.

Ann's days revolved around nursing Tina and milking Violet, feeding the sheep, and cooking for Robert. Just keeping everyone fed took all her effort. Some days she dragged through the hours like heavy boots in the sludge on the beach after a storm. Dreary gray often obscured the horizon, as the sea, the hills, and the rain merged into one. Ann's chief concern was her bairn, as Tina was often sickly, and though the thought was irrational, Ann feared she would lose her.

One day when Robert had been gone for several nights, Tina developed a fever. Ann walked her and rocked her but could not make her comfortable. When Tina cried, Ann fretted. The bairn's fever would not break, and Ann felt helpless and inadequate as a mother. She sat and hovered by the hearth, holding the fussy child on a cold afternoon, unsure just what to try. Should she wrap the child in more blankets because the air temperature was cool, or should she unwrap the child because her little body was so hot? Exhausted from worry and lack of sleep, Ann drifted into a stupor. Her eyes fixated on the peat fire, and then she stared beyond the red coals into the depths of her memory. The old image returned: there was Jamie again, burned like a charred piece of driftwood. Ann started to cry. She thought she had rid herself of that apparition. But there she pictured it again dominating her vision and building once again a burgeoning dread in her gut. Just then tiny Tina awakened, stretched her arms wide, and opened her eyes. Ann looked into her little face and, by surprise, discovered a naïve but true wisdom. And then she remembered her mother's advice. What was it? She just needed to reimagine the vision. With one hand she held Tina to her chest, and with the other hand she covered her eyes and willed the image in her mind to change. The blackened log softened and became transparent. A billow of smoke rose from the hearth and floated gently up and out into the sky. High above her, it dissipated into the clouds that chased each other across the horizon until they were gone, completely gone. Ann took her hand from her face and wiped her tears on the blanket that had slipped off Tina.

She stood up with her little girl, stripped her, and bathed her in a basin of lukewarm water. Tina's flesh cooled, and she smiled up at her mother. Then Ann patted her dry, dressed her in a fresh nightdress, and laid her in the box bed in the ben end. As Ann stepped outside to milk Violet and bring the sheep into the croo, she breathed in the cold evening air. Perhaps they would have a few sunny days. And Robert would be back at the croft before too long. Sheltie trotted into the cottage with her and settled himself by the warm hearth.

She sat, petting the sheepdog, and prayed silently . . .

> Dear God, make Tina well. Teach me how to care for her. Chase the demons away. I know I can do what I need to do; I just need you by my side, along with Sheltie. Bring Robbie home to me safely, and keep us all in your care. Amen.

5

Learning

"Now, TINA, MAKE YOUR letters properly, while the sun is still up, and you can see the page before you," Ann admonished her six-year-old daughter, who sat by the fire at the same wooden table where the family took their meals.

"Yes, Mam, I am writing all the names in the family: Mother, Father, Clementina, and James. How do you spell James, Mam?" She raised her eyebrows, so determined to be accurate.

Ann bounced little two-year-old James on her lap. "Why, J-a-m-e-s, like the brother of Jesus."

"I thought James was named after our brother Jamie, who died." She looked up at her mam, her young brow furrowed with questions.

"True, you remember correctly, darling." Ann returned her daughter's earnest expression.

"And Jamie was named after Grandfather, who was also called James," Tina added proudly for remembering.

She nodded. "Yes, again. 'Tis true indeed."

Ann leaned forward eagerly. "Did Jesus have a sister named Clementina?"

"Well, that's a good question. I dare say I don't know. The Bible doesn't tell us about the sisters."

"Well, why am I called Tina, then?"

"'Tis because when you were born you were so tiny."

"I don't want to be tiny."

"Well, Clementina means merciful, so that's what you are then."

"What is merciful?"

"It means loving and forgiving, like a good Christian." She smiled at her daughter whose intent eyes searched for more explanation.

"And have I no middle name, Mam?"

"Aye, but you do," she nodded. "You were baptized Clementina Helen, for Saint Helena born on your birthday, the twenty-first of May."

"Who was she? Was she Jesus's sister?"

"No, I'm afraid not, sweetheart. But she was the mother of Constantine, the emperor who brought the Romans to Christ."

"Did they go to the manger to see him?"

Ann chuckled. "No, darling. He was already grown and dead and gone to heaven."

"So how could they go to him?"

Patiently, Ann explained, "It means they believed in him, that he was God's Son sent to earth to teach us how to be good people."

"Mam, who were the Romans?"

"My, you have questions today! Such a big girl you have grown to be!" Ann put James down, who toddled over to pat Sheltie curled up by the fire. She turned back to Tina. "Well, the Romans were the ones who lived in the Holy Land and brought the gospel all the way to our islands."

"Was the gospel in the Bible then?"

"Yes, the story of the good news of Jesus Christ was written down for us by the evangelists, Matthew, Mark, Luke, and John, during the first century."

"I thought the Romans were the bad people who killed Jesus."

"Well, I suppose some of the Romans were bad people, when they crucified our Lord, but later—many years later—they changed their minds about Jesus and started to follow him."

"Was he dead then?"

"Yes, Tina, he was. 'Tisn't easy to understand, is it now?" She sat down beside her daughter and wrote with neat penmanship for Tina to read back to her. "Here, watch me write these words as I say them: Jesus was born in a byre. His parents were Mary and Joseph. They prayed to God and gave thanks for the bairn. Jesus grew up to be a strong lad. He loved to read the Bible and go to temple."

"What is temple, Mam?"

"'Tis like a kirk."

"I would like to go to a kirk, but we just have a chapel here."

"Yes, Tina. But we can worship God wherever we are, you know. We don't need a fancy building." She wrote on: "When he was grown up, he told people about God's love. But the Romans were the landowners then, and they were not always good to the Jewish people."

"Like our laird, Mam?"

"Well, yes, in some ways." She went on writing and speaking out loud: "Jesus became a threat to their power, and they put him to death on a cross. His followers buried him in a grave, and God took him up to heaven, where he still lives today."

"Does he live in a crofthouse, like we do, Mam?"

"I don't think it looks quite like this with an earthen floor and a thatch roof, but maybe." She gave Tina a pat on her back. "Now you read this back to me."

Tina tucked her feet under her and began. She stumbled over the word Jewish, and Ann added parenthetically, "You know, Jesus was Jewish. The Jewish people believed in our God—they still do. All the people in the Old Testament of our Bible were Jews: Abraham, Moses, Elijah—Esther and Naomi too. They were good people."

"Do we know any Jewish people, Mam?"

"Well, no, not here in Shetland. But there are Jews in Edinburgh and London."

"Are they good people?" There was so much she didn't know.

"Why, certainly, they are good people, created in God's image. But they do not believe that Jesus is their Savior, as we do." When Tina finished reading, Ann asked her to copy the story and learn to spell all the words. While she worked at making her letters neatly, Ann washed and chopped vegetables for soup. Looking out the window to the rise in the path where Robert would soon be appearing, she silently hoped her husband would bring home a fish to add flavor and nourishment to their meal. She was pleased they would be together tonight—all four of them—since Robert had been out in the sixareen for the last three nights. The children missed their daa. Ann knew how Tina loved to sit on her father's lap as he read from the family Bible for their devotions after tea. For tonight, Ann chose the Gospel of Luke, chapter 19, verses 1–10, about Zacchaeus and marked it with a piece of straw. She left Tina to her writing and took James and Sheltie out to milk Violet before the sun disappeared on the western horizon.

❧   ❧

Ann hummed one of Robert's fiddle tunes while she added chunks of sea trout to the broth. In the bedroom, Robert changed his heavy, wet clothes and washed for tea. As he joined the family, he said, "We started net fishing at the haaf this week, though 'tis still so cold. The salmon and trout are jumping, and we brought back quite a decent catch."

"Robbie, you must be exhausted. Net fishing is the hardest, my father always said." She wiped her hands and took his hands in hers by the fire. "Were you numb out there in this cold?"

"Yes, I'm glad to be home. 'Tis not only cold but lonely out on the water, and I worry for your well-being here." Ann glanced at two-year-old James eating his supper with his fingers. He was the same age as Jamie when he died. Was Robert anxious about James? She didn't know what he was thinking. But she hesitated to ask him to voice his thoughts right then at the table when he was tired and hungry. Sometimes it brought the spirit of their home down when she spoke of Jamie, like a lamp going out as the wick descended. She would talk to him later.

Robert ate his soup and oatcakes eagerly without further conversation, while Ann attended to the children and the dishes.

"Have you energy to read tonight, Robbie? Tina can follow along quite well if she sits with you and looks on."

"Come, tiny one." Tina climbed into her father's lap. He found the passage and began:

"And Jesus entered and passed through Jericho."

"Where's Jericho, Daa?"

"'Tis a town I think not far from Jerusalem."

"Where Jesus died, Daa?"

"Yes, that's right." He turned to Ann. "She's been learning with her mam, I can see."

Ann smiled and motioned for him to continue, as she lit the lamp for him to read by, and then put James down to bed. Finally, she sat beside her husband with a sigh, her body tired from the effort of the day and from carrying yet another child in her belly. She picked up her knitting and listened.

"And, behold, there was a man named Zacchaeus, which was the chief among the publicans, and he was rich."

"Who were the publicans, Daa?"

"Well, they were the men who collected taxes for the Romans."

"Were they bad?"

"'Tis not so simple as bad and good, peerie one. This lesson shows us that, you'll see." He finished to the end with verses 9 and 10: "And Jesus said unto him, 'This day is salvation come to this house, forsomuch as he also is a son of Abraham. For the Son of man is come to seek and to save that which was lost.'"

"Abraham was a Jew, Daa." Tina announced with pride to have remembered what her mother had told her earlier that day.

"Why, of course, they all were Jews—Jesus too."

"But what about the Romans, Daa? Were they Jewish?"

"No, honey, Zacchaeus was a Jew working for the Romans, collecting money, and keeping some for himself likely. But he changed and then promised to give half of his possessions back to the poor people."

"Why were they poor, Daa?"

"My, she has questions!" Robert smiled at Ann as she put down her wool and reached to rub his shoulder blades. He sighed and placed the Bible in his lap. "Well, love, first of all, being poor is not a bad thing. We are poor. We have no land of our own. We must fish and raise sheep for the laird to stay here in this crofthouse."

"Why is the laird not poor as well?" There was so much she wanted to understand.

"Well now, that is a hard question. Some people have power over others. 'Tisn't the way Jesus taught, but 'tis the way it seems to be. The Romans had power over the Jews. And the laird has power over us."

Tina pointed to the Bible passage and to the word salvation just above where Robert had left the piece of straw to mark where he had stopped reading. "What is this word, Daa?"

"Salvation, it means to be saved by God, to be found and not to be lost."

"Who was lost, Daa?"

"Well, Zacchaeus was lost because he was greedy and not living by God's teaching to love his neighbor."

"Are we lost, Daa?" She glanced toward her mother.

"No, we have the love of Jesus and enough to eat. We are not lost." Ann added, "Tina, dear, you know that God loves you, don't you, lassie?" Tina nodded, and Ann finished her thought. "So, 'this day is salvation come to this house.'"[1] She smiled and then added, "And 'tis time for bed."

---

1. Luke 19:1–2, 9–10.

They sang together a stanza of a new hymn they had learned at their class meeting, "Praise, My Soul, the King of Heaven."

> Father-like He tends and spares us;
> Well our feeble frame He knows.
> In His hands He gently bears us,
> Rescues us from all our foes.
> Praise Him! Praise Him!
> Widely as His mercy flows.[2]

Ann tucked Tina into her box bed after James had settled. "Goodnight, Clementina Helen. You know, Helena is also a Scandinavian name from our Norse ancestors."

"Norse?"

"Yes, the ancient people of Norway across the water were called Norse. They are also part of your heritage."

Tina's eyelids had dropped.

Ann prepared for bed and started her ritual of praying . . .

> Dear God, thank you for Tina and all her questions! And for Robert and his patience even when he is so tired. Keep us safe from all perils of life here in the Ness: the storms at sea, the poor soil on this rocky point of land, and all manner of illness and accident. Rescue us from these our foes, O God. Give us our daily fish and grain to strengthen our bodies to do your will. And send your mercy down upon us like the rain that never ceases. Make us worthy of your steadfast care. Bless us all and especially the peerie one yet to be born. Amen.

SPRINGTIME 1840

Robert pulled a chair close to Ann's by the fire one evening. "After the crops are in, Annie, I should like to go to Sumburgh to learn some new fiddle tunes. Andrew says there is a man there called Jacob who is a fine fiddler. He is getting on in years and wants to make sure the local tunes are passed."

2. Henry Francis Lyte, "Praise, My Soul, the King of Heaven," #66 in *United Methodist Hymnal*.

Ann's eyes twinkled as she looked up from her knitting and pictured Robert playing his father's fiddle. Then her brow creased as she contemplated his leaving again when he was already gone so much. With Tina, James, and now peerie Mary not even yet one, she had her hands full.

"Surely, we can make time for you to play fiddle. And perhaps the pleasure of music will help you through your other tasks." She looked up into his eyes. "I'll manage with the children when you go to Sumburgh; you needn't worry." Ann remembered how Robert had built the chapel at Durigarth and how it had taken him away from the family. The long evenings had offered him the daylight he needed to get the task done. He had carried the stones he dug by wheelbarrow along the pony trail toward Quendale. Each trip took an hour going and again coming, after all day fishing on the sea. At times Ann had resented his choice to make the chapel a priority. In this case, she knew how much amusement the fiddle brought Robert. She had her books, and he had his music. It was only fair. Life must be more than drudgery.

As soon as the ground was soft, Robert tilled the soil of their croft. Then he planted barley for their bannocks and oats for the animals, and Ann put in taaties, cabbages, and turnips for the household. The family eagerly awaited a summer harvest, for they had consumed most of what they had stored over the cold months. Fortunately, they had milk and fish, as well as a bit of cash when they sold Ann's hand-knit shawls to purchase meal and sometimes tea and sugar. Ann drank spring water from behind the cottage, and well water they carried from the community well, to keep her milk flowing, so that Mary could continue to nurse beyond one year. That way she could give Violet's milk to the rest of the family. They eked out a frugal existence, and Ann felt a measure of pride in their ability to make do.

After the crops were sown in the still-cold spring ground, Robert cut the peats from the bog on the hill behind their croft and set them to dry for the coming months' fuel. They had lived at the Boe already ten years, and Ann had learned how many peats they needed to bring into the byre each spring. The work was wet and tiring, but like all chores of a crofter, it had to be done. Ann took over all the other daily jobs when Robert cut the peats. There simply was no question about it; they would manage from day to day with God as their guide. When the peats were finally cut, Robert said he would spend an evening in Sumburgh each week after three days of fishing on the sixareen, to play his fiddle and learn the tunes of South Mainland.

Ann came to accept her life, bound fast to the croft and her bairns. One afternoon when the rains had stopped, she dressed the children warmly and took them to the tip of the island, to the outcrop overlooking the ocean. She held Mary wrapped in her shawl. Tina held James by the hand, and they walked along the voe and over the fields to the rocky cliffs of Sumburgh Head. Tina stopped to pick yellow mayflowers on the hill ground, and James pointed to the puffins they could spot on the crags that fell off steeply to the sea.

"Shall we sit here and rest?" Ann suggested. "'Tis a beautiful day that God has given us." She took out the Bible from the sling she wore over her shoulder, where she also carried water, brönnies, and a clean nappy for her bairn. She opened the Bible to Matthew, chapter 6, and read, skipping some parts of the longer sentences:

> No man can serve two masters: for either he will hate the one, and love the other; or else he will hold to the one, and despise the other. Ye cannot serve God and mammon. Therefore I say unto you, take no thought for your life, what ye shall eat, or what ye shall drink. . . . Consider the lilies of the field, how they grow; they toil not, neither do they spin. . . . But seek ye first the kingdom of God, and his righteousness; and all these things shall be added unto you. Take therefore no thought for the morrow: for the morrow shall take thought for the things of itself.[3]

"Tina, how does this reading speak to you?" her mother asked as she put Mary to the breast.

"Well, Mam, it talks about two masters. Have we not just one master, the laird?"

"Well, 'tisn't the laird about whom Matthew speaks. 'Tis God and money; they'd be the two masters." She turned to Tina and spoke emphatically, "And we must only have God as our one Master; we mustn't worry about money, so says Jesus."

Without any cares at all, James considered the pebbles at his feet and happily arranged them in rows on the flat surface of the rock on which he sat.

"But we do worry about money, don't we, Mam?" asked Tina.

"Yes, we do, but we mustn't. You see, that is why we read the Bible: to correct our sinful ways."

"What is sinful about worrying, Mam?"

3. Matthew 6:24–25, 28, 33–34a.

"Well, love, it says here that God knows everything we need and will provide."

"Then why do we pray?"

"Hmm, 'tis a good question. We pray to talk to God to remember that God is always listening to our needs." She tousled James's hair and smiled at Tina, so grown up and able to think for herself.

Tina asked, "Do we have lilies in Shetland, Mam?"

"We do. We have water lilies in our lakes, but they may not be the same as Jesus knew. Here in Shetland our favorite flowers are primroses, bluebells, and purple thistle, and, of course, our greatest island treasure is heather, as we'll soon see blooming in summer."

"Why does Jesus talk about flowers, Mam?"

She looked into Tina's serious eyes with a smile on her lips. "I suppose he wants us to stop and see God's beauty all around us."

Tina pointed to the passage. "At the end, what does he mean about the kingdom of God?"

Ann smiled at her daughter and her wise questions. "That is the whole point, I believe, that we should make God our king, not anything or anyone else. And when we put God first, then all else will be well."

"Do you believe that, Mam?"

"Oh, yes, darling. I do."

Mary had fallen asleep nursing, and James was ready to move about, so they climbed down from their perch on the rocks, back over the heather to return home by the path. Tina and James skipped ahead. The kittiwakes flew about until they perched at their nests on the sea cliffs. Ann breathed deeply. The whispering breeze, the peaceful moments of respite, and the arresting message they had just read from the Bible completed her day. A sense of tranquility washed over her with the assurance that indeed all would be well. She too felt free and unencumbered, even like the fulmars casting off from the cliffs and soaring without a care on the sea winds.

❧ ❧

That night in bed Ann prayed . . .

> Dear God, you have kept us alive and fed through the cold months. Thank you for seeing to our needs. I pray for a good summer harvest now to replenish our pantry. Help me be patient with Robert when he tries to do too much. I pray for his

safety and his happiness. And thank you for Tina's mind and
her growing faith. God bless all three children: Tina, James, and
Mary. And in heaven, God bless Jamie, too. Oh, and help me to
remember the lilies of the field. Amen.

SUMMER 1840

Summer began with torrential rain. It poured unceasingly as if the Norse-
men who invaded Shetland long ago were unleashing an arsenal of evil
forces. The downpour dashed the crops and turned the field behind the
Leslie croft into a mucky pond. Just when the oats and barley needed sun
to dry their kernels for harvest, overcast days and dark deluge persisted.
The family garden lost its rows and became a dreadful lagoon of mud.
Ann tried to salvage the taaties, but at first she could not even find the
plants to lift out their edible tubers, and when she did, the taaties were
soggy and mostly rotten. Robert could not fish for the laird, as gale warn-
ings kept the sixareen tied to the shore. He went out each day at low tide
alone and dug for razor clams, to bring at least something home for the
family's tea. They needed their milk, so instead of taking it to market,
Ann made kirn-milk and sparingly cut off slices to substitute for fish for
their meager meals. She knit as many shawls as her hands could produce
before she dropped asleep each evening, and Robert took the woolen
goods to Madge to sell in Lerwick. Sometimes Ann's mother met Madge
and sent Ann butter or bread from her larder.

Class meetings with fellow Methodists on South Mainland sustained
Ann and Robert through that stormy summer. One evening, midweek
between Sabbaths, they bundled the children up and walked to Madge
and Andrew's through a pounding hail shower. Between storm clouds,
the sky still wore its golden summer gown, and they hoped that time with
friends would lift their spirits. Madge had just returned from Lerwick
with tea leaves and sugar, and the kettle was steaming on the hearth when
they arrived. Ann peeled off the children's coats and draped them on the
stone floor to dry. As Madge poured them sweetened tea and then added
milk to cool the children's portion, the family joined the others who had
begun to sing a Wesleyan hymn:

> And are we yet alive, and see each other's face?
> Glory and thanks to Jesus give for his almighty grace!
> What troubles have we seen, what mighty conflicts past,

Fightings without, and fears within, since we assembled last![4]

The words could not have been more apt. It was indeed a comfort to be together and to find both warmth from the inclement weather and solace from its disastrous effect on their economic plight.

Andrew prayed for all the crofters: "Almighty God, protect your people on these islands from the stormy blast. Save us from hunger, now that the taatie crop has failed. In your grace, grant us courage to face this calamity." He paused. "And, O Lord, give us respite from the rain! May sunshine dry up our gardens and fields and salvage something of our ardent toil. We trust your faithfulness, O God of wind and sea. Breathe on us salvation from the perils before us, and grant us peace. We pray in the name of Jesus, our hope in time of trial. Amen."

Ann's eyes filled with tears as she took in the solemnity of Andrew's prayer. The blight had destroyed all their taaties. Dire trepidation flowed from her nagging fear that famine could even take the children's lives in the weeks and months ahead. Then as the group began to sing another hymn, she realized she was not so much afraid of death as she was afraid of hunger. She remembered how she had confronted Jamie's death and that she had somehow eventually survived its grasp. Now she was among friends who faced a common catastrophe on the island: scarcity. No one had died of hunger; they were "yet alive." As neighbors, if only they could rally hope and stand together in their privation! With God on their side, perhaps they could prevail through the hunger pangs. Nothing could shake their faith in Jesus, yet would the bairns starve? She did not think she could watch that. Ann's tears flowed first out of fear, then out of love for her children, and then finally out of a renewed assurance of community in the promise of God's providence.

Robert read the Bible story of Jesus calming the storm from the Gospel of Mark:

> He arose, and rebuked the wind, and said unto the sea, "Peace, be still." And the wind ceased, and there was a great calm. And he said unto them, "Why are ye so fearful? How is it that ye have no faith?" And they feared exceedingly, and said one to another, "What manner of man is this, that even the wind and the sea obey him?"[5]

---

4. Charles Wesley, "And Are We Yet Alive," #553 in *United Methodist Hymnal.*

5. Mark 4:39–41.

A profound silence ensued from the reading. Perhaps, as Jesus said, there was truly no need to fear. After days of panic, tightness in Ann's chest released as she leaned back and rocked Mary in her arms. She searched the faces of those sitting with her. No one spoke. Calm had descended on the group. It was as if the whole room let out a restorative sigh. After some moments of silent reflection, one at a time, the families began to speak to one another as they put on their coats and prepared to leave.

"Please know that you can always come here, anyone who needs a warm meal," Madge offered. "We always have enough for a neighbor."

Andrew added, "Yes, we still have taaties from our winter crop."

Ann said, "I have shawls to sell, and with the money, I shall buy flour and bake bannocks to share. And your children are always welcome at my hearth for lessons when you must work in the fields, or scavenge at the shore, or even go up to Lerwick for supplies."

The older neighbors proposed to watch the children so that husbands and wives could mend nets and get a head start on their next chance to go out fishing. Some offered to spin so that others could knit. As the community learned to trust its members, hope sprouted up from the hardened soil and then grew tall, like the golden grain they so missed.

As they walked home, Ann carrying Mary in a front sling and Robert draping James over his shoulder, Tina ambled along beside her parents and turned to ask her father, "Why was everyone so quiet after you read the Scripture, Daa?"

"God's Holy Spirit had come upon us, just like on the boat when Jesus stilled the storm."

Ann looked at Robert, proud of his strong faith. "You must be right," she said. "But at first no one understood, just like the disciples who 'feared exceedingly.' Then after the quiet spell, we knew that Christ was with us and we needn't fear any longer." Ann smiled first at Robert and then at Tina and saw in their faces a newfound peace. The rain and hail had stopped, at least for the time being, and the air was fresh. The coastal hill ground had been washed clean and smelled of roseroot, thyme, and heather. Clouds paid their respects across the sky and then departed. As the family arrived home, the gloaming spoke a gentle benediction.

In the ben end, with her children sleeping safely in their box beds, Ann prayed before she dropped off for the night . . .

Dear God, you have stilled the storm, and now all is well. Thank you for our friends and for your Holy Spirit that has brought us peace even in these times of grave uncertainty. We turn to you for comfort and strength. Amen.

6

The Valley of the Shadow of Death

AUTUMN 1840

THE CROPS FAILED, AS everyone had feared. A dreadful famine engulfed Mainland. Animals and humans all became foragers. Tina learned to sneak up on the limpets at the beach and yank them off the rocks at low tide before the sea creatures felt the vibrations of her steps and clamped down for dear life. She collected whelks and winkles and proudly brought her mother a basket of the snails to boil.

"Look, Mam, I got some big ones today!"

"Yes, darling! Such a good fisher you are!" She boiled them, and Tina helped pick the tiny bites of flesh out of their shells for tea.

The sheep were accustomed to grazing, but Violet, who had previously been pampered with harvested barley or oats brought to her stall, had rarely had to go looking for her feed. Sadly, the winter grain was gone, and in the devastating floods, the summer fields had reaped nothing. Violet had to scavenge on the hill ground along with the sheep. "Out you go, Violet," Ann said. "Don't be thinking of roaming too far now." Thankfully, Sheltie could keep the animals herded together, and Violet knew to come home for milking.

Times were lean. The family had nothing but milk for breakfast, so Robert sold a ram to buy oats for their gruel. Ann could almost taste the mutton stew they would never be able to afford. That afternoon when

Robert came into the house after chores, Ann asked, "Why won't the laird help us, Robbie?" She frequently lost patience with the inequities of life in Dunrossness.

Robert pushed back from the table, where he and Ann were having a rare quiet time for a cup of tea, and responded calmly, "All the crofting families are in the same boat. We are beholden for this thatch over our heads." He looked up to the rafters and thatch and then around the bleak but end. "We must be grateful for protection from the rain and for my work on the sixareen that pays our rent." He paused. "Let's hope the laird will take my hours as payment on our lease and not be asking for milk this month in addition."

"God forbid! We have not a drop of extra milk! 'Tis so, even now, I must stretch the milk with water. I only hope Violet continues to have a full udder, what with her measly diet of heather and wild grasses." Ann looked at her husband with a new worry. "And we shall either need to breed her so that she will have milk from another birthing, or else, heaven forbid, sell her."

Tina heard her parents' conversation and looked up from her knitting. "You can't take Violet!" she cried. "She is part of the family!"

Robert bent over to console his daughter. "There, Tina, darling. You know, our Violet is quite an old lady by now. I appreciate how much she means to you and to our family. No one has said yet what must happen. We shall wait and see." When Tina grew silent, Robert added on a brighter side, "The animals will come and go, lass, but our family is here with you. We must think of our blessings. For example, how fortunate we are that you have a mother who is an experienced teacher. You can stay right here at our hearth and learn without having to walk miles to school." He smiled first at his daughter and then at his wife.

"Which reminds me," Ann remarked, "we must make use of the daylight while we have it for reading." Ann saved the chores that she could do in the dark—like knitting and washing—and reached for her books in the afternoon when the young children napped and the sun still shone through the small windows.

❧ ☙

The Pilgrim's Progress was her favorite. She had read it many times, and each time she picked up new insights. On a gray afternoon, while Robert was tilling the field behind the barn, Ann immersed herself in the story with just enough light to read. Christian and his companion, Pliable, had entered the Slough of Despond. There Pliable abandoned Christian, and he was left alone with all his fears and guilt. Ann paused in her reading to account for her own life of despair. She too had to slug along through the boggy swamp, and often in her drudgery, she found herself alone. What had the Shetlanders done to deserve this mire? Surely God did not intend for human beings to suffer so. Yet everyone she knew was only scraping by this autumn. And what was more, the dark season would soon deprive them of nearly every ray of sunlight.

She put her book down as the last light disappeared into the gloaming, dissipating with it her good mood. If there had been taaties, she would have gotten up to chop them and boil them in the fish stock for the family's tea, but there were none. Their meal would be cold bannocks, with a few of Tina's whelks and winkles dropped into each soup bowl. The children were getting leaner each day. Ann's eyes filled with tears. She didn't mind if she missed a meal, but to watch her children go hungry was close to more than she could endure. She turned to God in anger and spoke under her breath, "Why? Oh, why?"

Her neighbor had told her how the minister at the Established Church had chastised his congregation for their sinfulness, which he said had surely caused the crop failure and island famine. When Ann asked whatever sins the people had possibly committed, her friend said he had accused them of drunkenness and infidelity, as well as sloth and failure to attend services. Ann could not imagine her neighbors to have been at fault in those ways. For all she could tell, they worked hard and certainly never had any money for drink, nor time for laziness. They never played cards or attended dances. Unlike the Methodists, the Calvinists prohibited fiddling and dancing, and their ministers even refused a cup of tea. With such strict living, surely the believers carried no guilt on their shoulders.

Ann considered whether she and Robert had in any way possibly caused the scarce times. Should they have prayed more often? Had they not helped their neighbors enough? But clearly, they had tried to lead Christian lives. Robert had worked on the building of their chapel, and she had taken neighbor children to her hearth for lessons. They had walked to church regularly and to class meetings and Bible study also. She could not honestly blame herself for the general plight of the people of Dunrossness, yet a nagging question persisted, and she paused to pray . . .

Forgive me, O God, if I have neglected your will. Show me what you want me to do. Bring us a good harvest, please, before the frost. Oh, dear.

She broke down in tears.

The children were still napping, so she walked outside to breathe in the fresh evening air. Sea mist sprayed her face, and she shivered from the chill. She relieved herself outside in the shed and heard Violet lowing. Robert would be starting the milking. His voice sounded warm and kind, like the deep drone a fiddle bow makes drawing across the lowest string. He was talking to the cow. She couldn't decipher the words, but he must have been saying, as he always said, "There, there. Easy does it. Let's just see what milk you have tonight." And Ann thought, these were the words she needed to hear: "There, there. Easy does it . . . Things will work out."

Ann washed her hands and face in the rainwater, wiped them with her apron, and walked back into the kitchen to stir the broth and set out the barley brönnies. Sheltie curled up by the fire. They had one another, and God would provide—at least that's what she wanted to believe.

Robert approached the table bent over with exhaustion, so on that night Ann said the evening prayer for the family . . .

Dearest God, you have given us a little something to eat to nourish our bodies and a good family to comfort our hearts. For these and every blessing we thank you. Watch over us, we pray. Amen.

Ann noticed that Sheltie didn't go out to round up the sheep that night. He stayed by the fire and let his head drop onto his paws. The children said good night to him with pats on the head, and he barely opened his eyes. They knew he was getting old and that he couldn't get up easily anymore. Before Robert went out to bring the sheep in, he gave Sheltie a long petting, "You've been a good dog, Sheltie lad. 'Tis a good life we've had together. Close your eyes now." When Robert came back in, he stooped down to pat the dog. Sheltie didn't move. Ann and Robert could tell that he had died. Ann cried as her husband lifted his beloved companion like a baby and carried him down the path toward the sea. She watched as Robert's tears fell onto the sheepdog's fur, and the rain whipped Robert's cap from his head.

Ann woke that night when Robert climbed into the box bed where she and baby Mary were already asleep. Silent tears soaked Robert's pillow until he cried himself out. He clung to Ann and finally fell asleep until morning. They knew they must tell the children.

The bairns could not be consoled. "We didn't get to say goodbye!" Tina cried.

"Why didn't you tell us?" James needed to know.

"We didn't know," said Ann as she prepared gruel for their breakfast. "One never knows when the end will be." That day it rained all day. Each time the children opened the crofthouse door, they expected Sheltie to greet them. The cottage was deathly quiet. No one could walk over the empty spot by the fire where the warm sand lay. The sheep seemed to know too; they wandered aimlessly and hardly knew to come into the byre when snow flurries fell later that day.

The early frost brought fear of a cold winter. Robert came home from the shore to find Ann downcast as she finished the chores and got the children ready for bed. James climbed onto his father's lap before saying goodnight.

"I miss Sheltie, Daa."

"Yes, James, so do I. He was a good pal."

"Why didn't we bury him, like Jamie, Daa?"

"The earth is too hard now that we've had a frost. And I needed to carry him off to the sea, where I spend so many of my days and nights."

"But who will take care of Sheltie now?" James turned his head to face his father.

"That would be God, son."

"Oh, that's good."

Ann was listening. She nodded toward Robert with loving eyes, tears flowing down her cheeks. Robert lifted his little lad and put him to bed, much as he had carried his dog the night before, lovingly in his arms.

That night, Ann whispered from memory the psalm she had learned as a child . . .

> The LORD is my shepherd; I shall not want.
> He maketh me to lie down in green pastures:
> he leadeth me beside the still waters.
> He restoreth my soul:
> he leadeth me in the paths of righteousness for his name's sake.
> Yea, though I walk through the valley of the shadow of death,
> I will fear no evil: for thou art with me;
> thy rod and thy staff they comfort me.
> Thou preparest a table before me in the presence of mine enemies:

thou anointest my head with oil; my cup runneth over.
Surely goodness and mercy shall follow me all the days of my life:
and I will dwell in the house of the LORD for ever.[1]

The next afternoon, as if in answer to their melancholy, missionaries from England came along the footpath with a cart filled with grain for the poor crofters of Dunrossness. They said prayers at each croft and promised the coming of "meal roads," which would mean work for the crofters building roads and, in exchange for their labor, sacks of meal for their families. The good news of grain buoyed Ann's hopes. She prayed that the barley from the missionaries would last until the meal road came to the Boe. Each fortnight, the days were shorter, and the nights were colder. Fear and hope battled each other in the ebb and flow of life on the edge. Which would be the victor?

SUMMER 1843

In these poor times, Ann and Robert relied on their Methodist friends for support. It seemed to Ann that faith became ever more important when there was little to eat. The rains were relentless, the crops failed, the seas were rough, and the laird demanded almost all their fish. Yet without fail, the couple walked with their now four children—Tina, James, Mary, and Annie—to Sabbath service each week. They prayed, sang hymns, and somehow found consolation in the words of Scripture and preaching. Ann often pondered why it was so.

As they trudged home from the chapel across the soggy hill ground on a misty Sunday morning, Ann asked, "Robbie, what is it exactly that happens at Sunday service? Even though the weather is dreadfully dreary, I always feel glad I came."

"I know what you mean, Ann. Today the preacher seemed to be speaking directly to me."

"Why? What was it that he said that spoke to you?"

1. Psalm 23.

"He was talking about Job, and then he read the part where Job says, 'I know that my redeemer liveth.'[2] Even after Job had lost everything, he still believed in God."

"'Twas a strong witness."

"Yes, and Job's great suffering makes ours seem less. Do you not agree, Ann?"

"Yes, that must be it. Our problems, in comparison, seem less heavy after hearing about those that came before us. And simply being together among friends always makes me feel stronger and better able to cope, don't you know?"

"Being together with friends and being together with God." Robert took her hand in his.

"Aye, Robbie, 'tis just that."

Some of their neighbors were in a state of discontent with their religious affiliation. Many criticized the Established Church for supporting the lairds. Congregations broke away and became "free churches." A call for Christian piety swept the Shetland Islands as ministers walked out of their former meeting places and worshiped in homes or on boats in what became known as the Great Disruption. Wesleyan Methodists, however, continued to practice a simple faith, believing in loving God and helping those less fortunate. Their preachers had never defended the ways of the lairds. The life of Methodists suited Ann and Robert. When they gathered with their fellow believers, they felt accepted and cared for. They were poor, but the community itself seemed to make hardship bearable. Ann thought about the people in the book of Acts, where everyone helped one another, sharing what they had and shouldering one another's burdens.

Then she remembered Jesus's words and spoke them aloud as they walked along: "Come unto me, all ye that labour and are heavy laden, and I will give you rest. Take my yoke upon you and learn of me; for I am meek and lowly in heart: and ye shall find rest unto your souls. For my yoke is easy, and my burden is light."[3]

"Your mother is good at reciting Scripture, bairns," said Robert. "'Twould be a passage to read this week as you study together."

Tina remarked, "I like those words, Mam. We are often heavy laden, especially with a kishie of peats on our backs."

---

2. Job 19:25a.

3. Matthew 11:28–30.

Ann chuckled. "Yes, 'tis true. And we genuinely need to find rest in our souls. I suppose that's why we go to chapel."

James grumbled, "But why must we walk all this way?"

His father laughed, "Well, today is the Sabbath, and we shan't have work to do! Perhaps you'll read to Mary and Annie this afternoon by the fire, James, after we've had our meal. They say the hearth is a crofter's altar."

7

Making Do

ANNIE HAD BEEN BORN in 1842, and John in 1845, every two or three years another child, and, yes, another mouth to feed. Ann nursed the peerie one until she ran out of her own milk and cared for all five bairns, weaving and knitting clothing, washing the worn garments, and preparing their meals. She fetched water from the well, carried the peats, hoed the garden, and spread straw in the byre for Violet's second calf, a baby bull. Violet's first offspring was by now a male yearling and would soon be ready to sell. Perhaps the next calf would be a milker, and Violet would be sold then too.

Ann taught the older children around the table they used for tea, and they chatted about their livestock and their chores. She and Tina busied their hands by knitting to sell the shawls that brought them valued coins from the Lerwick traders. James and Mary practiced their maths, while Annie drew her letters and played with peerie John. Never an idle moment. Often Robert came home from fishing and went straight out to plow and plant. By the end of the day, he was too drained to play his fiddle, and Ann lay down at night too weary to make love. "We mustn't have another bairn, Robert. There is simply not enough food. And I have no energy for being heavy with child again."

"But I love you, Annie, and if God gives us another bairn, he will also give us what we need to care for it." He drew her to him, and slowly she warmed to his touch and succumbed to his faith that they would manage somehow.

WINTER 1847

Robert had begun taking James out fishing with him. At age eleven, the lad was a help with rowing and hauling in the nets. He also kept his father company when they fished in a fourareen with another father-and-son team. One night in December, the four planned to sail up Mainland's west coast to Scalloway. There they would dock and spend the night at Robert's mother's home. Not since Stewart's wedding had Robert seen his family. Ann found herself waiting eagerly for their return. She longed for news. How were Stewart and his new family? Was there illness in Scalloway this winter? She was more than curious—anxious, really. She realized that James had never been away from home overnight. Had he been fearful of the sea and the dark night? She didn't usually worry about Robert on the water, but her young son, James—what if a storm came up and the boat were dashed against the rocks? Would they make it home by the evening? And if they didn't?

Ann calmed her apprehension by shifting to the needs of the other children. After the midday meal, she used the daylight to read to Annie and Mary from the Bible. With John sitting on her lap, she opened to the Psalms. Every other minute the lad got down to toddle about, and their new sheepdog they called Archie pushed his nose into her lap for attention and made her laugh. She thumbed through the Bible looking for a psalm for the children to commit to memory but then put it down and recalled one that she already knew by heart. She would continue teaching, even with distractions, by simply reciting the psalm to the girls. Annie was learning her letters, and Mary was focusing on vocabulary and spelling. The Bible was Ann's primer for all instruction, and her reading and life experiences, however limited, were the stuff of her stories.

Make a joyful noise unto the LORD, all ye lands![1]

Now why did she think of that psalm? Joyful was not at all how she was feeling. Well, perhaps she would feel joyful when her men came

1. Psalm 100:1.

home safe and sound. But now she felt preoccupied, more like an anxious sheep that wandered off from its flock into the heather. She needed Archie to nip at her heels to bring her attention back to the girls and her teaching. "Now say this after me, lassies: 'Make a joyful noise unto the LORD, all ye lands!' Mary, you may write this verse and then the next, line by line, with your best penmanship, and then check the Bible for the spelling of each word as you read it over."

Annie repeated the verses until she could recite them, and Mary recorded the full psalm in her most careful handwriting. Next, their mother asked them both, "Do you know what joyful means?"

Annie wrinkled her nose, trying to think what the word might mean, or another way to say it. "Is it 'loud,' Mam? Make a *loud* noise to the LORD?"

"It could be loud, but 'tisn't the meaning of joyful. It means happy, and with good cheer. We would say *canty*, in dialect. 'Tis how we are to approach God—with joy or full of joy—do you see?"

"Yes, I see," said Mary. "But why doesn't the Bible say canty, Mam?"

"Well, there are many languages, and this Bible is written in the King's English. Someday perhaps you'll translate it into our tongue." Mary groaned. "Now please spell joyful," Ann continued, "but not with that doleful face."

"*J-o-y-f-u-l*. But what does doleful mean?"

"'Tis another word for melancholy; now there's a word to spell!"

Meanwhile, Tina read her own book by the window, oblivious of the activity in the cottage. Ann glanced her way, remembering how, like Tina, she too had been the oldest in her family, a bit set apart from the others. She had always enjoyed watching the younger bairns learn their letters, and for as long as she could remember she had wanted to become a teacher. Tina, however, wrapped herself in her own internal world. She lived vicariously through the heroines of the books she managed to get her hands on. She was a dreamer, content to imagine herself in romantic English tales and ancient Nordic legends. Ann envied her—to be young and able to read and escape the worries of everyday life, which weighed so heavily on her and her husband, raising their brood on this tiny spot of rocky land. To have the luxury of postponing real-life problems with a story line that whisked her off to distant shores where fictitious characters worked out their own predicaments! Tiny Tina, that was her name as a newborn. Ann looked at John, the youngest, and remembered her bairns, as she had brought each to life: Jamie, Tina, James, Mary, Annie, and now another boy, John. Ann pulled her mind back to the table and the lesson at hand. When the daylight faded, she took up her knitting, and she admonished Tina to put down her book and prepare their tea by chopping the cabbage and onions while they still had a touch of gloaming. Ann noted she would have to light the kollie lamp for the family to eat by. And when would her lads return, anyway? The night sky was eerie, with hardly a bit of moonlight. How would they see their way home to the shore?

Ann prayed aloud over the supper . . .

> Dear God, bless this food and our evening. Bring Father and James back safely—and soon. We turn to you for assurance. In your holy name we pray. Amen.

Father and son burst from complete darkness into the lamplit cottage that evening. Ann stood up holding John, the youngest bairn, who had fallen asleep in her arms.

"Mam, you can't imagine what we saw! Last night the sky was green!" Robert smiled as James exclaimed about the nighttime spectacle. "We were coming up the coast. The sky was completely clear with only the hint of a crescent moon." He caught his breath and then went on, "Before we came to Scalloway, suddenly the black sky filled with color! First 'twas gold and then green. 'Twas already so dark out, but the colors moved before us like in a sunset!"

"Ah, so you have seen the merrie dancers!" Ann whispered with a twinkle in her eye. She kissed Robert, though he seemed not to notice, and then she sat back down.

"The what?"

"Didn't your father tell you, that's what we call the lights, the merrie dancers? Did you see the lights dance across the sky?"

Robert watched his son, proud to have him tell the story. "He just said it was the northern lights." He turned as if to ask his father more, then smiled to his mother again. "Oh, you should have been there, Mam!"

"I wish I had! I only saw the lights once as a child in Lerwick. Where I grew up, the town lights made it hard to see the colors."

James and Robert took off their wet coats and hats, and warming their hands, they sat down at the table, hungry for their meal. Tina ladled out the cabbage soup they had saved for the fishermen's tea, and she took two leftover brönnies and placed them beside the bowls. Ann stood up and passed baby John to Tina to hold, and she embraced her husband from behind, as he gulped down the soup. She laughed to herself that her husband appeared to be hungrier for food than for her affection. She tousled her son's hair and sat down beside the famished seamen to hear more news of their expedition.

Robert explained between mouthfuls, "The fishing was the best ever as we rowed north, so we put down the anchor off the coast, just past West Burro, out in the deeps. Our nets filled, and the boys pulled hard, along with the men, until we had the catch in the bottom of the boat." Ann nodded. She could imagine the young boys heaving with all their strength to be useful in the craft. "We were tired and ready for tea and a peat fire, that you can believe, but then the sky broke forth in jewels of light!"

"And we stayed to watch. First came purple, then orange, gold, and green!" exclaimed James, waving with his hands before his face as if he could still see the flames of color.

Robert continued, "Then a cloud just pushed the lights away, as quickly as they had appeared, so we rowed on north to Scalloway and docked in darkness. We carried the fish in sacks from the boat and left them outside in the cold at the home of church friends close to the harbor."

"And what of your mother, Robbie? Was she still up?"

"The door was open as usual, so we just went in and lay down in the common room with blankets she had left out. There were bannocks and kirn-milk on the table, so we helped ourselves, and then we turned in for the night, exhausted but excited for having seen such a show in the sky and having caught such a grand load of fish."

"Minnie made us porridge for breakfast in the morning, and we had tea with sugar."

"How pleased your Minnie must have been to see you grown up so," Ann added.

"Then Daa started work on gutting and salting the fish. We brought some of it home; 'tis outside." James was proud of the catch and that he had helped lug it from the water all the way up the path to the croft.

"Ah, there will be fish chowder for our noon meal tomorrow. 'Tis a mercy!" Ann smiled, glad of the nourishment after lean days and cold nights. "And how is your mother, Robert?"

"She is well, well enough. 'Tis hard without Father, and Stewart is busy with his own family now." Ann loved to hear about Stewart and secretly wished he had settled in Dunrossness, so they could have a brother nearby. "He came to see us and share a cup of tea. He helps with the garden and brings milk and fish when he can. We didn't get to see his wife and bairns, though. 'Twas too short a visit."

"'Tis too bad you didn't stay longer, but we missed you and are glad you returned safely." She gave Robert's forearm a gentle squeeze.

"And 'tis well and good we came home when we did, for there is consumption in Scalloway. Mother is worried they may have been exposed."

Ann let out an audible moan. Now what? With the news of contagious disease, she ascertained—as she had concluded so often—that moments of joy passed swiftly and occurred only infrequently. Illness and scarcity crowded out even the simple pleasures of colors in the sky. Why must there be such hardship in life? She didn't want to be pessimistic, but even the thought of losing Ross or one of Robert's nieces or nephews to contagious illness was frightening. This sudden new worry made her feel as if her boat were sinking and she could not bale it out in time. With a concerted effort, she pushed the fear of consumption out of her mind. No need to anticipate something that had not in fact happened and likely would not in the Ness—at least she hoped not. She inhaled deeply and imagined the floor of her boat dry and the craft once again floating high on the water. "We must pray for the people of Scalloway and trust God that your family will be spared."

When tiredness weighed upon her eye lids, she got up to check on the lassies. She heard Mary and Annie in the ben end breathing evenly, sound asleep. Tina had also turned in, weary from her long day doing the chores that James usually accomplished. No need to wake them, as father and brother would be able to greet the others at breakfast soon enough. Ann breathed a sigh that her boys were home again, safe under their thatch roof, by her peat fire. She put John down for bed and cleared away the dishes.

That night Ann closed her eyes in bed beside Robert and let the feeling of relief ease her extraneous worries. Black stillness engulfed her, and then purple, green, and gold leapt across the dance floor of her mind. How glad she was that she had permitted James to go with his father to Scalloway! She stretched and yawned, allowing her body to relax into the comfort of her bed. And then she let the merrie dancers lead her by the hand into the fairyland of Nod.

SPRINGTIME 1849

Another bairn was born in 1849. By then, Ann's namesake, Annie, was already seven, so it seemed only right to name this next one Robert after his father. Ann hoped this would be the last child. And it was a laddie, how lovely. They had been married twenty years, and she had given birth to babes, nursed them at the breast, and then fed them gruel throughout all those years. Sometimes she smiled to think how anxious she had been when she bore her first bairn, her beloved Jamie. How simple life had been then with just one child. By this time, she had brought seven children into the world, usually with a midwife or neighbor, but sometimes just with Robert present. Truth be told, she had endured the labor and managed the delivery mostly by herself. Even through hardship, all but Jamie had survived. She had indeed also managed by herself when Violet had a second calf, and when the ewes birthed their lambs that spring, for Robert, like all the neighbor men, was off fishing at the haaf.

Lambing was hard labor. Ann stayed up all night waiting for each ewe's time. Every mama sheep had its habits, pawing the ground or moving about apart from the herd as if drunk when the lamb was about to be born. Ann watched for the signs and then stood ready to catch the lamb and help its mother clean it and put it to its udder. Sometimes there were two in a litter, and one was smaller and weaker than the other. Often the smallest lambs would not nurse, and she had to bottle-feed the peerie things. By the end of the two weeks of lambing, Ann was worn out. When Robert finally came home from the deep sea, she retired to bed, exhausted. She thought she must be coming down with a cold from staying out in the damp air without rest or proper meals. Robert came to her as she lay on their bed. Too run down to complain to her husband that he had left her with all the chores and the lambing too, Ann dozed off without even undressing that night.

The next morning, she woke up feverish. Robert brought her tea and lay the palm of his hand on her forehead. "Annie, dear, you have worked yourself into a sickness. I did not expect to be gone so long. And it seems the lambs came early this year. As I walked yesterday from the beach, I saw them all over the grassy hills on each crofter's land. And I knew ours would already be born too." She did not stir. He looked up as if seeing right through the stone walls of their crofthouse. "Oh, 'tis quite a sight each year! Ewes munching spring grass and their young hopping about over the rocks and the heather." He turned to her, "But I am sorry that you were by yourself through the lambing. You did a fine job of it, lass." He gave her rosy cheek a pat. "How are the children? Did they help their mam?"

Ann tried her best to smile and welcome Robert home with conversation about the family, but she drifted off to sleep again, trusting Robert to take over the care of the children and the animals now that he was finally home.

By the next day the fever had broken, and though she still felt weak, Ann rose from bed, picked up little Robert, and walked to the door of their cottage. She breathed in the fresh air, relieved that her illness was clearing up—no consumption, thank God; her lungs felt fine. From the door, she watched her other bairns run after the ewes and their newborn lambs in the heather. It was her favorite time of year! She had made it through the hard part and participated in the miracle of birth itself. Each ewe produced one or two little ones—mostly white, but a few black or brown hardy Shetland sheep too. More mouths to feed, but also more wool for jumpers and shawls. Robert called to the children to help him in the byre with cleaning the stalls and milking Violet, and they came running, eager to please their father and work alongside him. There would be milk, and Robert had brought home fish, so all would be well. They used every part of the fish but the guts, which Robert had tossed to the gulls, keeping the livers to boil and the heads to stuff with oats. Though they were poor, Ann admitted it was a good life. God did provide. Purple shadows painted the hills as the late spring sun finally set over the western coast.

WINTER 1855

After little Robert, along came Margaret in 1852 and then Christina in 1855. They called Margaret "Maggie," and Christina sometimes "Chrissy," because they already had a Tina, who was by then twenty-three and like a second mother to the younger children. Ann smiled and noted how the children looked alike with fair skin, round faces, and brown or golden curls. One couldn't say they looked like her or like Robert exactly, but they all looked like each other. They were healthy bairns and happy, most of the time. John was sometimes a bit off, troubled somehow. There wasn't time to worry about him really, but for a ten-year-old, he was more serious than Ann would like. She figured he was the middle boy, not old enough to fish with his older brother James nor young enough to play with his younger brother Robert. He would probably grow out of that awkward age soon, perhaps when his voice broke.

Getting along was mostly about food. Some months, there was enough salted fish to sell at the market and enough knitwear between Ann and Tina to turn a decent profit. And Mary and Annie had begun to knit too. When father and son brought home plenty of fish, there was ample kollie to light the lamps, and so Ann found time to read in the winter evenings by the light of a smoky but steady flame.

The books she read became the stories she told her children around the peat fire. Charles Dickens had published *David Copperfield* in monthly installments a few years back, and Ann's mother had collected the episodes, so now Ann borrowed these when she was able to get them from Lerwick. She read the tales of David Copperfield, an orphan subjected to child labor and urban poverty. Each time she finished a thirty-two-page installment, she retold the story to her children, who were eager to hear what happened to this poor lad in London, very far from their world of Exnaboe, Shetland. John seemed to identify with the lonely plight of David Copperfield. Ann tried to help her children recognize how fortunate they were to live in a safe environment where both parents loved and cared for them. Young Robert, though, more than the others, dreamed of some place more alluring than Shetland, or even the British Isles.

Their oldest son, James, at nineteen was already a capable skipper like his father. When a German whaling ship came looking for young men to crew on the six-month sea voyage hunting for whales in Greenland, James asked to go. One evening when James was still out fishing at the voe, Tina was reading by the lamp in the ben end. After the younger children had gone to sleep in their box beds, Ann expressed to Robert her fears. "I cannot let him go, Robbie. What if he never returns? We lost Jamie long ago, and I cannot imagine losing our second James. He has grown to be strong like you and such a help to the family. I want him to stay here on Mainland, perhaps find a wife and settle nearby."

Robert replied, "Yes, I know how you feel. But he is young and wants adventure. And the pay is good on the big ships. He will come home with his own earnings and nothing to owe to the laird. He will see places where you and I will never go. We must let our young take the opportunities that come their way for a better life."

"I suppose 'tis not our decision. He is old enough to do as he wishes." Ann sighed with the same resignation as if she were watching a cloud obscure the last of the sun in a gloomy winter sky. Six months would be like living in the shadow of that cloud until James returned.

SPRINGTIME 1855

By this time, the laird of Dunrossness had built more cottages in Exnaboe, Quendale, and Sumburgh, where crofting families worked the land, raised sheep, and went to sea. When crofters could not produce sufficient wool or fish for their tithe, the laird moved them off the land. These evictions left families penniless. It was not possible for a neighbor to take such a family in, when the neighbor, though meaning well, could alone barely survive himself from season to season. When the laird's steward came and forced the family to evacuate with only a day's notice, a new family often moved into the vacated property, already beholden to the laird. In this way, new families occasionally moved to the southern tip of Mainland. Sometimes the laird built a second crofter's house on the same land, making it impossible for either family to live adequately off the turf—little that there was of it. In this way, the men and boys were forced to fish longer hours and for more days on end to pay their rent.

James met a lad whose family was new to Dunrossness. When he heard that he played the fiddle, James asked his father if he could take his grandfather's fiddle to meet the family and learn to play along. Robert had found little time for the instrument, so he agreed, and Ann knew he was secretly pleased that his son had taken an interest.

On his return from Sumburgh, fiddle under his arm, James arrived at the croft after dark. He spoke eagerly to his parents after Maggie and Chrissy had gone to bed. "You'll like Magnus. He's a skipper like you, Daa." Ann listened with curiosity.

"So." Raising his eyebrows, Robert looked fondly at his oldest boy, nodding.

"And his son, William, fishes with him, of course, but he also has a talent for the fiddle." Tina was listening in, interested that a new fellow had moved to the Ness. "He has already met Jacob, the old fiddler you know. They have even played together at a dance." James turned to see Tina's reaction. "Today William taught me a tune he knew from the village where his family had lived before, and I got to play along with him on a few tunes I've heard you play, Daa."

"Well, let's hear you!" Ann said, as she and Tina put down their knitting. "'Tis about time we had some music in the cottage."

James lifted the fiddle carefully from its case and laid it on his lap. Then he took the bow and tightened the hairs. He put the fiddle to his chin and tuned the strings until they sounded right to him. "What do you say, Daa, is it well enough in tune?"

"Yes, I think you have a good ear." Robert smiled and leaned forward, ready to listen. James was beginning to demonstrate skills beyond his father's, and Ann knew the look of delight in Robert's eyes, seeing his son so grown up and so capable. Ann too watched her eldest son, reflecting with pride on his good looks and new abilities. With his broad shoulders and strong arms, he was no longer a child. She recognized her Robert in James's light hair and wide grin. She smiled and surprised herself to feel an instant of attraction toward the young man. It felt a bit like years ago in Lerwick when she first fell in love with Robert. Where had the time gone? This, their oldest living son, was already a man. She would not be able to hold on to him much longer. Ann glanced about the room and noticed Tina watching her brother and her mother with a smile. Her daughter had caught her tender look, and Ann blushed for just an instant and then looked away.

James played the new tune as his parents sat back in their chairs and listened to the haunting melody. One song led to another, and the women resumed their knitting. Ann's fingers worked busily, but her heart rested, enjoying the pleasure of family and home. They were adults together; even John at ten and Robert at six looked up to James. She sighed and basked in the satisfaction of having raised bairns to become competent adults.

James played until he could think of no other melody. "Daa, now you play a tune!"

Ann turned to her husband, lifted her eyebrows, and nodded in encouragement.

Robert took up the fiddle and played a favorite waltz, and Ann smiled, remembering their wedding party, when Robert's father, James, played that tune for the dancing late in the evening before the guests finally left. Nothing could have pleased her more than to see the love of music passed from father to son, once again.

Young Robert asked, "May I try to play?"

"Why, of course. Here." Robert the elder passed the fiddle to young Robert, who held it to his chin as he had watched his brother and father. He played on open strings and grinned.

When young Robert put the fiddle down, James looked at his parents and, clearing his throat, he spoke in a deep but quiet voice, "William is going on the next whaling ship to Greenland, and I want to go with him." He paused. "A whaling fleet is coming from Aberdeen next week, and it will stop here at Sumburgh to pick up crew. The Scotsmen like having us Shetlanders on board; they say we are the best shipmates." He continued through the silence. "I shall likely be just an oarsman—but that suits me. Later I might learn to use the harpoon."

Ann's hand shot to her mouth. Her eyes darted to her husband's face before she spoke. He breathed out the air he had been holding in and then turned to his son. "'Twill be dangerous work, you know, James," he said.

Ann wrinkled her brow and paused before saying, "Many whale-boys never come home, James." But she knew that her son had been working up to this announcement, so she stopped herself from adding more.

"I know, but I am strong, and the pay is good. I'll learn new things. 'Twill be good for me."

Tina looked on with interest to watch her brother stand up to their parents.

Robert regarded Ann and then spoke to James calmly. "We will pray for you every day while you are gone."

"And I will pray for you," said James, smiling at his sister, as well as back and forth at both parents.

Ann remained silent as she blinked away her tears.

Seeing her glistening eyes, James comforted his mother, "You needn't worry about me, Mam. I can take care of myself." Chilled by the news, as if a gale had dropped the temperature to a winter freeze, she wiped away her tears with her apron. James moved to touch her arm. "Think of it, I am already three years older than Father was when he proposed to you. At sixteen, he was not only an independent fisherman but a husband and soon to be a father!"

"True tale," said Robert. He and Ann nodded and smiled at each other. Yes, 'twas so indeed. They were once young and adventurous. But Ann reflected that they had migrated only south on the same island, not across the sea to Greenland! Still, she remembered her mother's tears that

day when her parents said goodbye and watched her depart with Robbie
south for Exnaboe.

Ann lay awake that night, visualizing James's departure, her clinging
to him and his pulling away. She thought about another woman in the
Scriptures, wishing to hold on to a young man, the one who would as-
cend and leave her standing there. "Touch me not," he said.[2] Ann prayed
silently, moving her lips . . .

> Dear God, give me the courage of Mary. I cannot hold him; he
> will go away from me, no matter what I do. So it has been writ-
> ten in the book of life.
>   I will pray for James. Keep him safe from harm, and bring
> him home again, O God. Amen.

Tina stayed with the children when Robert and Ann walked with James
to the south shore on the morning when the whaling ship put out its
anchor in the cove by the lighthouse at Sumburgh Head. John had packed
only a change of clothes and extra socks, which Ann had knit at the last
minute the night before. It was early dawn on the Sabbath, so the men
were anxious to get on board and out to sea before true light, for fear that
the ministers of the Established Church would chastise their families for
taking up work on God's holy day. Theirs was a God-fearing island, but
the people were poor and had to work when they could, sometimes even
on the Sabbath, the seventh day. The kirk gained no popularity among
the crofters for its constant chastisement on breaking the Fourth Com-
mandment. There would be prayers at sea and singing on board later that
day, no doubt, for the men had promised their wives and mothers to keep
their faith while away, and, after all, they too relied on God to survive
the perils of the sea. But surely such fears were far from James's thoughts
now. Ann could see that her son hastened his pace as they approached
the group of young Shetlanders assembled at the shore. They were all
so tall and broad shouldered. What a handsome lot, and her James was
among them.

2. John 20:17a.

"The wind has picked up," Robert said as he turned his face into a squall blowing off the sea. "The sailing should be good." Robert and James pulled their stocking caps down over their ears as they watched the seamen lower a small dinghy off the schooner into the waves. A lone oarsman rowed the tender through the surf toward the strand. Ann tightened her shawl around her head and shoulders. Her stomach nearly lurched as the dinghy rode the waves. She could not imagine life on a ship, up and down, rolling with the sea. Surely, she would be forever hanging overboard! How would James fare? Robert had assured her that their son was a born sailor and, for sure, that he had not only the muscles of a seaman but the stomach as well. She leaned on her husband, taking his arm, as if drawing confidence from her grip.

The dinghy reached the shoreline, and the men, who had gathered on the sand, said their last goodbyes. Ann embraced her son, and with tears collecting in the corners of her eyes, she whispered, "Stay safe, James, my love."

Robert clapped him on the back. "All the best," he choked out and then added shyly, "We love you, you know that."

As James waded into the surf and climbed into the boat, he turned to his parents and waved, calling above the roar of the wind for a last time, "Until September!" James settled in the dinghy with his back to the shore. He did not look back. Ann imagined his eyes would be fixed on the mighty sailing vessel and the open sea before him. His life would be an adventure with thrills and dangers quite unknown to her. Ann and Robert watched as the men picked up oars to row out to the big whaleship, with sails ready to hoist and embark on her voyage.

So, this was the break. She would no longer feed and care for her son. He would no longer rest under her wings, as a young bird clings to its mother's warmth. He would sail away, far away! Perhaps it was just as well; life at the Boe was not the best, for the family had so little. Likely James would get more to eat on the whaling ship. But then Ann thought about what they would be given—hardtack and fish. Oh, dear! Not scurvy, God, no! Don't let him get sick for lack of fresh vegetables! She smiled at her own thoughts—a mother always worried about her child. All the island boys grew up to be seamen; what else could they become? Why had she not prepared herself for this? But was there ever such a notion as being prepared for trial? No, never; it came "as a thief in the night."[3] Her

---

3. First Thessalonians 5:2.

thoughts turned back to James, and, through the mist, she watched the distance grow wider and wider as he rowed away.

When the men on board had pulled the tender up the side of the ship, Ann lost sight of James. The wind off the water had dried her cheeks, and sand stung her eyes. She sighed and turned to Robert. He put his arm around her, and they pivoted to face home. Their steps sank heavily in the loose sand. Only the seagulls cried out, until Ann broke the couple's silence and asked, "Oh, Robbie, what if this becomes his life, the life of a whaler?" It was more a lonely lament than a question, like the deep toll of a mighty fog bell sounding over the water. In that moment, nothing mattered more to her than the safety of her precious son.

"Annie, we mustn't worry like that. What will be will be. In God's hands he will make something of himself, and we must accept that."

"We'll just have to pray that September comes soon."

They tossed quick smiles to each other, as if to bolster their spirits, and then they hurried home to get the family ready for Sabbath service. Along the way, Ann turned back to glimpse the lighthouse. The light burning from that familiar promontory would steer her son's ship home, and, in the meantime, it would become her light in the darkness, a single white light burning by oil, but truly, in her thinking, fueled by God.

8

Ebb and Flow

AUTUMN 1855

ROBERT AND ANN HAD sold Violet when her third calf was a female. She was too old to give much milk, and they thought it better to sell her than simply let her die on the croft. Her bull calf had brought a good price, and a neighbor still had a good steer to service the new calf when she was ready. Ann was thankful Robbie had handled the livestock while he was home at the croft. So much of crofting was left to the women, and though the day-to-day routine was tolerable, Ann found the moments of important decisions and crises to be more than she cared to manage alone.

James was still away in Greenland, and Robert was gone again at the haaf. After a day of chores, Ann and her children settled into their evening time together. Annie was holding her baby sister, Christina, and singing a lullaby her mother had taught her, while little Maggie danced by the hearth:

> Hushaba my peerie ting
> Cuddle closs ta Mammie
> Cuddle closs an hear me sing
> Peerie mootie lammie.[1]

---

1. "Shetland Lullaby."

When Christina fell asleep, Ann lifted the bairn from her daughter's arms and put her to bed in the ben end of the crofthouse. Back in the but end, where life revolved around the peat fire, Tina sat reading, while Mary and Annie passed the evening knitting. On the floor Maggie and Robert played a counting game with stones, and John repaired a small fishing net by the hearth. When Ann sat down and picked up her yarn, Annie stopped knitting, removed her kerchief from her hair, and began to comb out the tangles from the day's wind. She asked her mother, "How was it that you married Father when he was only sixteen?"

Ann smiled, causing wrinkles to gather about her eyes, as she remembered running to Robbie's embrace by the loch each day after teaching at the schoolhouse. She looked at Annie and recalled how at her same age she was first interested in a lad who lived in the closs between her family home and the Lerwick harbor. Annie would soon start her monthly bleeding, and then, goodness, she would already be able to carry a child. Some Shetland lasses married that young, but Ann hoped her daughters would wait. There would be many years of bringing bairns into the world. She answered matter-of-factly, "We wanted to be married, 'twas simply that."

"But James is already nineteen and he's never had a lassie, has he?"

"No. But I suppose he could meet a lass in Greenland!"

"Oh, no, he wouldn't do that!" Mary interjected. "I want him to stay here with us."

Ann lifted her eyebrows as if to say, who knows . . . "I hope he is well. The ship is due back any day now."

Tina looked up from her book. "What did your parents think of your marrying when Father was only sixteen?"

"I suppose they thought he was too young, yet they didn't stand in our way."

Annie glanced at Tina and back at her mother. "And Tina is already twenty-three, what about her?"

Tina blushed. The conversation stopped, and everyone looked at their feet or at their knitting mid-stitch.

Tina raised her voice, "And who is to say that all lads and lasses should marry and have children?" Then she breathed deeply, straightened her back and continued her defense. "Not everyone accepts a marriage proposal, you know. Think of Jane Austen, and her Lizzie Bennett in *Pride and Prejudice*—she turned down marriage proposals more than once."

"Well, 'tis important to find the right person, surely, and there's no perfect age to marry. But the two should be mature enough to take on responsibility," Ann explained. "'Tisn't easy raising up you bairns, you know."

"And what if I never do marry, Mam?" asked Tina.

"Well, then you will have a different calling. What, do you suppose?"

"I could never become a teacher or a nurse. There's no training here in the Ness. And, besides, I can't see myself always doing things for others, anyway."

"So that's it, well, we are all called to serve in some way. Perhaps you would work for the laird as a servant at the hall. I hear the lady of the house is kinder than her husband, and you are already a decent cook. I dare say, you can knit and sew. Perhaps you should look into a position at Sumburgh."

Ann liked the idea of Tina finding her own position. Though the housekeeper would expect long work hours, certainly there were books in the hall library, and perhaps she could borrow one to read now and then. Being employed by the laird might not be so bad. "You know, Tina, each of us must contribute to our family's livelihood. You are a help to us now, but it wouldn't hurt if you had wages to bring home and perhaps, for yourself, better food to eat."

Tina opened her book again. Ann recognized Tina's stubbornness. But she also surmised that Tina must have become newly aware that the family's circumstances required something more of her.

By then, the prime milking cow was Violet's third offspring—Lily, they called her. It was a good Shetland name and a flower too. In the early morning as Ann fed and watered her outside the byre, she saw their friend Andrew walking toward the croft. Robert was away fishing, and John and young Robert were cutting peats. Andrew breathed heavily as he approached, and Ann reflected how he lately showed his age. Yet, with long strides, he rushed toward her, shouting out with effort as he came within her hearing, "The Greenland schooner has returned!" When he reached Ann and stopped to catch his breath, he broke into a grin and announced, "The men will be disembarking on the beach as we speak!"

Ann dropped her bucket of oats and turned and called out, "Bairns, come! James's ship is in!"

Tina wrapped Maggie in her cloak and shawl and put on her boots. Ann grabbed a blanket and fashioned it into a sling in which to carry Christina. "Too bad Father is still out at the haaf. Perhaps he'll have heard that the whalers are back." She called to Robert and John, and they came running with Archie, their affectionate sheepdog, at their feet. "Come along, Mary and Annie, don't you want to see James? Tell Archie to stay and mind the sheep," Ann admonished John. "Robert, come help me with this bucket."

The sun rose over the eastern horizon and threw pink ribbons onto the sky. In the distance, the voe shed its indigo cape and, in another instant, donned a gold and lavender shawl. Ann felt her heart warm as if she had slipped into a fine wool frock. Her son was coming home!

That night James unpacked his bedroll and presented his brothers with a knife-handle carved of whale bone and his sisters with a pair of whale-bone knitting needles. "I carved these for you on the way home. I hope you like them."

Robert eyed his big brother with pride. "How many whales did you catch, James?"

"We hunted down a good number, twenty in all."

Robert listened eagerly. "How do you get the blubber onto the ship?"

"Well, the harpooners go for the whale in the water from small boats. Once a harpoon sticks, the whale tries to escape and drags the harpooners in their boat through the water. It can go on for hours until finally the whale tires out." Robert and John hung on every word. "We drag the dead whale with ropes to the side of the ship, and then with spears and long-handled spades the men cut off big chunks of bloody blubber with its whale flesh, and the oarsmen hoist it onto the ship's deck. Then we flense the blubber from the meat with long, curved knives. 'Tis ice-cold work. My hands froze many a day."

"What is blubber, Mam?" asked Maggie.

"'Tis the whale's fat, don't you know?" Robert answered quickly, and Ann smiled to note how much he had learned about whales from his father. "They sell it for oil for burning in lamps."

Ann knew that whale oil was cleaner than the fish oil they used to light their lamp. She kept her eyes fixed on James as he explained further.

"The blubber is as thick as the breadth of a man's shoulders. We boil it down on the ship and then pour the oil into barrels—hundreds of them."

"'Tis used for soap, right, James?" added Mary.

"Yes, and then we grind the flesh into whale meal to eat and stack the bones. Every bit of the creature is sold." James began to yawn.

Ann sent the children to bed so that he could wash and go to sleep finally in the comfort of his own home once again. Drowsiness came over her too, as she put the baby down and tucked blankets around each child. Her anxiety over James's safety had disappeared as suddenly as a shifting wind. As she had embraced her son on the beach path, she detected an old gladness light up his face. Her lad back on Mainland and glad to be home with his family meant clear skies! It was better than purple heather on the hills or a full bowl of steaming broth on a cold night! She realized then that part of her own self had been missing in the past months—like an arm or a leg cut off—and now it was attached again, connected, and moving easily with all the other body parts. She could relax her limbs once again and pull up a blanket around her body to feel complete. Even without her husband beside her, her eight children rested happily under her roof—all but Jamie. Love filled her up to overflowing, and the feeling of abundance assured her that nothing else mattered. Like a mother seabird, she had all her chicks hatched and securely tucked under her wings, out of the mist and wind.

❧   ❧

In bed, with the house finally quiet except for the soft rain at the windows, she prayed . . .

> Dear God, thank you for bringing James home to us. Bless each of my precious bairns. Keep them fit with food to eat and free from illness. And God, be with my Robbie too. Bring him home to me. This bed is cold. Amen.

9

Gone to Sea

WINTER 1857

ROBERT ORDERED HIS OWN boat from Norway. It came in a kit with planks that were numbered and marked. Robert chose a sixareen, bigger than the traditional Ness yoal. His was made of Norwegian pitch pine and seasoned oak, strong enough for the far haaf. He knew a fisherman who no longer went out to sea but took work as a boatbuilder. This man collected the materials in Lerwick off a ship that sailed from Bergen. He chiseled the wood and beveled the planks in his boat shed. Each clinker plank had to fit just right so that the craft would be watertight. The boat was a beauty.

Robert was skipper of his own sixareen, and James was first mate. The son, at twenty-one, was physically even stronger than his father, who was by then forty-four. James could haul in the nets and raise the sails quickly while his father captained the craft. They put out to sea for themselves with a few other local fishermen as crew whenever they could, rather than sail for the laird and forfeit the fish.

In the last year, fishing had been plentiful, and they had been able to sell enough ling and cod, also some herring, to save fifty pounds Scots. Robert kept the money in a crock in the barn with a thick piece of driftwood wedged into the top. By January, the family larder was empty, and, with Ann's urging, Robert decided to take the money to Lerwick to buy goods for the rest of the winter and spring. Ann watched as her husband carefully counted the coins and paper money and dropped them into a soft leather pouch.

Men rarely sailed from South Mainland as far as Lerwick without fishing gear and the aim of bringing home a catch. This time they would set sail with two of Ann's cousins and a few neighbors—ten in all, men who also wanted to buy sugar, tea, tools, and perhaps a new teakettle for the wife. Before dawn, Ann walked with Robert and James to the pool of Virkie, just south of the Leslie croft where Robert's boat was moored, and there they met the others. They dressed warmly, for it was windy, and the sea was rough that morning. Robert tossed his knapsack into the hull, with brönnies and dried cod to eat and tea to quench the men's thirst. Ann handed Robert a cloth bag of knitwear, which she and her girls had produced over several months. The shawls would bring good money if Robert sought out the big ships docked in the Lerwick harbor with German merchants who sold goods to European markets. Wealthy German clientele valued the delicate lacy patterns, which Ann loved to knit from her finest, whitest wool. After Robert and the men launched the sixareen, waves pushed them back again toward the shore, but when James hoisted the sail, the wind augmented the human effort of six strong men at the oars, and Robert was able to steer his boat swiftly out toward the open sea.

Just before Ann turned to walk home, the sunrise of pink and orange lit up the sky enough for her eyes to lock on Robert, standing at the helm, patting his chest. The thickness of his pouch bulged from the inside pocket of his peacoat. She knew he was proud of the money and pleased to be able to acquire the provisions she needed to keep the family fed. She would also be glad to have a new pair of wool combs, so that two family members could work side by side to prepare the fleece to make good-quality worsted. Now that James was twenty-one, he was a strong second man in the economic life of the croft, fit for plowing the fields and rooing the sheep when it came time. Indeed, he had become a capable crofter as well as fisherman.

Ann left the shore to head home, wrapping her shawl tightly around her head and neck in the whipping wind. She hoped Robert would know what to buy and that he would find good bargains. They had no more savings since buying the sixareen, and they rarely had money to spend. She feared that he might not get what they most needed. But the boat had sailed off. She turned to look once more as the sixareen left the lagoon and entered the whitecaps of the unprotected sea. They were gone. And, as in so many life situations, she had no control over the outcome. Although she was very used to being left at home when her man went out to sea, on this day, with both her husband and James aboard, and their precious earnings with them, she had trouble shaking her worries. A rain cloud appeared from the horizon. Of course, as always, the woman's task was to do the work of two at the croft while her husband was at sea and then wait for the skipper's return. Such would be her duty. She certainly would not be idle.

Fortunately, Tina would return home after midday, when the housekeeper sometimes released her from her duties at the hall. Tina had also contributed to the money in the family crock in the last months, as she received wages for her work as a servant. She was a cook and reported to the housekeeper, who was rather strict.

As Ann entered the crofthouse, she found John, young Robert, Maggie, and Christina sitting by the hearth. No one was dressed. No one had done the morning chores. Well, it was the Sabbath, so the family would undertake only the necessary croft duties before leaving for chapel. Ann hoped that her children would mature and start taking on duties that her husband and oldest son usually accomplished. Her oldest daughter, Tina, had matured in her time away. She mused that Tina seemed more self-confident and considerate of others since working at the hall. The laird's wife didn't care for Tina's Shetland tongue, and she made a point of correcting her pronunciation with her own Highland brogue whenever she heard the cooks in conversation. Ann hoped Tina would read aloud to the other children when she came home later that day. The children always laughed when Tina imitated the missus's accent. Robert hated that his daughter was employed by the Scottish laird, the very man to whom he resented paying his tithe for the family's crofthouse and the tiny plot of land that came with it. But what other job was there for Tina? At least this way she ate well and brought home something to contribute. Ann smiled as she thought how Robert scowled when he heard his daughter rolling out her speech like the laird's wife. But it was time to get ready to leave—no more ruminations.

"John, won't you put another peat on the fire before we go?" asked Ann. Then she led the children off to church across the hill ground. They walked together and met up with other women and children arriving from another footpath also headed in the direction of the chapel. Ann asked one of the women, "So your husband is gone to sea then too?"

"Yes, he has been out whaling now for two months."

"Well, I dare say he'll be home soon, and with earnings for you and the bairns."

"'Tis our prayer, that he will be home soon. And your husband?"

"He and my son James have sailed to Lerwick, only just this morning. We expect them home tomorrow night."

"The whitecaps are rough, we heard. How big is his craft?"

"'Tis a sixareen, with ten men, and on the way home they will be heavy with provisions. 'Tis a new, steady craft. I'm grateful for that."

"'Twill be a happy hour when they unpack it all!"

Ann smiled as they walked. Then a fleeting premonition caused her to pause in her gait, drop the corners of her mouth, and turn to face straight into the woman's countenance. "I shall pray your man comes home soon—and safely."

"I thank you for your thoughtfulness. 'Tis a hard life, doing without him, and with my five bairns, all peerie, and needing their daa as well as their mam."

It had started to rain by the time they could see the chapel in the distance. In an instant, dark clouds obscured the little sunlight of the winter sky. The youngest children drew close to Ann, who led them forward by the hand in the direction they knew the chapel to be. Ann dared not let them run for fear of tripping on rocks and slipping in the mud. Even through their tightly knit wool hats and scarves, the downpour blew into their faces and drenched them to the skin. With relief, they arrived and entered the shelter of the chapel hall, then shook off and dropped their wet outer clothing, creating pools of water on the flagstones. Other crofting families who had arrived before the deluge made room for the newcomers on their benches, and Ann and her children huddled together shivering from the cold and wet.

Reverend Nichols began the service with familiar hymns. How good it was to sing and feel the warmth of one another's breath. Ann wished Robert were beside her, his strong voice emanating from their family group. She liked it when people turned to see who was singing and smiled at Robert as he nodded in his friendly manner. His bass notes created chords of harmony, rich and full, and she could imagine him with Christina on his lap, singing while rocking to the rhythm of the hymn tune they sang.

Dark and cheerless is the morn
unaccompanied by thee;
joyless is the day's return,
till thy mercy's beams I see;
till thy inward light impart,
cheer my eyes and warm my heart.[1]

The tune did warm Ann's heart. Or was it God, or the good people around her that comforted her like the welcome donning of a dry
woolen mantle? Being in chapel was simply a boon to living otherwise
in darkness and uncertainty. She glanced at each child sitting with her
in the row. Christina, the youngest, leaned tightly against Ann. Her little
legs stretched forward on the wooden bench, and Ann draped her arm
around her shoulder. Next to Christina was Annie and then Mary. At
fifteen and eighteen, the young women perched on the edge of the bench,
leaning forward to see who else was at chapel that day. They whispered
to each other and giggled about the way the people's clothes were soaked
through. Maggie sat on Mary's lap, so that the five-year-old could see
the Reverend Nichols in his long black robe. On the other side of Ann
were the boys—Robert, eight, and John, twelve, already squirming. Ann
knew neither was very happy to sit still for two hours. They had taken off
their shoes to rub their feet dry, and Ann worried that they didn't smell
very good. Although she tried to get the children clean for the Sabbath,
she never had enough time or enough hot water. Well, at least they were
all there, except, of course, Robert and James. And Tina would be home
soon.

There must have been at least sixty people in chapel that day. They
turned to Reverend Nichols attentively; in stormy weather and with men
gone to sea, everyone felt a palpable yearning for warmth and hope.

The text for the day was Psalm 107. The Reverend Nichols read it
from the Bible in a deep voice that commanded from everyone holy silence. Even the young ones learned to keep quiet, or else their parents or
older sisters would elbow them and promise punishment later that day.
The littlest drifted off quickly, as the minister's voice droned on through
the Scripture.

As Reverend Nichols launched into the middle of the psalm, Ann
sat up to listen intently.

1. Charles Wesley, "Christ Whose Glory Fills the Sky," #173 in *United Methodist Hymnal.*

They that go down to the sea in ships, that do business in great waters;
These see the works of the LORD, and his wonders in the deep.
For he commandeth, and raiseth the stormy wind, which lifteth up the
waves thereof.
They mount up to the heaven, they go down again to the depths: their
soul is melted because of trouble.
They reel to and fro, and stagger like a drunken man, and are at their
wit's end.
Then they cry unto the LORD in their trouble, and he bringeth them
out of their distresses.
He maketh the storm a calm, so that the waves thereof are still.
Then are they glad because they be quiet; so he bringeth them unto
their desired haven.[2]

The Reverend Nichols put his Bible down and looked out into the people's faces with a kind and gentle expression. Ann scanned the congregation. Women stared forward with bright eyes and gaunt cheeks. Men with soiled sweaters and sunburned faces cleared their throats and settled into their seats. Her focus returned to the minister, who waited, it seemed, a full minute before he began to deliver his commentary. "Men have always sailed the great waters. Without God's mighty ocean, where would crofters be? We thank God for the fish of the sea that nourish our bodies and provide us oil for our lamps and income for our daily needs." Good, he was going to talk about the island people. Ann was thinking that the Bible should be about them. "People of Shetland, brothers and sisters of Dunrossness, have faith in God's abiding protection in the great waters! Many of our men are now away at the far haaf, or in Greenland whaling, or off in the waters beyond the Shetland Isles somewhere else. Trust in the Lord!"

Ann so wanted to accept the minister's words. She exhaled a cleansing sigh and let the impact of the psalm wash over her like flowing rain. She was thirsty for the good, sweet water that came down from heaven and the grace of God that stilled the storm at sea. Had Reverend Nichols known it would rain so hard that day? Ann wondered how he had picked that psalm. Although she had read all one hundred and fifty psalms more than once, she had never thought about these particular verses that spoke directly to her that day. She wondered if Robert and James had arrived in Lerwick yet. Were they caught in this same storm at sea that the worshippers were now experiencing here on land? Ann could visualize their craft

2. Psalm 107:23–30.

rolling in the railing waves. Would Robert be able to steer the sixareen if a major gale came up?

Ann breathed deeply and turned from her thoughts of the tempest back to the minister's comforting words: "Have faith, my people. Lean on God and on one another. Be constant in your prayers. Never cease believing in God's haven at the end of the storm, and in the hope of the rainbow and the dawn's new light."

Soon they were singing again, and then it was time to depart. The rain had stopped, and thankfully the wind had died down, such that they carried their wet wraps without putting them back on.

Shortly after noon, when Ann and the children got home, Tina arrived. The scant winter daylight had already dimmed and departed. It was only one day past the solstice, not a good time to be gone to sea. Ann expected Robert and James to stay with her parents in Lerwick one night and then return by boat the next day. They would have a hold full of goods, covered in old sails to keep them dry. She would go to the shore to help carry the bounty as soon as she heard the boat had docked.

But for now, Tina's arrival provided them a ray of hope. Robert and Maggie watched their big sister unpack a bread pudding and set it on a grate to warm over the fire.

"Do you eat like this every day, Tina?" Annie wanted to know.

"Well, yes, if there is dessert left from tea the night before, I get to have a serving the next day in the morning, when they let me have a break for a cuppa. Usually, I am the one who made the treat, so I know 'twill be good!"

"What else have you made?" Robert looked at the pudding hungrily.

"They have a great big cookbook, so I can read the recipes and choose. I have made nut bread, apple cobbler, and, of course, shortbread and scones, they call them, for everyday."

"Where do they get all the necessary ingredients?" Mary asked.

"Well, they have servants who take the laird's boat to Lerwick, and they buy whatever they need. Money is no concern when you are rich. Sometimes a merchant or a relation sails from Aberdeen with even more goods, like plum and currant jelly, or lemon curd—that's very tasty! And they use only white wheat flour for their scones, not barley like in our coarse brönnies."

Ann steeped the tea, and John brought in the fresh cow's milk. They all sat together around the table, Tina dished up the warm pudding, and Ann added a bit of Lily's still-warm milk to each bowl. Christina plunged her hands into her dish and began the feast, licking her fingers with delight.

The girls and Ann spent the long dark hours of the afternoon and evening knitting by the fire. The boys mended nets and ground barley with a hand mill by the light of the oil lamp. The ministers of the Established Church would call it sinful to do such work on the seventh day, but Ann knew they had to accomplish something every hour, at least indoor tasks, or they could not eat. They hoped for a water mill, someday, to grind their grain in larger quantities. Basically, though, life was agreeable. The crofters were hardworking people. Even the animals played essential parts: Lily gave her milk, and Archie rounded up the sheep. Why hadn't they named the pony? Well, he was a stubborn fellow and required more kicking than talking to. He would rather be wild on the island moors than tethered in the byre. But he carried the peats and pulled the plow; Ann was grateful for his assistance. Of course, her Robbie did the most. He was her mast, holding the rigging and spars together, always piloting a strong and reasonable course. He was her mainsail, forging a clear angle on sea, land, and air—her life. In his wisdom, he stabilized her moods and steered her orientation to God. Without him, untethered, she could not imagine the rough voyage of living.

Robert looked up from grinding the grain and broke the silence. "When will they be home?"

Ann lit a lamp. "By tomorrow night, I think," she replied. "But they could spend a second night in Lerwick, if the goods are not available today. Or if the waves beyond the harbor are rough, or if the boat needs repair, or if someone were to fall ill."

"Who would fall ill? Daa is never sick, nor James."

"Well, we can never know what may happen. I like to think of reasonable explanations for a possible delay, so that I shan't worry about something serious happening." Ann returned to the task before her. Where was she in the knitting pattern? She turned the piece over in her lap and began another row. Needles clicking, she glanced about the room. Now, where did John go off to? And what would she prepare for their evening tea? "Robert, dear, can you and John catch a fish with your lines at the voe?"

"Where *is* John?"

"Perhaps he is there already. Fetch your fishing gear, and take the lantern." Ann frowned. "You know, I worry about John when he seems so far away in his thoughts, and then he wanders off like this after dark."

"Don't worry, Mother," Tina said. Ann put down her yarn and stood up to fill the teakettle with water. Then she went outside and, by feel, brought in the damp clothes that she had been drying on the line.

❧   ❧

"Where were you, John?" Ann asked as she set out dishes and food for their meal.

"Just walking at the voe."

"How can you see where you're going? 'Tis a thick mist out tonight." She shook her head. "Well, I'm glad you met up with your brother and came home with fish for our tea." She tried to be pleasant. "And you mustn't forget your milking, or Lily will be lowing." When Ann fried the two cod in a pan on the fire the smell of fish oil wafted through the cottage and drew the children to the table.

"When will Father be home?" asked Annie.

"We shall just have to wait and see. Did you hear any fishermen talking about the weather, John?" Ann asked.

"No, 'tis windy, though, that much I can say." John liked to wander along the shore from their nearby voe to the open sea at Sumburgh Head.

"Did you see Madge or Andrew about?"

"No, no one."

"I thought perhaps one of our friends would have heard about the sixareen and whether it had departed from Lerwick."

Young Robert wished he had been permitted to accompany his older brother and father. "They'll be staying more than one night in Lerwick, I'm guessing. I could have helped make the purchases, had they taken me along. Or at least I could have stayed with the boat."

By the time they sat down for their tea, the sky was dark, without a moon or stars in sight. Tina took a lantern and left for Sumburgh to go to bed and get up early to start the baking for another week. They finished their chores in the byre by lantern and cleaned the cooking area before bed. Archie curled up on the warm sand by the hearth, and Ann tucked the little ones in their box beds in the ben end and prayed aloud . . .

> Dear God, keep Father and James safe on their way home. Still
> the waters and the wind. Bless all the children: Jamie in heaven,
> Tina, James, Mary, Annie, John, Robert, Maggie, and Chris-
> tina—did I get them all? And bless Father, and bring him home
> tomorrow—oh, I said that already—well, bless us all. Amen.

Ann got up well before dawn and walked down to scour the coast. An unremitting torrent of wind blew off the voe, and Ann stretched on her tiptoes to search the lagoon for any boats coming in from Sumburgh or Lerwick. Just whitecaps, no boats. And what a squall! Could it be a gale such that no boats would go out today? Ann turned around to head home up the path. The airstream at her back pushed her body uphill like the billowing wind on a sail. From the lighthouse, the fog bell sounded its mournful call. She glanced back to face the sea and watch for boats. Were any visible? None. The sandy wind stung her cheeks. It would have been the time for the fishermen to go out, but there were no boats about.

When Ann returned to the croft the animals were stirring, and a curl of smoke rose from the chimney. Mary had stepped into Tina's role of assistant to Ann for cooking and already had brönnies baking and oatmeal simmering on the fire. Ann went into the ben end to help Chrissy get dressed for the day. She was still in nappies and, even at two, liked to suckle at her mam's breast.

"No, not now, sweetness. We'll have oatmeal with Lily's fresh milk. That will fill your tummy!" She tickled her and kissed her soft skin as she dressed her in a clean linen nappy and woolen undershirt. Ann wondered, would Christina be her last child? It was about the time she might expect the next one. Though she loved these moments with each peerie bairn, it would be a relief not to have to wash the nappies. She rubbed her chafed hands together and yawned, letting out a long sigh. She wasn't getting any younger, and nine births had made her a tired woman. Perhaps she could get Robbie to understand. Just having him next to her in bed was enough for her.

The day passed like any other winter day. The boys tended the animals in the byre. The women spun and knitted as they supervised the young ones learning at the hearth, where the peat fire kept them warm and fish dried in the smoky air. When darkness made it hard to see, they readied for tea and then bedtime, so as not to burn more oil until Robert and James returned.

The sun rose from the eastern horizon and tossed a rosy glow onto the island the next morning. As Ann sat eating breakfast with the children,

Archie barked and clawed the front door of the crofthouse. John went to open the door, and Andrew burst into the common room.

"Andrew! Come in. Sit down." Ann's eyes searched his face and quickly queried, "What is it?"

He took off his hat and sat at the hearth, breathing heavily. "Ann, I've just come from Lerwick. I saw your mother at the fish market. She told me Robert and James spent Sunday night at your parents' house. Then the crew made all their purchases in the morning, and they sailed out again straight away at midday yesterday south for home. Your father saw them off at the dock." He paused. "They should be back, but they aren't, are they? We haven't seen them come into the lagoon or unload. You know the trip from Lerwick should only take two to three hours with a good wind. And that we have had."

"Oh, dear, I thought perhaps they had spent a second night in Lerwick. Well, they didn't, so, where are they?"

Andrew spoke up quickly, "I'll take my boat and sail up along the coast. 'Twill be safe now since the winds have died down. Perhaps they put down their anchor for some reason along the way."

"John, run down to the beach by the lighthouse and ask whether a sixareen has come around the head yesterday or during the night."

Robert said, "Mother, let me go with Andrew up the coast."

"No, son, you are needed to watch at the voe and then come for us when Father's boat comes in," she said, trying to think of what possibly could have happened. "Thank you, Andrew, for coming to tell us, and for offering to go search."

Andrew set his hand gently on Ann's shoulder. "Don't worry, we'll find them." He pulled his stocking cap back on and turned to the door.

At dusk Andrew returned to the crofthouse with his lantern. This time, he knocked on the door with one slow thud and then another. Ann put down the knife she was using to peel the taaties and called to him to come in, as she wiped her hands on a towel. Andrew stepped inside and removed his fisherman's cap and let it hang at his side. Ann gasped. Andrew was holding Robert's knapsack. "Where did you find it?" she asked.

"'Twas on the rocks just south of Sandwick. 'Tis his, am I not correct?"

"Aye, 'tis his."

"Look inside."

Ann untied the laces and opened the stiff, wet bag. She reached around in the sack and pulled out a leather pouch. "Oh no! Yes, 'tis his, no doubt about it." She opened Robert's money bag, and inside, her fingers located just a single one-pound coin. "He spent all but this. But where is he?"

Andrew wiped his brow with his coat sleeve and looked at Ann with a painful tenderness she had never seen on his face. "His knapsack would have been in the hold of the boat." He looked at his boots, and then back up to her face. "Ann, the sixareen is lost, and the men with it."

"No! 'Tisn't true! He's made that sail so many times! And James? He would have helped in the gale."

"I know. I know. But my neighbor and I rowed my boat all the way to Lerwick scanning the rocks and the coastline. The seawall at Lerwick was even damaged by the storm; 'twas a mean one. When we turned around to come back home, we moored at Cunningsburgh, and I spoke with fishermen there. They had spotted the sixareen heading south yesterday. There was a gale blowing, they said, and the craft was reeling, but it was following the coastline due south, as would be expected. But then at Sandwick, no one knew anything about Robert's boat. The waves must have knocked it over, or it hit rocks between Cunningsburgh and Sandwick, and the knapsack washed ashore. Everything else in the boat was too heavy—the men and the goods."

"No men? No boat?" Ann started to grasp what had happened. She dropped into a chair and collapsed.

"So far, nothing more has been found." Andrew sat down at the table. "The water is deep there off the shore. There have been accidents by Sandwick before—drownings and shipwrecks."

"They shouldn't have returned so soon. They should have waited another day for a calmer wind." Andrew nodded as she continued, "But I know Robert. Every day is a day to work. He wouldn't like to be gone long."

"And your parents said the crew had made their purchases already that morning."

Suddenly, Ann began to fathom the desperate situation she was in. Her husband was lost at sea, and the provisions purchased with all their earnings had gone down with him. And James! Her son! He was gone too! "But why haven't they been found?"

"If the knapsack went overboard, so must have the men. Perhaps the boat was too weighted down with goods. It may have been poorly balanced."

The girls entered the room from the ben end where Christina was still napping and where they were knitting when they heard voices. Robert was still waiting at the voe, and John had not returned from Sumburgh Head. Mary had heard enough of the conversation to take in the dire situation and spoke up first, "Shouldn't we get the lads? Perhaps they've seen or heard something. What if just the knapsack went over, and the sixareen sailed on?"

Annie grabbed the leather pouch and shook her head. "Father would have kept his last pound tucked safely in the hold. The boat must have capsized."

Ann sat numb, as if frozen suddenly by a wind off the Arctic ice. Disbelief turned to dread, and questions dashed her brain like frozen hail stones: if they had died, how did it happen? Did they hit rocks that tossed them into the ocean? Where was her James? Was he now lying at the bottom of the sea? Why could Robert not have saved him? And the others, why had they not regained control of the craft? Had they not bailed enough? Had they not taken the sails down?

"'Tis what happens in a gale," Andrew explained. "The waves overcome the small boats. The winds come up without warning, and there is no turning back to shore. No time left." Andrew knew too well how many fishing boats were lost every year off Mainland.

"But they were so close to home! Father has sailed much farther, and he has always returned." Tears flowed down Mary's cheeks.

Maggie's eyes filled, and she went to climb into Ann's lap. Christina woke from her bed, crying as she often did after her nap. Mary went to get her. Shaking her head, Annie continued to try to piece together the sequence of events, "We usually hear of winds at sea off the *west* coast; 'tis that not more common? Was there a gale warning on the *east* coast yesterday?"

"I don't know. Today no boats went out in the morning from Virkie." Andrew scratched his head. "Yes, 'tis generally more dangerous on the west coast, by Scalloway, in a bad gale. But the sea has a temper, and it lashes out wherever it chooses." He shook his head slowly from side to side. "I'll find young Robert and John and send them home. Shall we fetch Reverend Nichols?"

"No. I just want to be with my children, those that are here," Ann replied. She rubbed her forehead and realized unexpectedly that her head pulsed with a plodding ache.

Andrew left the family huddled together in silence by the hearth. "Come, Mother, I suppose we must eat something," Mary suggested, and she got up to finish making tea. At least peerie Chrissy would want to eat.

John and Robert came home in the dark. They had nothing to report. No one had seen the sixareen. There were no sightings of a boat that had washed ashore. The boys were not ready to accept the conclusion Andrew had drawn. They went out to the byre to tend the animals and moved about without speaking. Night crept over the family, and a deathly silence entered the hollow space of their home. There was nothing more to say. Ann could not eat the taaties and brönnies Mary had prepared. She put the youngest to bed and lay down in her clothes, with her windblown hair still uncombed. A cold void engulfed her and separated her from the reality of what had happened. Nothing penetrated the empty space, save an ache that squeezed her heart and pounded in her temples. If only sleep would take her in its arms.

❧ ❧

The next day passed as if in a dense fog. Ann did not know what force possibly propelled her from bed to perform her daily tasks. Something as basic as the tidal force between the earth and the moon maintained the rhythm of life. They had to eat. They had to sleep. On the day after hearing the news, Mary walked to Sumburgh to tell Tina that Father and James had not returned. The sisters came home together, arriving to find Ann downcast, crouched by the fire rubbing her hands.

When Ann embraced Tina, her chest heaved with sobs. Tina cried too and told her mother, "When Mary said Father and James were lost at sea, I went to ask the laird what he might have heard. He said that a bit of a boat had washed up onto the beach at the head. He sent for his steward to take us there, and when we saw it, we agreed it was Father's sixareen. The man knew the boat and recognized the broken planks of wood that had been brought from Norway."

Mary added, "Only part of the boat came ashore. It was torn and ruined."

"Our family had saved for that boat," Ann remembered. "Father ordered the kit from Bergen, and you know how it was constructed in Lerwick. Not many crofters could afford such a craft. It was his prized possession—that and his fiddle from his father." She broke down crying. "Oh, how will we manage without them?" Tina hugged her mother again until she caught her breath. "Tina, can you stay with Christina and Maggie? I should go to the beach. I must see for myself what is left of the boat."

"Yes, of course, Mam." She turned to her sister. "Mary, will you stay here with me?"

Mary nodded and sat down, tired from walking to and from the south end of the island. She said to her sister, "'Tis surely a shock to comprehend. Even now, a day after Andrew brought home Father's pack, I cannot believe they are gone."

The others stopped what they were doing and entered the but end when they heard that Tina was home. John and Robert wanted to go with their mother to see the boat. Ann agreed, for they could help carry home whatever wood from the sixareen had drifted to shore.

"May I come also?" Annie asked.

"Yes, come along. The other girls can finish making the bannocks and keep the fire burning." It was a relief to speak of something tangible. Ann directed Tina and Mary, "Our neighbors brought us food, so eat, and you'll need to feed your peerie sisters too."

"Go, Mother. We'll take care of things," Tina said.

They dressed warmly and headed south through the soggy heath toward Sumburgh. The boys leapt ahead, and Ann and Annie hurried behind them. It was the first time Ann had ventured beyond their croft since the news. The wind chilled her face, and she crossed her arms and tucked her hands in her armpits for warmth. The sky was misty, but it was clear enough to see the lighthouse, and she wondered whether Robert had seen its light in the fog and rain when the wind and waves downed his boat. How far from the coast had they sailed? She wondered if the wreckage could give them any answers.

When they had mounted the bluff, they spotted the hull of the sixareen on the beach. The tide was out, so it sat on dry ground. Another boat was pulled barely onto the sand, and the fishermen had walked up the beach to survey the wreckage.

"'Tis our boat! See the clinker planks?" John shouted back to his mother as he reached the shore first. "'Tis only the broken bow, but look, the fore head is still intact." He stooped down to open the compartment where sails and tackle were kept. Inside was the square sail, folded and still wet, the one he had helped mend more than once. "They must have taken the sail down when the storm came on."

"That was James's job, to take down the sail. Father would have been at the tiller," Robert explained to his mother and sister.

Ann lifted the heavy sail and let it unfold from her arms onto the sand. The fishermen came to her with bowed heads, asking how they could help. She knelt down on the beach and ran her hands over the rough fabric, with its hooks and ropes still attached. Tears streamed down her face. Annie sat with her mother and let her cry. Then Ann stood up and blew on her chilled hands and rubbed them on her coat. Without a word, the fishermen helped her double over the stiff flax. Together, and with the aid of the men, John and Robert hoisted the remnant of the hull of the boat onto their shoulders, and Annie supported the bow to share some of the weight. They waited for their mother before starting up the rise toward home. Ann carried the sail in front of her between her outstretched arms. She led the silent procession. Annie followed, leading with the point of the bow, as the boys carried the main weight of the broken hull behind her. Mist settled over the sail and the hull of the boat, as if speaking a solemn prayer for the dead.

There would be no bodies. The sail would be the burial shroud for both her beloved Robert and her dear son James. The two had been together in the boat until the last. And now, they were together still.

10

Mourning

SPRING CAME LATE THE year Robert and James were lost at sea. Patches of snow and ice covered the Ness even on the first day of May. Christina was sleeping, and Ann had sent the other children to the beach in their winter clothes to gather shellfish. A pounding on the door roused Ann from the hearth where she kept warm, knitting on this cold, gray morning.

The laird's steward stood outside stomping snow from his boots. "Good day, ma'am."

Knowing she must be polite, Ann offered, "Will you come in from the cold?" She moved from the doorway to allow the man to pass her and enter the but end. "So, what is it, sir?" She knew it would have been more polite to invite him all the way inside to sit in the resting chair offered for company.

Standing in the middle of the common room, he said, "'Tis the rent I've come for, ma'am. I have received no fish from this croft for a month."

"We have no fishermen and no boat, sir. You know my husband died at sea, and our son James with him."

"Yes, we know," he said gently, and Ann thought his words came out with at least an ounce of compassion. But then he diverted his eyes from her face and spoke further in a low voice, "The laird must have the tithe for the cottage, you see. He's sent me for it. You'll have to leave the crofthouse if you cannot pay the rent in fish, or crops, or sterling." He seemed to tower over her in his heavy wool coat and herringbone hat, looking down at her feet as they stood by the fire.

Ann shrank and collapsed into her chair with a sigh. "You know we have no crops, for 'tis still freezing, and everything we had of value we lost overboard on the sixareen from Lerwick."

"Will you move out then?"

"Sir, have pity on us. We have nowhere to go. This is our home. My husband worked for the laird every day since we married." She started to cry. "I am alone with six bairns, and Tina working at the hall. The boys are too young to fish for the laird. My daughters and I can knit, that's all we can do. We have only a bit of barley left now."

"But you have the animals. I shall take the cow for this month's rent. Already, in his mercy, the laird gave you a free month, you know."

Ann could form no words in her mouth, for it was dry and clamped shut. Salty tears crossed over her pursed lips. The man hesitated and then saw himself out the door, leaving it ajar. Shortly, Ann heard the cow bellow as he lashed her in a harness and tugged her out from the straw in the byre onto the icy ground. Ann threw herself onto the door, opening it fully, as she wailed. A gust of wind accosted her and flung her hair in her face. Trapped in a rage of misery, like a madwoman, she screamed at the steward and pounded the air with clenched fists as he shoved the willful cow up a ramp into the back of a horse-drawn cart. Ann could only bellow like an animal in protest. In seconds, the cart had pulled away, leaving her bereft of all her human dignity.

Christina woke from her sleep and came out of the ben end to see why both her mother and the cow had been howling. "Mam!"

"We've lost Lily. Another one gone."

❧   ❧

Rains came and then wintery spring finally acquiesced to allow the sun to announce the time for planting. Ann worked through the lengthening daylight hours, and thus she barely sustained the family's croft life. She plowed the cold, hard earth, harrowed the field, and scattered the seeds. Once the sowing was done, she carried the peats in a kishie on her back from dawn until twilight, rain or shine, both for her own family and for her neighbor, Agnes, who paid her with taaties. Ann's shoulder muscles grew hard, and the skin of her hands formed calluses. Every day, she bent over each task, without lifting her eyes beyond the path in front of her. At the end of her toil, she trudged into the crofthouse and instantly collapsed by the hearth to knit.

But one day, come June in the gloaming, after four trips to the peat hill, Ann unloaded her kishie, piled the peats in the byre to dry, then straightened her back and massaged her shoulder blades. She looked out over the croft. The sheep were grazing on the grass close to the cottage. Archie, though getting on in years, still nipped at their heels when they dared to wander. The youngest children—Robert, Maggie, and Christina—would be learning their lessons with Mary in the but end by the simmering pot of turnip broth, and Annie and John, she hoped, were collecting clams at the voe. This day, before entering the cottage, she faced into the cool wind and let it blow onto her sunburnt face. The lustrous colors at the horizon, where the heavens met the dark sea, surprised her. How could the sky be so lovely? Did it not know that life was dark and cruel? She thought of her Robbie. Why had she not cried more when he died at sea? Why had James's death not pushed her to tears, as little Jamie's had? Had her heart so hardened that she had no capacity left for sorrow? Red and gold blended into a warm blaze before her eyes.

She thought of her youngest, Christina. It was for her that she could not give up, and for the other children too. She had to keep the family fed. She looked out to the horizon over the water. How many other women labored with their husbands gone fishing for herring at the haaf, or sailing on whaling ships to Greenland, and those women too worked the land through every daylight hour to feed their bairns? Like all the crofters she knew, Ann fought an endless battle against hunger. It hovered near like an enemy laying siege. Yet when the foe advanced to threaten, she refused to surrender in defeat. She must keep the croft, which meant they had to produce sufficient grain and hand-knit hosiery to pay the laird. Soon John would be able to go out with the men on a sixareen. Ann wished fervently, God be with them! And let the sun and rain partner to yield good summer crops to satisfy the laird! Ann looked to the ocean and the sky for a shimmering ray of hope.

Weary with these worries and exhausted from toil, Ann bowed her head and asked herself, which was it that drove her, fear of starvation or anger at her station in life? When she looked up again, the colors had dissipated and darkness had closed in on her. She breathed in the sea air. The wind turned cold, and mist descended onto the croft. Momentarily, she was able to put fear to rest for the night. And if she had felt anger, it too had drifted off. She looked up the path, hoping to make out Annie and John returning home with shellfish for tea. Then she let her shawl drop from her head onto her shoulders and opened the cottage door to join her children.

That evening, Mary read from the Bible, from Psalm 95:

> O come, let us worship and bow down: let us kneel before the LORD
> our maker.
> For he is our God; and we are the people of his pasture, and the sheep
> of his hand.[1]

Mary repeated the lines and then asked Maggie to recite these verses from memory. She did, and Ann drew her into her lap and praised her, "Indeed you have learned your lesson today, darling. Good lass."

Robert smiled and said, "The new lambs are getting big now. They're eating plenty of grass and jumping all about! They don't even need a shepherd, Mam."

"Oh, but they do. And so do we. 'Tis God who is watching over us each day, you know. I can tell, for our Provider painted the sky for us tonight with a brilliant palette."

❧ ❧

After supper, Ann turned in for the night, and just before dozing off, remembered to pray . . .

> Thank you, God, for the clams Annie and John dug today, and for the brönnies Mary made, using the last of the barley. We haven't tea, but we can survive without tea; our ancestors certainly did. Tomorrow will be fish broth, for we haven't any milk, of course. And no more oats, as well. No matter what befalls us, keep us in your care, O God. And thank you for the sky tonight. It helped me think of you. Amen.

1. Psalm 95:6–7a.

11

Tears in the Heather

AUTUMN 1862

TINA CONTINUED TO WORK for the mistress of the manor, bringing home a few coins each month. Wages were hard to come by, and Tina was fortunate to have a position. At thirty, it seemed she would not be marrying. Fine, thought her mother—just as well! To marry and lose your man at sea is no bliss. Tina wished for a different life, but Ann tried to help her see that she contributed more to the family than she could in any other way. And besides, she ate well at the laird's, and that was worth something.

With Tina's earnings, Ann went to Lerwick with Madge in Andrew's boat. She bought worsted, as well as tea and sugar. Ann made more money by knitting fine jumpers with quality wool than by growing meager crops. The constant wind had eroded the fertile soil, and even the grass was so thin that the sheep had not produced as much wool as she would have hoped. Each year, the earth had less bounty, and Ann carried the weight of uncertain survival like a heavy kishie that caused her back to stoop and her legs nearly to give out.

Arriving back in Sumburgh, Ann spotted Tina doing an errand for the housekeeper in the village. Tina asked eagerly what her mother had seen in Lerwick.

"Well, women are gutting herring at the dock. And they make decent wages."

"Should I leave my position and take a job on the waterfront?"

"No, Tina. You mustn't give up working for the missus. She likes your cooking, and I have a notion you make it possible for us to stay here. You know, we haven't paid our full tithe since Father and James died."

"Yes, Mam, I believe you are right. The laird is clearing out crofters to the west. He sends his steward, and then the families must move out in less than a fortnight. There are more and more people now without homes and livelihood here in the Ness." Ann shook her head. "This trucking system is unfair. We Shetlanders are the deserving people of these islands, not the Scottish lairds! Why should we have to pay whatever rent the laird demands?"

"'Tis the way, darling, since we don't own the land. I never expected to be rich when I married a crofter-fisherman."

"But, Mam, you have worked all your life! And what do you have for it? Peats on your back and piltocks in your belly!"

"I do not complain, Tina love. God has given us enough, not plenty, but enough."

"You used to grumble about the laird to Father, don't you remember?"

"Yes, and he spoke as I do now: 'tis our station. We are humble crofters. We should not expect more . . . And you must get back to the hall."

"But I want more for our family!" Tina continued. "Perhaps 'tis too late for me now that I am thirty. But if I cannot have a husband and a life away from here, at least I would wish it for my sister." Tears formed in her eyes. "Mother, will you let Mary go to Lerwick?"

Ann studied her daughter's face. "Well, we might be able to do without her here. If she's to marry, she should be finding a lad, better sooner than later. There's no one for her here in the Ness." She regarded her oldest with sympathy. "Tina, your life is not what I would have chosen for you, darling. But it could be worse. You have a bright mind, and you can continue to learn by reading in spare moments. And perhaps you will be able to travel to Aberdeen some day on the laird's ship. Wouldn't that be something?"

Ann admonished Tina to run along and went back up the path to home. She found Mary in the ben end, where she had been reading to Christina. Ann knew Mary would be eager to go to Lerwick and earn her own wages, and perhaps even find a husband as well.

The next day, Mary left early for the Virkie dock, where she planned to take a sixareen up the coast to Lerwick and apply for work at the harbor. Ann finished clearing away breakfast and sent the children into the field and byre to tend to their chores. Duties crowded her head: the washing, the garden, the animals, the field, the peats . . . Annie and John would have to take on Mary's workload. Robert, Maggie, and Christina were already doing all they could, with learning their letters and figures on top of crofting. And John went fishing on the days when he managed to join a sixareen.

Ann sat alone by the hearth. The fire needed fuel, but rather than fetch more dry peats from the byre, she sat staring at the ashes. How she wished for a cup of tea, a comfort to hold in her hands on this cool morning! Now both of her two oldest daughters would be gone from her. She sank into the chair and stared blankly into the embers as she counted the losses in her life: Jamie gone in the fire, and James and Robbie drowned at sea. One by one, her family was leaving her. Her parents had died from influenza the previous winter, and she had not even been able to return to Lerwick for their funerals for fear of falling ill herself from the stubborn disease that still lurked in the town. God only knew where her brothers were. Only her sister was still in Lerwick, as far as she had heard.

Mary returned at dusk, tired from the journey by boat to Lerwick, five hours of gutting herring, and the trudge up the path from the southern tip of the island at the end of a long day. She was red in the face and panting when she appeared at the door.

"Mother, they hired me! I am to start full days next week. Look, I already earned a few pence!" She handed the coins to Ann and peeled off her boots and shawl.

"Oh, Mary, you reek of fish! Even more than your father did! Go wash yourself! Then come inside and tell us all about it."

There was herring from Lerwick that night for tea. While ladling the pungent fish soup, Robert asked his sister, "What was it like? Were there lads gutting too?"

"No, just young women. The boys do the salting, but mostly off at the shore where the deep-sea fishermen dock. The lads stay there in a camp overnight through the season, unless, of course, like you and John, they are needed at their crofts."

Ann looked around the room. "Where is John? He hasn't come home for tea."

Robert answered, "He was walking south at the voe earlier today. I haven't seen him since."

Mary asked, "Why does he go off like that? Doesn't he know that he is needed here?"

"I worry about him, off alone at night," Ann added. "Take the lantern and go look for him, will you, Annie?"

"I'll go too," said Robert.

"But 'tis late, Robert. Annie may need to go all the way to Sumburgh."

"No matter. We'll go together."

Ann waited up after the others went to bed. Finally, when the moon had risen to the top of the peat-black sky, Annie and Robert returned home. In hushed voices, Annie related to their mother, "We didn't find him. We walked all along the voe and then on the path to the lighthouse and over to the beach. He wasn't anywhere."

"Did you see anyone to ask?" Ann asked.

"We stopped at Madge and Andrew's, but they hadn't seen John at all, not for a day or two, they said. It's been damp, and there's been heavy mist to obscure visibility."

"Not for a day or two? What then? What was he doing when they last saw him?"

Robert answered, "They said it seemed he was returning from the lighthouse."

"From the lighthouse? Why?"

"They didn't know." Robert frowned and asked his mother, "Was he doing something wrong? Something he should not have been up to? Or else, why didn't he speak to us about it?"

"I don't know." Ann shook her head and frowned. "I don't know at all." She crossed the room to the door, opened it, and looked out. Wind whipped her face in the dark. They wouldn't be able to search for him any more at that hour. "We shall have to wait until morning." Or perhaps John would return by dawn, she thought. After all, he was seventeen, old enough to watch out for himself.

But by morning, John had not returned. Ann and Mary left the younger ones and went to search. If John had been seen a day or two ago near the lighthouse, then perhaps they should inquire at Sumburgh Head. For all they knew, there was only a lighthouse keeper there, and Ann reminded the others it was rumored that he had a daughter, though no one had ever seen her.

Ann and Mary wrapped their shawls tightly around their heads and shoulders, and they walked briskly along the footpath toward the south end of the island. They had never approached the lighthouse keeper. Only a few times had they even walked up the path to the lighthouse, just to watch for whales and seabirds from the high lookout point. It was a remote destination, beautiful, but a place laden with ancient tales of shipwrecks and danger.

The fog bell sounded its mournful toll as they approached. Ann knocked on the lighthouse door, and when no one answered, she called out, "Is the lighthouse keeper about? I would speak with him!"

After a good minute, a middle-aged man opened the door and looked sternly into the women's faces. "What do you want?" he grunted. "I am working."

"Yes, excuse us, please. We are looking for my son, John Leslie. He was seen coming from the lighthouse in the last days, and he didn't come home last night."

"John is the name?"

"Yes, he is seventeen. Have you seen him?"

"The head has seen too much of that lad! Come in, and I'll tell you, I am mad as hell at that lad."

"Why? Where is he?" They entered the lighthouse. The keeper made no indication to take the stairs, so they stood awkwardly inside the narrow entrance by the closed door.

"Where he is now, I do not know, but he'd better finish what he started."

Ann looked at Mary and paled as she waited to learn more. "What do you mean?"

"Your son has been meeting secretly with my daughter, who is only fourteen. I just learned he left her with a bun in the oven."

Ann gasped, and her shawl fell from her head. "Can this be true? We had no idea he was seeing a lass."

"My daughter had never left this lighthouse. I have kept her under my watch here since her mother died. When I saw her creeping out one evening, I brought her back by her hair and lashed her with my belt. But it was too late. She was already with child."

Mary said, "We'll find John, and he will do right by her, if he is the father."

"Oh, he is, all right. You can be sure of that. She told me his name when I asked her."

"But where is John now?" Ann insisted. "Does your daughter know where we can find him?"

"He was acting crazy, like an animal, the day before yesterday."

Ann asked, "Can we talk to your daughter? Please, we must understand."

"No, she is staying here until your John comes for her with a vow to marry and a home to take her to."

"We will search for him, but we have no idea where he would go. Did he tell her he would return?"

"No, she said he left her outside on the rocks when she told him she was carrying his child. He was the only man she had ever laid eyes on, really just a lad, the scoundrel. My daughter was unknowing of these things, and he took advantage of her."

"How long had they been meeting?" Ann asked.

"Weeks, perhaps, since summer. Sometimes I take a break in the long bright evening when no light is needed, and I leave to get provisions. She must have slipped out then. She knew it was forbidden; that puts her also at fault."

"'Tis shameful of our John. I am deeply sorry." Ann wiped tears from her eyes. "Of course, your daughter can live with us, and we will raise the bairn. 'Twill be baptized and have a good home."

The keeper continued, "If your son does not return, I shall keep her here to myself until the bastard is born. I can say no more." He looked up. "I must return to the light now."

❧ ❧

Ann and Mary stopped by Madge and Andrew's croft and found Madge cooking in their common room. She took their wraps and invited them to sit down. Mother and daughter pulled up chairs and began to peel the taaties and turnips that Madge had washed for the next meal. Madge asked right away, "What brings you both here with such worry spilled across your brows?"

"'Tis John. We cannot find him. He didn't come home last night."

Mary turned to her mother. "Tell Madge what the lighthouse keeper said."

"We have just come from there. He said John got his daughter in the family way." Ann gasped as she heard herself say it. "The keeper is terribly angry, as he should be. But no one knows where John is."

Madge looked away and then back into Ann's eyes, shaking her head. "We suspected something like this, Ann."

"What?" Ann asked incredulously.

"John has a way of wandering about, we all know that. He has been here in Sumburgh alone frequently since summer. We hadn't known what he was up to, or we would have spoken to you, Ann. But everyone knows that the lighthouse keeper has a daughter. 'Tis rumored that she has never seen another man besides her father, never once in her life. He keeps her locked up for fear of just such an incident, I suppose. We could not imagine what John was doing. We just figured he liked to walk alone along the coast. But in recent weeks, he has come and gone in the gloaming, always to the lighthouse and back. He made it a pattern."

"Did you then suspect this?" Ann needed to know.

"We spoke of the chance of it, Andrew and I. But you know how we love your family. We prayed about it and hoped that John was just growing up and needing to be away from home. Perhaps he was lonely, and we reckoned he could still be in a dark way since his father and James died. We didn't want to worry you without true knowledge of his behavior."

Ann put down the vegetables and knife and took out a handkerchief from her pocket. She wiped her tears and spoke feebly, "What should I do? Where should we look for John?"

Mary assured her, "Surely someone will know where he is, Mother. We'll ask the laird and then the local preacher."

Madge gave them brönnies to take with them. She hugged them and then sent them off in their misery, "God walks with you, you know that, Ann. And John too is not alone. This will all work itself out in God's time."

The autumn winds came up as the women walked to the laird's manor and then through the village at Sumburgh, knocking on doors. Had anyone seen him board a boat? Was he hiding at some deserted croft in shame, they wondered? Had he left the island? But hadn't he slept somewhere? Not to anyone's knowledge. Questions fell upon their path before them, like stones to stumble on. No one knew the whereabouts of John Leslie.

It started to rain as Ann and Mary eventually gave up the search for John and neared their crofthouse. A fleeting hope quickened their pace. Perhaps they would find him sitting with the others by the fire. Perhaps they had eaten together. Had he remembered he was needed to tend the sheep? Or had John by now returned to the lass at the lighthouse? The wind whipped Ann's hair out of her shawl as she looked once more down the path from whence they had come. Mary urged her mother inside, into the warmth where the others were waiting.

But by the next morning, John had still not come home. Nor had anyone seen or heard from him in the last three days. Ann gazed across the room as she stirred the oats over the fire. Did he love the lass? He must be sorely afraid, she thought. Was he hiding with a friend, someone the family had not known? She wondered how much of his life he had kept a secret from them. Why hadn't he come to her? In fear, he may have run, she thought. By now, John could have left the island, perhaps to work on a ship or travel far from Shetland. Oh, where was her lad? Ann sat down at the breakfast table and broke down as she served herself oats. She stirred her porridge aimlessly, breathing in its steam as she wept. There was no way she could leave the croft again to search for him; there were too many chores, and the young ones needed her. Tina had returned to the laird's house, and Mary was preparing to go to Lerwick where she would sleep weekdays with Ann's sister. Her Aunt Mary, Mary's name-sake, had offered her a bed in her home while young Mary worked at the dock. Without the oldest girls, only Ann and Annie would be home to run the croft and care for Robert, Maggie, and Christina. Without John, Robert would have to fish, though he was not yet a grown man, and Annie would have to push the plow and plant next season's barley. There wouldn't be much time for Maggie and Christina to learn their lessons by the hearth. Maggie would need to carry the peats and knit, and Christina would do the wash and the cooking with her mother. They had to eat, and they had to pay the laird their tithe. Ann wiped tears away and spoke to the family with resolve, "We shall continue, as always, to be a family, and to help one another and make it through, God willing."

"Father would say, 'God is always willing and ready to carry us through,'" said Mary. "And I will come home on weekends with fish and provisions from my wages."

Ann went out to check on the sheep. She shook her head, thinking, "How will John manage? What will become of him?"

That night after everyone had gone to bed, Ann left the house to walk alone on the hill ground. The October hunter's moon shone like a gold coin illuminating the dark sky. She stepped into the thick heather, not caring that her shoes would get too wet to dry by morning. The spongy turf welcomed her steps and seemed to draw her into the comfort of Mother Earth herself. A large rock blocked her path, not that she had found a real path or any direction in particular. But the rock was there, and so she sat on it to rest. She breathed in the scent of damp heather and closed her eyes, inviting the breeze to caress her face. Tears drained from her eyes and dropped onto the heather around her ankles. How she longed for her mother's embrace—even now at her advanced age—or for Robbie's caress. But instead, she found herself with only the earth and the sky for companions. She wept, perched there alone on the rock. After some time, she wiped her eyes and blew her nose on a handkerchief. Then taking courage from the firm rock and the wide expanse of moor and sky around her, words of prayer formed from a deep place in her throat . . .

> O God, you are my mother and my father, my husband, and my rock—my only hope. Forgive me for not coming to you in prayer before now in my desperation. Pardon me, O God.
>
> Our John has gone away. I fear he is out in the cold with no shelter, alone and sorely troubled. If you can speak to him, tell him that I love him and that we will forgive him of his transgressions if he would just come home. Perhaps he has been afflicted these many months, and I have paid no notice. Truly, he has been acting strangely, now that I ponder it. He often has not spoken but has disappeared early in the day and returned not until late at night. Help me to understand. Why did I not see his behavior as a warning that all was not well? What kind of a mother does not watch out for her bairns? Forgive me, O God.
>
> I pray for the lass at the lighthouse. She is so young and now with a bairn on the way. Care for her, O God, and protect the peerie one. Bring John back to the lighthouse or to us here at the croft. Give us a chance to help him at this crossroads in his life. Do not let him despair!
>
> And soften the heart of the lighthouse keeper, O God. Keep him from harming his daughter or the child—my grandchild! Guide him to treat the lass with love, and the bairn in her belly as well. And if John returns to them, may they accept him into their family, as we surely will take him back into ours.

Now 'tis when I miss my Robert so. If he were only here, he would know what to do.

Ann broke off in sobs. Usually by the end of her praying, she felt better, but this time, voicing her concerns only augmented her fear and loss. Finally, she pushed her hands against the rough rock and lifted her tired body from the cold stone. She trudged back to the croft. Quietly, she kicked off her shoes and undressed in the dark. Shivering, she crawled into her cold bed. She buried her face in the pillow and surrendered to the comfort of the blankets as they slowly warmed her damp skin.

Mary gutted fish at the dock in Lerwick and returned each weekend to Exnaboe on Friday evening. Tina came up from the laird's house to see her sister whenever the housekeeper permitted her a few hours off. Then the sisters sat together in their box bed and whispered into the evening about the skippers and fishermen Mary met at the Lerwick wharf.

One weekend in the late autumn, Mary came home Friday night after dark and walked up the path from the voe by herself. Coughing, she entered the crofthouse where Ann and Annie sat quietly knitting by the fire. Ann stood to meet her at the door and with the lantern scanned her flushed face. "Are you ill, Mary?"

"I am tired, 'tis all," Mary said with a raspy voice.

"Come, sit by the fire. I'll put the kettle on for tea."

Annie felt her forehead. "She's burning hot, Mam."

Ann got a cloth and wet it with cool water and laid it on Mary's brow as she sank into the resting chair. Mary shivered. "I'm afraid she has a fever. Here, Annie, help her off with her coat. She should sleep out here in the but end, and the rest of us in the ben. We cannot risk catching whatever she has."

"Could it be typhus, Mother?" Annie whispered.

"I hope not, good Lord." Mary dozed off even before the tea had steeped. Her hoarse cough caused her to toss from side to side, unable to get her body comfortable. Ann sent the family into the other room and to bed. She helped Mary lie on blankets on the floor by the fire and covered her with a clean quilt. Having done all she could for her daughter, she joined the others in the ben end and tried to sleep.

By morning, a scarlet rash covered Mary's chest and back. She complained that her head pounded, and her fever soared. Ann knelt beside

her daughter, urging her to swallow sips of cool tea. Annie made the porridge and got the children up and ready to do their chores outside. Ann
knew she must get help. She sent Robert for the minister. Perhaps he
would know what to do after seeing many parishioners suffer from fever.

Robert hurried back from the manse where he had met briefly with Reverend Bentley. "The Reverend won't be coming. He said rash and fever
surely mean 'tis the typhus fever Mary has, and for that there is no cure.
He said just water and rest, and we are to stay away from Mary, so no one
else catches it. He'll be praying for her, of that he assured me."

Ann threw her hand to her brow. "Oh, dear. Well, I'll tend to Mary,
and the others of you stay clear if you can. I shall do the cooking, and you
do your chores outside, and take your meals there too, if 'tisn't too cold.
We'll pray that she recovers and can soon return to Lerwick."

Though Ann tried to be hopeful, when Mary's rash spread to her
hands and feet, she began to fear the worst. Mary slipped in and out of
restless slumber. Her waking moments were tormented by nausea and
aching that overcame her like powerful demons. Ann moistened a cloth
and wiped her skin, helpless to know what more she could do.

Tina did not come home the following weekend. Ann had asked
her to stay away for fear of exposing herself again to the fever. But after
two weeks, Tina returned despite her mother's admonishment. When
Tina entered the crofthouse, Ann cried out as she beheld her daughter's
blotchy red face. "Oh, Tina! You have it too!"

"The housekeeper sent me away to keep the fever from the other
servants."

"Oh, Tina! We'll watch over you!" Ann could not hide her premonition. Her brow tightened and her hands kneaded the creases in her
forehead. She took Tina's shawl and hung it on the resting chair.

Mary lay on the floor. Tina gasped when she watched her sister's
chest heave and heard her uneven and rattling inhalations. Ann made a
bed for Tina by the hearth on quilts covering the earth floor next to Mary.
She tried to think of something positive: perhaps the sisters could give
each other strength. But truly it appeared that Mary had given her sister the sickness, and it threatened to engulf them both mercilessly. Tina
would not be returning to the hall; that was clear. More than a usual mist,

a treacherous hurricane had swept into their home, and the eye of the storm hovered now ominously over the sisters.

Light withdrew behind threatening clouds, and autumn, the season of dying, darkened the next days. Torrents of rain pounded on the barley just before it was to be harvested. When Ann should have been storing dry grain for winter, instead she nursed her daughters by the peat fire and listened to the storm slash away the family's hopes in a downpour of despair.

Mary died first, and then Tina two weeks later. The neighbors dug one grave and then another, side by side in the churchyard where Jamie was buried. When they laid Mary to rest, quickly without a coffin or a minister, they figured Tina would be next, and she was. The two sisters had lain beside each other in life, and they would lie beside each other in death. Ann feared the soggy earth would wash away and expose Mary's body, so they piled stones on the grave until sometime later they could pack the earth down and properly mark the grave. Proper or not, the sisters would lie there together for eternity.

They lowered Clementina into the second grave, and men took turns shoveling the rocky earth over her body. Reverend Bentley faced Ann, Annie, Robert, Maggie, and Christina, as the bedraggled family stared at the makeshift graves. As if frozen, they stood speechless in their worn coats and disheveled hats and scarfs, soaked through with rain. Tears flowed down their faces. All were silent, except Annie, who sobbed in anguish, voicing the despair they all felt. Reverend Bentley read from the Bible:

> Remembering mine affliction and my misery, the wormwood and the gall.
> My soul hath them still in remembrance, and is humbled in me.
> This I recall to my mind, therefore have I hope.
> It is of the LORD's mercies that we are not consumed, because his compassions fail not.
> They are new every morning: great is thy faithfulness.
> The LORD is my portion, saith my soul; therefore will I hope in him.
> The LORD is good unto them that wait for him, to the soul that seeketh him.
> It is good that a man should both hope and quietly wait for the salvation of the LORD.[1]

---

1. Lamentations 3:19–26.

He led them through the Lord's Prayer, and concluded by saying, "Clementina and Mary, children of God, may you rest in peace." Maggie and Christina put sprigs of last summer's heather on the rocks where their sisters' feet would be. Then Ann wrapped her shaking arms around her children and let fall a downpour of tears, as if God had been holding back a cloudburst until the minister's final words were spoken. As they embraced, she whispered, "Oh, my children!" The wind howled, and Reverend Bentley urged them all to retreat into the church building and wait until the skies ceased their crying. There would be another time for more words of consolation. Two sisters cold in the ground were enough for one day.

The house was quiet that night. The hard reality of the long, anguished hours of sickness and the inevitable dying of her two eldest daughters lashed Ann like a lightning storm. They were now down to five. The family should have counted eleven. Five were gone to be with God: first Jamie, then Robbie and James, now Mary and Tina. And John was gone too, perhaps with the others in heaven, or maybe in his own hell on earth. Ann cried silently as she knitted. The stitches formed steadily without thought, and her mind drifted into a dark realm of regret. If only it could have been she who died—not her precious daughters, Mary and Tina; not her sweet sons, Jamie and James . . . If only John had come back. He didn't even know that his sisters had died of the fever. Oh, dear! Well, perhaps better that he wasn't home to catch the illness. But where was he? Would he ever come back? She couldn't begin to entertain losing yet another child. Would he ever know his own bairn, or would the child too be lost to him? Ann closed her eyes and listened to the pounding rain. So many loved ones, washed away.

Ann willed her eyes to open. She knit another row, and another, and then she regarded her living children one at a time sitting beside her at the hearth, like stiches of yarn in a row. There they were: Annie knitting. Maggie and Christina turning yarn into skeins. And Robert leaning back in the resting chair, having just checked on the sheep in the field. He wiped away tears from the corners of his eyes. "Now I'm the only lad left. I wish I had at least a dog to keep me company."

"Oh, Robert, yes. A new sheepdog would be fine, now that Archie too got sick and died," replied Ann. "Shall we see if there is a pup from a neighbor this spring?"

"I'd like that. I wish John were here. But more than anyone, 'tis Father I miss. He would have something to tell us on a day like this."

"What do you suppose he would say, Robert?" Annie asked.

"Well, he'd say, 'God will provide.'" Robert's gaze lifted to the thatch above the rafters overhead where they sat, as if he could see into the heavens beyond. "And he'd tell the story about how Jesus wept too when his friend Lazarus was dead."

"But then Jesus brought Lazarus back to life, remember?" added Annie. "That's not going to happen with Mary and Tina." Annie broke down again in fresh tears.

"You'll be missing your big sisters, now, won't you, Annie?" Ann whispered, as she stood to embrace, now, her oldest.

"It was canty when Tina came home with stories to tell about the hall, and when Mary came back from Lerwick."

Her mother nodded and sat down again.

"Now 'tis just five of us left, with too much work for five," Annie spoke the words that hovered in all their minds as she looked around the group.

Resuming her knitting, Ann sighed. Stiches, at least, marched forward in a line despite the family's sorrow.

Christina offered with resolve, "I'll do the work of two. I can cook now, and I've begun to knit. I'm not as fast as you, Mam, or Annie, but I'll get faster."

Maggie nodded, cognizant suddenly that she too would need to work harder. "There won't be as much time for reading now—just when I've got up to speed with my letters."

"We'll make time for reading, children. Life must be more than toil. Just wait until spring when we have more light. But now 'tis time for bed. Shall we pray first?" The children bowed their heads. She inhaled deeply to gain composure and then prayed aloud . . .

> O God . . . God of love and God of life, take Mary and Tina into your eternal care. Surround them with everlasting peace. Shield us from illness and give us comfort, for this has been a trying time. Provide us with what we need that we may not despair. Bless John, wherever he is. And bless Father and James—and

Jamie. Unite them with our girls now, O God. Give us hope in
this dark time. We pray this in Jesus's name. Amen.

There should have been more to say, but Ann had no more words
to give. Grief had emptied her gut and squeezed her heart until it ached.
Silently, she pushed herself from the chair to stand. Then she bent to each
child and planted a kiss on her children's heads, one by one. Four sets of
eyes stared at her in sorrow. She withdrew to bed quietly and succumbed
to deep slumber.

12

Birth

ANN GOT UP WITH the sun and walked out to the pasture before the others woke. The ewes had been acting strangely the day before, not eating but restlessly pawing at the ground. This morning, some were bleating. As she approached, the heavy ones retreated, and Ann suspected they were ready; in fact, lambing could start at any moment. She must bring them into the byre. She called to Max, the young sheepdog they had accepted two months earlier from a neighbor's litter. He was yet small for herding sheep, but she needed all the help she could get. She whistled and Max came out from the byre. "Bring them in, Max!" She stretched her arm out toward the sheep in the field.

Herding instinct kicked in, and the sheepdog trotted around the grass, urging the sheep into a smaller circle. They moved as if in a daze. Did they know they were ewes about to give birth, or did they think they were sheep headed to their slaughter? Ann hurried into the cottage to wake Annie and Robert. She would need their help to see that when the lambs dropped, they were cleaned and put to their mothers' teats. Maggie and Christina could take their turns later, after they had their breakfast. Of course, the family hoped for only live births, perhaps even a few sets of twins.

Robert watched his dog round up the sheep. "Good lad, Max!" He went to him and petted him fondly. Annie pushed the ewes that looked

145

ready into the byre. Then Robert brought his dog a dish of fish scraps from the night before. "You're a good laddie!" he beamed with pride.

Ann called to him, "Here's the first one! A fine, peerie lambie!" Annie held the lamb by its front legs and dropped it by its mother to lick it warm from the nose on down its face and neck. Then they moved them both out to pasture together, so that the newborn could suckle, and birthing would continue in the byre.

Lambing took two weeks. By the end of it, the newborn lambs were already steady on their feet, toddling about the verdant pasture. Ann was exhausted from watching over the ewes and protecting the young. Every year she worried a lamb would be rejected by its mother and a seabird would swoop down and trap it in its beak. At the end of a long night in the byre and pasture, she retired into the house to rest. Robert set about trying to milk one of the ewes, for the family had no other milk.

Just as Ann drifted off to sleep in the resting chair by the fire, she was awakened by a knock on the door.

"Good morning, Ann!" called Madge.

"Why, Madge! What brings you here?"

"'Tis no worry. I just wanted to tell you what we heard."

"What is it?"

"The bairn's been born at the lighthouse, just yesterday. 'Tis about the right time, is it not?"

"Yes, yes. Oh, my. I have been praying for the bairn. But now what will I do?"

"Well, I suppose you'll want to see it, will you not?"

"Oh, yes, indeed. Do you think he will let me, the lighthouse keeper?"

"Well, you'll need to ask, of course."

"How did you learn?"

"The midwife near us was called, and when she returned home, I went to ask so you would know."

"Is it a lad or a lassie?"

"She said a lass."

Tears of joy ran down Ann's face. "Oh, a peerie lassie, my granddaughter!"

"I brought a soft blanket you can take to her as a gift, provided the peerie one's grandfather and mam will let you in."

"Oh, thank you, Madge. Thank you for coming and telling me. And for this gift and sharing my happiness. Here, take a cup of tea while you are here, and I'll fetch the wee clothes I saved from when Chrissy was peerie. I'll walk back with you."

Annie overheard their conversation and wanted to come along. Ann told Robert to watch over Maggie and Christina and the sheep while the three women walked to Sumburgh. "I cannot say when I shall return today, Robert. But you will manage, will you not?"

"Yes, Mam, go. The girls will only wish they too could see the bairn."

"Well, we hope there will be other times. Take care, now."

The women set off together. Though it was foggy and cold for a spring day, Ann's eyes gleamed like sunshine on meadow buttercups. Annie wanted to know everything: "When was the bairn born? How long was the labor? What did the lighthouse keeper say to the midwife?"

"Hold your questions, Annie! We'll know more after we get there. Just wait." She turned to Madge. "I only wish our John were here to be a proper father and to love the bairn as his own."

"You haven't heard anything about him at all, have you?" asked Madge.

"Not a word. We ask the minister in Sumburgh at every opportunity."

They parted from Madge, thanking her again, and walked up the path to the head and the lighthouse. Ann knocked at the keeper's cottage. They waited, then she knocked again, and the lighthouse keeper opened the door.

"Good day, sir. We heard the bairn has been born. We've come to welcome it and offer to help."

"She doesn't need your help," he said, starting to close the door on them.

"Who is it?" asked a quiet voice from inside.

Ann answered in a strong voice, "'Tis the Leslies, John's family. We have gifts for the bairn."

"Daa, let them in. 'Tis only right."

Reluctantly, he opened the door and let Ann and Annie enter the living space at the base of the light tower. The young mother looked small, sitting with a shawl around her shoulders in a straight chair holding the tiny bairn. She turned to see who had come.

"I'm John's mother, Ann Leslie, and this is his sister Annie."

"I am Rachel. And this is Hannah," she said as she gazed back down at the sleeping bairn in her lap.

"Oh, Rachel. She is bonnie." Ann looked from the bairn to the new mother. "How are you?"

"I'm well. 'Twas painful, but look at her!"

"Yes, 'tis a miracle!" Ann whispered.

Rachel's father held back, then awkwardly he said, "Lass, you needn't speak to them, you know."

"'Tis all right, Daa. I want Hannah to meet the family of her father."

"Perhaps we should have come sooner. We feared you wouldn't want to see us. We have prayed for you since we knew you were with child." Ann looked lovingly at the baby. "Is the bairn well? What did the midwife say?"

"Yes, she's perfect. I'm just to put her in the sunlight."

"Well, 'tis a blessing for 'tis spring."

"Daa, you'll have to let us go out, you know. We won't find any sunlight here in this old lighthouse!"

"I suppose," he said.

Ann turned to him. "This hasn't been easy for you. What name may I call you, sir?"

"Thomas Haley, if you must."

"Mr. Haley, 'tis a pleasure to meet you now formally," Ann continued. "I want to apologize on behalf of my son. We haven't heard from him since before that day when I was last here. Have you?"

"No, ma'am. Not a word. Time has curbed my temper a tad, but I was fit to kill the lad!"

"Indeed, it does not surprise me. We have been ashamed of our son and heartily saddened to lose him altogether over this."

Annie added to Rachel, "If my brother were in his right mind, he would never have left you. 'Tisn't what our parents taught us."

"Well, I am glad to be over these months, and I already love this peerie lassie," Rachel said.

"She is truly God's blessing!" Ann said, smiling.

"May I hold her?" Annie asked, but her mother frowned.

"Yes, certainly," Rachel replied. "Here." She wrapped the bairn in her shawl tightly and handed the bundle to Annie.

Ann handed Rachel the blanket from Madge and the bag of baby clothes she had brought. "Here are a few things for the bairn. Gifts from us to welcome her." She didn't dare say "into the family."

Rachel thanked them and seemed not to know what else to say.

Ann had a thought. "Would you like some assistance? Perhaps Annie could stay and help you wash clothes and cook for a bit, while you recover in your confinement."

Annie smiled, "Yes, 'twould make me so happy to help in any way I can."

"Oh, to have another lass here, that would be so nice. 'Tis terribly lonely here with only my father."

Her father blushed, knowing he had confined her all her life to the lighthouse property. Ann guessed that he was realizing that things would now surely change, as Rachel would come into her own as a woman and mother, and the child would want to go out for fresh air on walks and then eventually to the nearby school. Ann thought perhaps Mr. Haley would be more generous with his granddaughter than he had been with his daughter. After all, his daughter had lost her mother, leaving him in grief after she was born. This birth might bring him happiness. A new season of life.

Ann motioned for Annie to give Hannah back to her mother, and she spoke softly to her, "Stay and help as long as you are welcome. I shall go back to the others. Then come home, and let us know how mother and bairn are faring."

Thomas led Ann out and nodded to her as she departed.

"Thank you, Mr. Haley, for letting us see Hannah and Rachel. I will pray for you all."

❦ ❦

On her way home, Ann took the longer path along the voe. By then the sun shone through the clouds, and she hoped Rachel would take the bairn out and keep her color rosy. She smiled as she remembered each child she had given birth to, all nine of them. By the last, she had mastered her fear, but she recalled the first time when she anticipated the pains and caring for the child alone in the crofthouse. She breathed deeply and walked with confidence to know she had done the right thing to go to see the newborn that day and to apologize for John. It wasn't the way she would have aspired to become a grandmother, but much of life was not as one would expect or hope. If there had been any life lessons in her thirty-four years since marrying Robert and leaving home, this was it: what a person expects seldom happens. Trust God and accept what comes.

With that thought, a mother duck with nine baby ducklings, all in a row, swam along the bank of the voe.

When she returned home, she found Maggie and Christina cross that they hadn't been permitted to go to Sumburgh with Annie and their mother. Robert was having trouble getting them to do their chores, and the pleasant calm of her walk along the water evaporated abruptly.

13

Signs of Life

ONE SEASON ROLLED INTO the next. Some things did not change. The new grass sprouted, and the winter gray turned green. Ann tended the lambs and put out plants for a spring garden. The sun rose each day—earlier by the week—and with the light of every new day, chores beckoned. When Ann came inside fatigued, she perked up to notice that Maggie already had set the porridge to simmer and a pot of tea to brew. She reflected how each chore persisted in the same way; only which child performed it altered as the years rolled by. The children were nearly all grown up; it seemed that time passed more quickly than ever.

Maggie sat at the table staring into her unfilled teacup. Her face, usually so full of sparkle, appeared as empty as her cup. Ann joined her, and Maggie raised her eyes, without lifting her head. Her daughter's cheeks lacked their rosy hue; and at that moment, her red eyes imparted the only color in her otherwise pale face. "What is it, Maggie?" Ann reached to touch her arm, and tears rolled down Maggie's cheeks.

"I have blood on me. Is it the curse?"

"Oh, Maggie, darling." She paused. "You are thirteen. It's the right age to start having your monthly time. Let me help you." They went together into the ben end, and Ann found clean wool she saved for her girls for this purpose. "Here, wash yourself and then use this. I haven't need of it anymore. You can always get more from our sheep, especially at rooing time. The wool absorbs the blood and keeps your clothes clean."

"Why did Annie call it the curse?"

"Well, it's an old name. Perhaps an old wives' tale. 'Tisn't any shame, you know. We girls all have it. Though at fifty-four now, I'm too old. You'll have it every month from today on, unless you come to carry a bairn—and you know that is forbidden until you marry." She sighed. "Then when you get on in years, like your old Mam, 'twill stop."

"I don't like it."

"Hmm, well, I suppose no lass does. But it means you are healthy, and now all grown up." Maggie went out to clean herself and change her undergarment and skirt. Ann smiled and thought to herself, 'tis a sign of life, not a bad thing.

Many days, Ann struggled to keep her children progressing with their studies. She wanted them to have the education she had had, but she was occupied with so many chores, and without Robbie and the older children, all the work fell to those remaining. Annie, at twenty-three, was a capable teacher, though she lacked patience. And her siblings did not always take advice from their big sister. So, Annie shared the physical jobs at the croft, and Ann tried to squeeze in her own reading and teaching every day with the younger members of the family.

Ann felt it was important for Robert and his younger sisters to learn about the world beyond the shores of Shetland. One day in Lerwick, after selling her shawls to traders at the dock, she bought *The Scotsman*, a newspaper from Edinburgh. The family would use it as teaching material, for they had no textbooks.

Ann showed the newspaper to Robert. "It seems in America the people have been embroiled in a violent civil war, the War between the States, they call it." She handed him the paper.

Robert looked at a map of America, which the Scottish newspaper had printed, with a line called the Mason-Dixon Line separating the northern from the southern states. "The land is so big compared to Shetland," he noted.

"Yes, the size is quite hard to fathom. See the scale? The country is, what, two or three thousand miles across?"

"How big is Shetland, Mam?"

"Heavens, I suppose only ten or twelve miles across! Your father walked from Scalloway to Lerwick for our wedding. That was nearly from coast to coast! And here from Sumburgh in the Ness, 'tis some fifty miles to the north tip of Mainland."

Robert eagerly read the news about America—a new country with a wide frontier. He discussed what he read with his mother. "The nation has been fighting to stay together—the northern with the southern states—under the leadership of their president, called Abraham Lincoln. It says just last week, on April 9, the South surrendered."

"That will mean the union of the states will remain, and President Lincoln will abolish the enslavement of African people. We learned in chapel that Wesleyans oppose slavery, you know."

"What about in Scotland, Mam, do we permit slavery?"

"No, son. I think before the 1830s, though, 'twas permitted in the British colonies. Of course, 'tis how the American states got started, as British colonies. But John Wesley had argued a century ago against people owning other people as chattel. We can be proud of our own Methodist tradition."

"Why do you suppose the Americans kept slaves so long?"

"Well, they were divided on that subject, it seems. The white folks in the South wanted the Negro slaves for their labor in the cotton fields. The land is so big, a family needs help to run the farm. But I see this news from America as a sign of liberation. Unfortunately, though, many people died in the war to emancipate the black people."

"But at least life will be better for them now, right, Mam?"

"Yes, and for their children. If the Americans can only learn to love each other."

Ann thought about the trucking system in Shetland, for though the crofters were not actually slaves, they were oppressed unfairly by the lairds, much like slaves.

Robert asked, "Will our trucking ever change? Perhaps we need a President Lincoln."

"Well, that would be something, now. I doubt the queen would like that. We Shetlanders don't think she has the welfare of the crofters in mind as she sits eating fancy food in Buckingham Palace. She did travel to Scotland some years ago, though I don't believe she came all the way north to our islands."

"What do you suppose she is like, Queen Victoria?"

"Well, I cannot say. She did give birth to nine children; so, we have that in common. I imagine that's about it, though."

"Well, her husband died too remember, only a few years ago, Prince Albert."

"Yes, it was typhoid fever, like our girls. Some things know no class or station." They entertained their thoughts, and then Ann continued, "They say the queen likes Highland tartans."

"But we don't wear them here, do we, Mam?" Maggie who was listening wanted to know.

"No, we Shetlanders are more Nordic than Scottish, don't you think?"

"And besides, who could afford them?" Christina chimed in.

"Well, we can always read about tartans, and that's a pleasure. Remember Bonnie Prince Charlie in his kilt?"

Robert read on in the paper and then asked, "Tomorrow, can we go to see if the puffins are at the head? It says here they have been spotted nesting."

"Oh yes!" cried Christina.

"We could stop and see Rachel and Hannah on our way home," added Maggie.

"And Madge and Andrew may have news from Lerwick." Ann always looked forward to a visit with Madge.

Before bed, Ann prayed with Maggie and Christina, while Robert continued reading in the but end, for it was still light . . .

> Dear God, I thank you for the children and the ways they are growing and becoming good Christians. We thank you that Christina writes her poems and reads from the Bible. And we thank you for Maggie's helpfulness in cooking and keeping house, and that she is becoming a woman. We pray that both girls will continue to enjoy their friends at church. Don't let them grow up too soon. And thank you for Robert's interest in America. We pray for the freeing of the slaves there. And remember to bless peerie Hannah. Help us all to see the good in life and to give thanks. Amen.

She thought of Mr. Haley, the lighthouse keeper, and wondered if he saw the good in life.

14

The Laird

WORD SPREAD THAT THE laird was clearing families from their crofts. Agnes, a neighbor down the row of houses in Exnaboe, lived alone after losing her husband to typhus. With no man in the family and no children to help, she could not pay the laird her tithe. Ann heard that Agnes would be cleared from her cottage and land, with nowhere to go. She asked the family and then went to Agnes and invited her to come live with them. Gratefully, she moved in right away. Ann hoped the laird's wife would take young Annie in as a servant, just as Tina had worked at the manor for several years before the fever took her life. The lass was more than old enough to provide some income, and with her gone, Ann would have another bed to spare. In her absence, Agnes became an additional woman to help with chores and knitting. Besides, she brought with her her cow.

The laird's steward came to Ann for her rent and stood shifting his weight inside the door. "I shall take your knitwear now and your milk after tonight's milking, Mrs. Leslie. I know you haven't fish, with the men gone. We'll be needing your field then too, as the laird gets both fish and corn from his other crofters."

Ann frowned and declared bravely, "Sir, we have taken in Agnes Leask, out of Christian charity, since she lost her husband. The laird will have her croft, but please do not take our field. We need it for our sheep to graze, so that we have wool for the knitting we do for you, sir. And I am thinking the missus may be able to use our Annie now at the hall as a servant. She'll be a good one, like Clementina was."

"I shall consult with Mr. Bruce, Mrs. Leslie," he responded.

"Who is Mr. Bruce?" whispered Christina to her sister, listening from the hearth.

"Shh," mouthed Maggie back to her sister. "'Tis the laird, don't you know?"

"I never knew he had a name."

The steward took a sack of jumpers and shawls that Ann and her daughters had knit. He put the woolens in the cart, and then he went to the byre to wait for Robert to finish milking. Ann followed. When Robert had emptied the udder, the man pressed him aside, stepped in his place by the cow, and poured the fresh milk from the family bucket into his milk can. Robert spoke up, "But this is our family's tea, sir. We'll be having only milk and brönnies, sir." The steward drained the bucket into the pail without looking Robert in the face and carried it out to his cart. Ann put her hand on Robert's shoulder and then, leaving Robert downcast in the byre, walked out to the cart, helplessly trying to come up with what she could say or do.

The steward called to her as he pulled gently on the reigns and hissed to start the horse and cart moving, "That lad is old enough to fish, ma'am. You'd better send him out to the haaf this spring, if you want to keep this croft."

Ann turned to see that Robert was listening from the door of the byre. With tears in her eyes, she rushed to him and pulled him to her. "Oh, Robert, not you, not yet."

"'Twill be alright, Mother. You needn't worry about me." Then they strode slowly into the house for their brönnies.

Ann shook her head and sighed. Then she bowed her head and prayed at the table . . .

> God, give us the bounty of your love, for we have only scarcity here tonight. Teach us acceptance for that which we cannot change. Bless these brönnies, O God, and may they satisfy our hunger. Amen.

That night, in the ben end, the younger girls were reading aloud from a new book of poetry their aunt had sent from Lerwick. In the but end, the others sat by the fire heavy with thoughts of the laird. Robert broke the silence and asked, it seemed out of nowhere, "Mam, may I play Father's fiddle?"

"And your grandfather's, Robert. Remember, 'twas your daa's father's," Ann explained.

"We haven't heard it played since Daa and James died. It has been, what, nine years? I was only eight when they were lost at sea."

"Yes, love, we haven't heard any fiddle tunes these years. And, yes, you may play it. 'Twill take some learning, to be sure, but you are old enough now."

"Where is it, Mam?"

"I've hidden it."

"But why?" asked Robert.

Annie whispered, "I know, so the laird won't take it," as if the laird or his steward were lurking about the croft.

"Well, you are right. So 'tis. I couldn't bear to lose your father and James—and the fiddle as well. I shall get it out, but not while Maggie and Christina are still awake. I don't want them to see the hiding place in case the laird's steward should ask for it."

"But how would he know we have a fiddle?" Robert pressed his mother with yet another question.

"Oh, that man is a spy. He would remember that James played the fiddle in Sumburgh, and of course, if you take up playing, you'd better be careful the laird doesn't hear music coming from this croft again."

Ann went to say good night to Christina and Maggie and asked them to share a line from the poem they had been reading by Robert Browning.

"This is my favorite verse, Mam." Maggie read, "'God's in his Heaven / All's right with the world!'"[1]

"I shall write a poem like that tomorrow," said Christina.

"What lovely thoughts, lassies. I think that counts as your bedtime prayer tonight." She kissed their foreheads and took the lantern into the but end.

With the kollie lamp, Robert read from where he had left off in *The Last of the Mohicans*. Ann smiled when he shared his fascination with

---

1. Browning, "Song from Pippa Passes," in *Selected Poems*, 21.

Indians. "Mam, I like to imagine Hawkeye hiding behind trees in the North American wilderness. We haven't any trees in Shetland, have we?"

"No, Robert. It must be a very different place."

"When did this story of the Indians take place in America? Was it during the War between the States that we were talking about a little while ago?"

"No, earlier. In the 1700s there was another war between the French and the Indians. That is what Cooper wrote about."

"It tells about redskins and whiteskins. We only have whiteskins here in Shetland, right, Mam?"

"Except for traders on the ships, I reckon you are correct."

Once Ann was sure that Maggie and Chrissy were sound asleep, she slipped into the ben end and retrieved the fiddle case from inside her box bed. There was a small compartment, just large enough for the fiddle. She brought it out to Robert.

Robert put down his book and opened the old case, fingering the rough leather and then the soft cloth in which the old fiddle and its bow lay wrapped. He tested the strings; the tones sounded familiar to Ann. Could it be Robert remembered? He lifted the fiddle awkwardly, not knowing how to hold it exactly, but then he must have recalled James putting it under his chin with his left hand and taking the bow with his right. The horsehairs were frayed and loose. He set the instrument down and took the bow in both hands. He twisted the screw on the bow and stretched the hairs as tight as he dared. Then he lifted the fiddle once again under his chin and with his right hand pushed the bow across the strings. A scratching sound pierced the quiet. Tears slid from Ann's eyes as she remembered James, the last to play. And her Robbie was just Robert's age when she married him and his father played at their wedding. If Robbie could only see his youngest son, his namesake, now.

SPRINGTIME 1867

The dark evenings brought the family to the hearth where they knitted and Robert played the fiddle. Ann sang the tunes she remembered, and Robert picked them up. She smiled to see he had his grandfather's gift. One tune she recognized by name, "Is Jack Still Alive." Jack, for John, she thought. I wonder if our John is still alive. The music cracked open her stored-up grief, and in her private thoughts she mourned again for the children who were gone.

As Robert played his tunes into the night, Ann's melancholy lifted. She recalled the poem her girls had been reading by Robert Browning:

> The year's at the spring,
> And day's at the morn;
> Morning's at seven;
> The hill-side's dew-pearled;
> The lark's on the wing;
> The snail's on the thorn;
> God's in His heaven—
> All's right with the world![2]

The words echoed from a distant time into the present quiet evening. Ann smiled that her children enjoyed poetry and music as she did. Tunes and lines of verse were nearly as satisfying as good things to eat.

---

2. Browning, "Song from Pippa Passes," in *Selected Poems*, 21.

15

Changes

THE POPULATION OF SHETLAND grew rapidly as people looked for work and Lerwick became a proper town. Women outnumbered men because the men either drowned at sea or were nearly always gone fishing in the deep ocean beyond their shores. The lairds cleared many crofters from their land to make sheep farms and bring in more income. Many women then desperately moved to Lerwick where they could find work gutting fish. Those with a room to spare took in boarders. Conditions were crowded. Sickness took many lives. The changes were not good.

Ann was glad her Annie was working at the laird's manor in Dunrossness, like her older sister Tina, before the fever. She hoped Annie would thereby be spared the diseases that spread rapidly in the town. Ann's sister Mary still lived in her parents' house in Lerwick, but the brothers had moved out. Ann did not go to visit, for she had too much to do at the croft. The laird had spared the Boe from clearings, thank God, except for Agnes. Ann and her children could still walk their grain to Quendale to the mill, though many of the crofters in Quendale had been cleared from their land.

It was time for Robert to leave home for the haaf. Ann knew she couldn't hold him any longer. She needed more income to pay her tithe to the laird, and, at eighteen, Robert sought independence. First her husband had been the crofter, and then young Robert assumed the role. But now that he would leave, truly she herself was the crofteress. More and more, there was such a thing. Women stepped into men's jobs and kept island life afloat.

Ann prayed that Robert would be in a safe boat with a sensible crew and that he would come home after each trip to the haaf. She packed his food and drink much as she had packed meals for her husband when he went off to fish in the first years of their marriage. Although Ann guessed Robert knew how his mother worried about him, he expressed no fear at all for his own future. He was like his father that way. Ann surmised, without a wife, he would have preferred to go all the way to Greenland on a whaler, but he compromised his wanderlust to placate his mother and remained closer to home.

The day came when Robert took a fourareen up the coast to meet up for the first time with a seafaring sixareen on its way to the far haaf for the summer months. Tears stung in Ann's eyes as she waved him off at Virkie. His leaving was inevitable, and like all partings and losses, she could do little but make the best of it. As she walked home, she remembered how her Robbie had told her the men would often sing together on the boat. She figured her young Robert would at least enjoy the music and the camaraderie.

Another change came to family life at the croft at Exnaboe as Agnes had settled in. With Annie at the hall and Robert out at the haaf, just Ann and the young girls remained at the Boe. Agnes fit in comfortably, like an aunt to Chrissy and Maggie and an older sister to Ann.

Ann and Agnes walked side by side to the peat hill with their spades propped in their kishies, knitting with their free hands as they walked. Fortunately, Agnes had her own tools, so, between them, work could move at double pace. They cut the peats and stacked them to dry. On another trip, they loaded the pieces into their kishies and brought home the heap on their backs. After several trips, they could no longer stand up straight, and they thought their bodies would surely collapse. At fifty-six, Ann began to think she was too old for this. But her girls were only fifteen and twelve, and Ann wanted them to stay close to the hearth and learn their lessons while they tended the stove and the animals. All the females of the household knitted throughout the day whenever their hands were idle and into the evening hours as well. Their hosiery brought in by far the most income they could earn.

Sitting by the hearth, Maggie put down her needles and yarn and tossed another piece of peat onto the fire, just enough to keep it burning and the cottage warm.

Agnes spoke, "'Tis very good of you to take me in. I don't know what I would have done. Indeed, you are more than good neighbors. I am much obliged."

"You are certainly most welcome here, Agnes. I am glad to have your company, and you are a right good help."

"The times are uncertain. If I were a man and had steerage, I might consider making the journey to America or Australia. But how could I afford to go? Alone and at my age?"

"This is our home. I cannot imagine another." Ann looked about the cottage and into the faces of the women there with her.

Maggie imparted, "You know Annie wants to find a husband. But there are so few men, especially in the Ness. She'll be asking to go somewhere."

"Well, I am just as glad she is not in Lerwick where the men come off the boats and drink their wages away."

"There is enough sorrow to go around without marrying a drunk," said Agnes.

"True tale. We Methodists don't believe in drinking, you know. 'Tis a vice. The minister says we are to abstain."

"Not a bad practice." Then Agnes added, "May I go with you to chapel on Sunday?"

"Why, yes, of course. Annie will be home, and we'll leave here at eight. The service will go from nine o'clock until eleven, and then there is a women's class meeting until noon. You'll be most welcome."

"I thank you, Ann."

The girls always liked the Sabbath because they had fewer chores on that day, and they could see their friends at chapel. Nowhere else in the Ness did people gather in large numbers but in church.

On Sunday, the household of women rose, washed, and put on their cleanest skirts and blouses. They wrapped their heads and shoulders in their nicest shawls and walked to the chapel, which contained wooden benches with places for four hundred to sit. Often it was full, mostly with women and children. The new minister assigned to Durigarth Chapel,

Reverend Roberts, greeted each member of the congregation by name. As they arrived, the women shared with him their latest woes, about the sickness in each hamlet and the accidents at sea that a livelihood of fishing inflicted on them. He nodded to each person and spoke a word of hope.

"Young Robert has now gone to the haaf for the summer, Reverend Roberts. We ask that you pray for him."

"Indeed, Mrs. Leslie, I shall, and for you as well, and the others in your household."

"Thank you, Reverend," Ann replied and remembered her guest. "Here is Agnes Leask, who now lives with us."

"I am pleased to make your acquaintance, Mrs. Leask."

"Thank you, sir. The Leslies have been most kind to me." They moved on into the chapel to allow others to greet the minister.

The text for the day was about the boy Samuel. Reverend Roberts read from his Bible, 1 Samuel, chapter 1. Then he addressed the congregation:

"Samuel's mother had just left her son at the temple where Eli, the priest, was to teach him. She put her faith in God to care for Samuel." He looked out at all the mothers and at the few fathers present. "'Tis no easy task to let our young ones go. We must trust that God will provide, whether it be in Greenland on a whaler or in an open boat in the haaf. And furthermore, many of our sons and daughters are leaving for America and for even farther countries, like Australia and New Zealand. They go for the chance of a better life, but we grieve for them." He looked into their eyes. "I tell you, we must let them go. God has a purpose for them.

"Then when his mother departed, entrusting her son to Eli, young Samuel was not alone. In the night he heard a voice calling to him, 'Samuel, Samuel.' He thought it must be the old priest, but 'twasn't Eli. Samuel heard his name again, and then again, until finally he realized 'twas the voice of God calling to him, 'Samuel, Samuel.' And finally, he replied, 'Speak, for thy servant heareth.' And then, the passage ends with a statement of Samuel's faithfulness: 'And Samuel grew, and the LORD was with him and did let none of his words fall to the ground.'[1]

"Are we so faithful? Do we answer God's call, such that God will bless our every word and our every deed?"

---

1. First Samuel 3:10, 19.

Ann thought about what it could be that God would be calling her to do. She did not feel able to take on more than she already was barely managing: her children, her croft, and her tithe to the laird. She believed, though, that the one thing she could do would be to brighten her disposition. And she could clean her thoughts of judgment. For instance, she could try again to visit her granddaughter Hannah, John's bairn, and demonstrate to her mother and grandfather unconditional love, that is, if Mr. Haley would allow it. She could refrain from holding anything against Rachel, having the bairn without a husband. And, above all, she could forgive John. There was some aligning herself with God to take care of.

Ann wondered what the others got out of chapel. For her, it was a morning of respite from the ordinary duties of life and a time to set to right anything that was somehow amiss. While sitting in the gathered community, she inhaled a mysterious calm and then was able to exhale her worries. In and out, simply breathing gradually restored her soul. The music buoyed her spirit, and the words of Reverend Roberts moved her to savor God's tender care.

By the end of the service, the preacher's benediction settled on her like a downy quilt:

> The LORD bless thee, and keep thee. The LORD make his face shine upon thee and be gracious onto thee: The LORD lift up his countenance upon thee, and give thee peace.[2]

When worship was over, the women and men met separately in small groups in corners of the chapel, in the minister's manse next door, and in a neighbor's house. Most stayed because they wanted to discuss the sermon and simply be together. That was what the Sabbath was for—rest and spiritual renewal. Their founder, John Wesley, had taught the first Methodists to worship regularly and to commit themselves to a small covenant group. In the band that Ann and Agnes attended, each woman was asked to account for her time during the past week. Ann told of Robert leaving for the haaf, and then she explained how she had tried to visit Hannah, her only granddaughter, in the past week, but that Mr. Haley and Rachel did not invite her in. She shared for the first time with these women that Hannah was the bairn by her son John, born out of wedlock. Tears streamed down her face when she acknowledged that he had been missing ever since he knew there would be a child.

2. Numbers 6:24–26.

"How long has it been?" the leading woman asked.

"Now, over four years."

"Oh, my." One woman sat forward in her seat. "Let us pray about this." The women bowed their heads. "O Lord, we bring before you the sorrow of the Leslie family. If John be living, we pray for his health and his safety. Give him the courage to come home, for he is missed. We pray also for his daughter, Hannah. May she grow in your likeness. Comfort Ann and her family. Strengthen them in love and kindness toward the bairn, and also toward her mother. May they walk with Jesus. Amen."

Ann glanced into the faces that had turned to her. "I thank you all," she said. Some of the women listening would, no doubt, scorn her for the behavior of her son. But their eyes at that moment were accepting. After the women had prayed on her behalf, she felt a tightness loosen in her chest, and she breathed more freely.

On the trek home, Maggie and Christina shared news from other crofter families.

Maggie asked, "Mam, they are meeting on Wednesday for hymn singing and prayer. May I go?"

"Who, darling?"

"A visiting minister is to hold a midweek class meeting for youth."

"Well, the days are long now. If you finish your chores, yes, by all means, you may go. Only take along your knitting."

"Of course. Thank you, Mam." The girls knew they should never knit outdoors on the Sabbath, but at every other occasion their fingers had to stay busy.

Christina asked, "May I go too?"

Maggie frowned and her mother caught her expression. "Let just Maggie go, Chrissy. 'Tis a time just for the older children, love."

"I never get to do anything. I am always the peerie one."

"Yes, 'tis so. But you needn't worry, you too will be old and wise some day!"

Christina groaned.

"And besides, summer evenings are best for reading, and now you can start *Wuthering Heights*, which Maggie is just finishing! Perhaps you can read it aloud to Agnes and me. I am anxious to hear it for myself, after what Annie and Maggie have said about that man, Heathcliff."

Christina accepted the idea and seemed pleased that her mother would include her in reading among the grown-up women.

Ann asked Maggie, "Will the neighbor youths go too? I shouldn't want you to walk to the chapel alone."

"Yes, Mother, I'm quite sure the Andersons will be going."

The women took out their brönnies to stave off hunger on the way home. As they ambled along, their feet swept through the high grasses that had emerged just in the last months since the spring rain. In the wind, those grasses created undulating patterns like the configurations of waves on the sea. In the distance, the ocean heaved its ceaseless rhythm, in and out, and white foam rolled in never-failing reprise onto the coastline. A landscape always changing, and yet, for centuries, so much the same.

Ann recalled her minister telling how Irish monks had first brought Christianity to Shetland long ago. That was even before the ancient settlements, back when only the sky and the sea had yet made acquaintance with these islands. "Remember, lassies, when Reverend Roberts spoke of St. Ninian's Isle on the west coast, where the first Catholic monks landed? 'Tis a sacred green off the coast connected by only a thread of land."

"Could we see it?" Chrissy asked.

Ann replied, "Perhaps. 'Twould be interesting to see where Christian missionaries arrived and worshipped long ago."

⬥　⬥

Later that night, Ann prayed . . .

> O God, I am grateful for your sacred day, and for the early fathers who brought us the Christian faith. And for the Reformers and the Wesleyan missionaries, too . . . for otherwise, we would not have a chapel and a minister to preach the gospel to us.
>
> Thank you for giving me the courage to share with the women today about John and Hannah. In the telling, you have touched me with good news. Help me to accept the situation as it is. I ask your blessing on the peerie lassie, on her mother, and on John, wherever he may be. Keep him safe and show him your love. O God, may he know that I forgive him.
>
> Now, give me the strength to do what must be done this coming week. We are all in your hands. Amen.

16

Love

SPRINGTIME 1870

ROBERT WAS HOME FROM fishing, and his personality filled the cottage from earthen floor to timber rafters. Ann had almost forgotten what it was like to have a man at the croft. In the early dawn, lying under covers in the ben end, she could hear him in the but end, humming a tune as he opened and shut the door and stomped his feet. She smiled. He would have already tended to the morning chores in the byre and barn. Next he would stoke the fire, and the cottage would be cozy enough to rise and dress. But she lingered in the comfort of her covers. Robert so reminded her of her husband! When her Robbie was home, he would come back to bed after being out in the morning air. His neck would be cool against her chin, and the beard on his cheeks would nestle into her forehead. Desire washed over her as she had not felt in years. Surely, she was too old to feel this way, and yet, she welcomed the sensation.

Agnes stirred and stretched. The day before, Ann had observed how her housemate had tried to rub away the stiffness in her back and how she had limped with pain in her knees as well. Not surprising. She was well into her sixties and would be slowing down, Ann conjectured. Maggie yawned from inside the girls' box bed, and Ann guessed Christina would plant her pillow over her head to block out the morning sounds. Perhaps Ann could let them sleep on a bit, for there would be more than sufficient hours of daylight to finish the family's work, especially with Robert home. She rubbed her eyes and, before rising, allowed her thoughts to drift to her grown-up children. Her youngest, Christina, already fifteen, and Maggie at eighteen, both accomplished chores around the croft now more efficiently than she. Annie at twenty-eight, working at the hall, had fashioned a secure life, but, unfortunately, at her age she would likely never marry. There simply were not enough men, and she was no longer a young lass. Annie seemed content to bake and cook meals for the laird's family, even though she had long hours. Luckily, the housekeeper kept her on, perhaps because the laird's wife seemed to favor Annie, and that was fortunate. The income was what kept the family able to pay the laird. Thank the almighty God for that.

Robert brought back decent wages from the haaf. While he was home, he was indeed the man of the croft, though Ann knew the life of a fisherman-farmer was not his choice. He would prefer to study or play the fiddle. He was her dreamer, much as Tina had always been. Robert had told the family about a new ship that was to sail by steam as well as sail, called the *Oceanic*. Built in Ireland, she would embark on a cross-Atlantic voyage and carry more than one thousand passengers to New York. Imagine!

But was Ann not also a romantic like Robert and Tina, for there she was in bed, musing away the morning? With that thought, she rose, pulled off her nightdress and donned her everyday long skirt and blouse. She closed the door to the ben end to let the lasses get up as they pleased.

"Good morning, Robert, dear. You have already been out and about."

"Yes, Mam. 'Tis the way of the crofter, no?"

"'Tis good to have you home, son." She put on a pot of water for oatmeal and tea. "Thank you for stoking the fire. 'Tis a help to have an early riser."

"Mother, sit, while we wait for the water to boil. I've got something to ask you."

She sat at the table and leaned toward her son across from her. "What is it?"

"Maggie's been wanting me to take her to Quendale. I think she has her eye on a young lad there."

Ann's interest piqued. "Who is that, then?"

"I had trouble getting it out of her, but I believe he is called John Eunson. She met him with some lads at a church meeting."

Ann poured the hot water over the tea and set oats in the pot to boil. "Well, it doesn't surprise me. She has always been a bit of a flirt around the laddies."

"I could take the grain that is left and have it milled at Quendale Mill. And while I wait on the milling, she could meet with her fellow. Would you approve, Mam?"

"I will speak to her at breakfast. She's eighteen. There is no reason to stand in her way if she has fallen for this lad."

Maggie entered the but end, followed by Christina and Agnes.

"So, the sun has finally coaxed you lassies to get up! Come and join us. The tea is now steeping." They pulled up chairs; five fit nicely around the table. "Maggie, love, Robert says you wish to walk with him to Quendale."

Maggie blushed and replied, "Yes, Mam, may I?"

"Well, tell me why you are so interested in Quendale."

"I met a lad, John Eunson, on the way home from chapel, and he asked if I could come meet him at his family's croft."

"She's sweet on him, Mam," added Christina with a giggle.

Ann ignored her youngest and continued in a serious tone, "Do we know the family?"

"I believe the miller is their relation," Maggie told her.

"So, they are not Methodists, are they, or we would know them by name?" Ann asked.

"No, I think they are Baptists," Maggie replied.

"Well, believers, at least. That is important."

"Yes, Mam, I think they are very strict: no dancing, no cards, that sort of thing."

"That can't be much fun," Christina concluded.

"And how old is this John?" As she said his name, Ann thought of her John and wondered for a fleeting moment whether he had another lass by now. Or was he even still alive?

"I'm not sure, Mam. I shall ask him." Ann nodded. "His family has a croft, like ours, I suppose. They have sheep, I'm told."

Robert suggested, "Perhaps we could go to Quendale tomorrow, Mother. What do you say?"

"Well, if you both get more than a day's work done today, tomorrow should be fine."

"Oh, thank you, Mam! I'll work hard today."

Agnes added, "And I can do your chores tomorrow while you are gone."

Ann reminded the girls, "I must take our knitwear next week to Lerwick and buy oatmeal. We are short on grain for porridge. Can you finish your shawls tonight?"

"Yes, Mam," Maggie and Christina assured her.

"The grain that you mill, Robert, we shall use for bannocks. With luck, we'll have enough until harvest time comes again."

They finished their breakfast, then Christina cleaned up, while Maggie started the wash and Agnes tended the garden. Robert took nets to the voe to haul in some fish for the family's supper. Ann walked to the bog and dug more peats and, after depositing them in the byre, settled herself to knit by the fire.

Together, the women had knit a stack of fine wool shawls ready to sell. Ann wanted to finish the last one she was working on by nightfall. But it was a lovely spring day, and the sunshine called to her. Perhaps she would go to the voe before lunch and help Robert tug on the net to bring in some seafood. It would be nice to have mussels with their lunch, as well as a fish for supper.

An hour passed, while the peat fire warmed the crofthouse from within and the May sun shone down on the thatch roof from without. As the embers died down, Ann laid her knitting on her chair, fetched a bucket from the byre, and set out to find Robert at the shore. On her way, she remembered the times she had met her husband Robbie part way along the path as he walked home from his boat. She recalled the anticipation of seeing his smile, feeling his kiss, and basking in that special sensation of being loved. If Maggie grew to love this fellow, John, as she had loved her Robert—also when she was eighteen—tomorrow would be an auspicious day. Mother and son strolled home together with clams and a good-sized cod in the bucket.

That night in bed, Ann prayed . . .

Dear God, accompany Maggie as she meets John and his family tomorrow. I pray that he is a decent lad and that if she fancies him, he will be good to her. I am grateful that Robert is home and can accompany her. May they use good judgment. Oh, dear, don't let happen to Maggie what happened to Rachel and our John. Keep her chaste, I pray. I remember well when I was her age.

Bless our Chrissy too, O God. She always feels left out. I pray that she will stay with me a few more years. I will need her company, especially when Robert has gone back to sea. Bless them all, dear God, and also those who have already departed to live with you—Jamie and James, Robbie, Mary, and Tina.

She drifted off before finishing her prayer.

Robert and Maggie returned the next evening as dusk was falling. Ann had left out oatcakes and kirn-milk for their supper. She rose eagerly from the hearth as they entered with windblown hair and rosy cheeks.

"We're home, Mam," Robert spoke first as he closed the door behind them to keep out the wind.

"Well, how was it?" Ann asked, searching their faces for a sign.

Taking off her shawl, Maggie smiled. "John asked us both to stay for supper, so we did."

"'Tis a respectable family, Mother." Robert went out to the byre to check on the animals and to clean up.

"So, Maggie, tell us about John." They sat down, and Ann smiled at Christina, who put down her knitting, impatient to hear the details.

"I cannot say much, Mam," she answered shyly. "Just that he is nice, and his mam let me help her with the dishes."

"How old is John, Maggie?"

"I reckon he's a few years older than I."

"Does he fish, or does he farm?"

"His mam needs him at the croft. His father is a whaler. When he returns from Greenland this time, they'll be having a wedding."

"Oh?"

"John's sister Alice met a trader in Lerwick, and they'll be getting married. John said he would like to invite me." Maggie smiled, and then she yawned. "It has been a long day, Mam. We can talk in the morning." She got up to wash before bed. Christina and Agnes followed.

Ann waited up for Robert to come in. "So, Robert, do you approve of John Eunson?"

"Yes, Mother. 'Tis a good family. Mrs. Eunson prayed before eating, and she invited you to visit too."

"Thank you, Robert, for going today. And the barley meal?"

"Yes, 'tis all in the barn. You can make your bannocks now."

"Thank you then." Ann retired for the night, content that her family had grain stored and hope alive.

The summer solstice neared, and the days stretched long. The Eunson wedding was to be held at the Dunrossness Baptist Church, followed by a party at the Eunson croft. There would be no alcohol or dancing, but the family permitted music. John had invited Maggie and her family to attend, and he asked Robert to bring his fiddle, for the young people fancied a lively evening.

Ann, Robert, Maggie, and Christina headed out from the Boe in their finest wear. They would meet Annie at the church, for she had the afternoon and evening off from her work at the hall. Nothing was better amusement than a wedding, when all the young people looked forward to seeing one another. Any young man from South Mainland was welcome at a wedding in the Ness, as there were never enough men for the women. Ann knew that Annie hoped to meet a whaler, perhaps from Mr. Eunson's ship, or a trader whom the bridegroom might bring along.

They approached the church with other guests arriving. Ann's little clan made a handsome group. The women wore lacy shawls, the kind they usually sold to German traders in Lerwick. The evening was warm, and Robert had combed his hair back and wore no cap. The girls were glad the wind had not blown their hair about, as they had taken time to comb and braid it. Annie waited for them outside the church.

"Annie, dear! How lovely you look!" Ann exclaimed. She took in Annie's new skirt, a soft purple linen, so unlike the drab wool skirts the women from the crofts wore.

"The housekeeper lent me her most delicate outfit to wear today. Wasn't that kind of her?"

"Aye, Annie, 'twas indeed."

"It reminds her of the Highland heather of her childhood, she says."

They entered the large stone church and sat together in a pew. Robert set his fiddle at his feet, also the family lantern, brought along in case the evening went late into the night. The roof loomed high above them, and they scoured the faces to determine if they recognized anyone. John Eunson took his place beside another young man and the minister in his black robe in the front of the church. Maggie hardly let her eyes stray from John's tall figure, even when Mr. Eunson entered from the back of the chapel with John's sister, Alice, the bride, in white lace. Ann's eyes searched for Mrs. Eunson and recognized her in the front row as she turned her head to watch her daughter walk down the center aisle on her husband's arm. Young women stole glances at Robert shyly. Ann figured the young man next to John must be the bridegroom, the trader. The ceremony was short except for the preacher's sermon, which droned on a bit too long. Finally, the couple exchanged vows and received the blessing from the minister. The congregation stood as the newlywed couple exited the chapel and led the way down the lane to the Eunson croft.

The Eunson family had prepared roast mutton and loaves of barley bread with tea and shortbread for dessert. After supper, Mr. Eunson asked Robert to play, so he took out his fiddle and tuned it, apologizing that he knew only a few jigs and reels. Others had brought their fiddles too, so the lads tuned their A strings together. Ann watched as the young people settled in the barn, which was cleared for the gathering with bales of straw propped up to sit on, leaving the older adults in the ben and but ends of the crofthouse to sip tea. She knew that Maggie would want to sit with John and would just as soon not have her mother watching over her.

Ann wished her husband, Robbie, were there, for she did not know the people from the west coast of the island. Mrs. Eunson chatted with her to make her feel welcome, but she naturally had other guests to attend to also. As the evening drew late, Ann yawned and stood up to find her children. In the barn, Maggie was sitting in a corner holding hands with John and did not want to leave. Nor did Annie or Christina. Robert put his fiddle down and assured his mother he would see that Maggie and Chrissy got home safely, but that it would surely be quite late. Reluctantly, Annie left by herself for the hall. Ann had hoped that one of the children would walk home with her, but she understood that Annie had to get back south, and they all they had few occasions to enjoy a party. So she bid her adieus and walked home by herself, heading off before complete darkness obscured her way.

The fiddle tunes wafted into the evening air along the track, one reel merging into the next, as the music descended on the cluster of cottages she passed as she headed toward home. She hummed the tunes and paced her step to the beat. Every few yards, she turned to watch the sun setting behind her: ochre melted to scarlet, vermilion, and crimson. It had been a canty day. Alone with her thoughts, Ann reminisced about her own wedding more than forty years before. She remembered Robert's father playing his fiddle and the guests leaving also as the sun set. And then she had had Robert to herself, finally, after a long but perfect day. Perhaps this bridegroom would not spend the night there at the bride's croft as Robert had, but take John's sister to the townhouse in Lerwick by the harbor, which he had leased. Ann's mind drifted then to Maggie and her lad, John Eunson. Would they marry, and if so, would they live with John's family in the crofthouse where the wedding party had just taken place? Perhaps Maggie would soon leave her to start her own family.

When she arrived back at the Boe, Agnes was still up. Ann shared with her impressions of the wedding and the meal and music that followed. "Luckily we took a lantern along, for the children will be walking back late in the dark." She thanked Agnes for attending to the chores, and then the women said goodnight.

Ann pulled the covers up to her chin and said her prayers silently . . .

> O God, I thank you for this day. Bless the union of John's sister and her new husband. Keep Robert, Annie, Maggie, and Christina safe tonight. Who knows how late they will be? Give them a bit of moonlight to walk by. I do trust Robert to escort them home safely. Help me accept that Maggie is grown now and that she will want to spend her evenings with John. Oh, to be young again! Thank you for the love that Robbie and I shared and the precious years we had together. God bless him, and also the others. Amen.

SUMMER 1870

John Eunson came courting Maggie on evenings when he could get away. If Robert was out fishing, John cleaned the byre and carried water for Ann. Then he joined the Leslie family for tea at their table.

Maggie dished up the turnip and potato broth she had made, and Ann passed oatcakes 'round the table. "John, would you like to say the blessing tonight?"

"Certainly, Mrs. Leslie." He looked at Maggie and took her hand in his. "Good Lord, we thank you for this food. We ask that you would strengthen our bodies with it, and that you would also strengthen our souls to do your will. Be with Robert on the water and bring him back safely, we pray in Jesus's name. Amen."

"Thank you, John. You have a way with prayer. You truly believe in it, don't you?"

"Yes, I do. Don't you?" He looked from Ann to Maggie and back to Ann.

"Well, I do pray every day, but, honestly, sometimes I do not grasp for sure that it makes any difference," Ann confessed. "I always feel better; 'tis the benefit I recognize. But whether asking for anything truly does any good, I cannot say."

John responded, "I get a warm sensation in my chest. Then I know that God is listening." As he spoke, Maggie gazed into John's eyes. Ann could tell that he was a serious lad and that Maggie admired him.

They broke the oatcakes and dipped them into the soup. It wasn't a special meal, but it was filling and pleasant to have John fill the role of man of the croft. Ann smiled as she watched John and Maggie looking relaxed together and content.

Maggie glanced at John with a shy grin. She took a breath and began, "Mother, we are planning to be married."

"Oh, Maggie!" Ann exclaimed. She turned to look around the table. "I am so pleased for you both!"

Christina stood up and gave her sister a kiss. "Congratulations!" She hugged John too.

John cleared his throat. "My father will be going back out on another whaler before the end of the summer. We thought we could marry before he leaves, that is, if we have your permission."

Ann could feel tears well up in her eyes. "Oh, 'tis a canty day, your sharing this news. I only wish Maggie's father were here."

"Of course, I would have asked him first," John added.

"But I have no doubt, he would be proud to have you as a son-in-law, John."

"Thank you, Mrs. Leslie."

"Well, it sounds rather formal now for you to call me Mrs. Leslie. Shall I be just Ann, then, or Mam?"

"Mam, 'tis well, for I call mine 'Mother.'"

"Where will you be living?" Ann asked. She didn't think a newly wedded couple would want to live in their crofthouse.

"My uncle works at the mill, and he has a house in Quendale he has offered to share with us."

Maggie explained, "I shall do the cooking for him, as well as for John and me."

"I will continue to work the fields and care for the sheep at my parents' croft, and then when I learn the miller's trade, I shall be ready to take my uncle's place." John glanced at Maggie, who beamed with pride.

Christina said, "We'll be missing you here at the Boe."

"Yes, and I you," added Maggie. "But Quendale isn't far, and we can come to help you when Robert is at the haaf."

Darkness fell before John left for home that night. He and Maggie had taken a blanket and gone outside, or to the barn, Ann wasn't sure. And she didn't want to find them wherever they went. Ann and the others retired to the ben, but Ann thought she heard Maggie slip in at early dawn.

❧ ☙

Maggie and John were married in the Methodist Chapel in Dunrossness in late summer, just before John's father returned to Greenland. Maggie asked if her niece, Hannah, by now eight, could be a flower girl in the ceremony. But Mr. Haley and Rachel said no, Hannah should not be considered a member of the Leslie family. To Ann, it felt like a door slammed in her face. Maggie tried to make her mother feel better, saying, "We wouldn't want them to be uncomfortable, now, would we?"

❧ ☙

Maggie moved into the house next door to the mill. There she cooked for John's uncle, cleaned the flagstone floors, and pursued her regular knitting and gardening. John came home in the evening after shepherd duties at his father's croft and also learning the mill trade at the waterwheel. Ann expected not to see much of the young couple, but they managed to catch rabbits and string them up to bring to Exnaboe sometimes for a fine meal Sunday afternoon.

Ann scolded John for catching the rabbits on the Sabbath, but he said he got up before daybreak, so surely God wouldn't mind. Robert skinned the catch with nearly the skill Ann had seen him apply to a four-foot-long ling. The women boiled the meat and chopped garden vegetables for a tasty rabbit stew. Robert watched his new brother-in-law put his arms around his bride as she stirred the stew pot and smiled at him affectionately. Ann wondered if Robert would be as lucky to find a wife and settle nearby.

But Robert responded to his sister's marriage with his own rest-lessness. The croft was small, and though his labor was needed, Ann surmised he felt confined at the Boe with, other than him, only women under one roof. He left at the end of the summer for the haaf, lured by the memory of sea chanties and his own need to stretch his legs. Ann figured he sought freedom and independence. He was testing the current to find his own course in life.

17

Comings and Goings

MAGGIE'S FIRST BAIRN WAS born in Quendale after a long and difficult labor. Ann went to help as soon as she heard the child was on the way. They called the lassie Mary Ann for the two grandmothers, Mary and Ann. Ann wished she could stay longer to cook and clean while Maggie nursed, but her own croft needed her, as always. For four days Christina had tended the animals and crops alone at the Boe. Agnes was too poorly in the joints to work outside by then and could barely knit with her gnarled fingers. The others were gone: Robert at the haaf and Annie at the hall.

Ann walked home from the Eunsons', proud to be the grandmother of such a winsome, peerie lassie, but sorry to put her own needs before her daughter's and granddaughter's. The bairn was born a bit late, and because the wee one was ever so plump, her mother needed to mend from pushing her out into the world. Ann wished she could be with her daughter as she healed and regained her strength. Oh, and to hold the bairn, 'twas such a delight! If only her Robbie had lived to see his bonnie granddaughter, actually their second, counting Hannah.

Ann spotted a flock of whooper swans sailing in a V across the sky. As she watched, they landed in the voe beside her path and swam in loose formation with necks held tall and proud. She followed along the shore, admiring the grace with which they glided. Had they just arrived back for the winter, and would they stay here on the west coast of Mainland? Ann wished she could float home with such ease and not mind her tired body.

She arrived at the crofthouse at dusk and found Agnes asleep in her chair at the hearth. She heard only her soft snore. Ann shed her coat and shawl, stoked the fire with the poker, and then put a kettle on for tea. As she eased into the resting chair, she rubbed her feet and hands, numb from her walk across the island. Perhaps Christina was at a neighbor's or still working in the field behind the cottage. The door of the byre opened and then shut. Christina entered the but end, bent over with her kishie still on her back after carrying peats from the bank. She let drop the heavy basket beside the hearth and sank into the chair by her mother's side.

"Chrissy, you've been working hard."

"Well? Was it a boy or a girl, Mam?"

"A bonnie lassie! And they're calling her Mary Ann."

She smiled. "How is Maggie?"

Agnes woke up and joined the inquiry. "Did you get there in time, Ann?"

"Yes, the bairn didn't come for fifteen hours. Maggie struggled in exhaustion, and John had a case of nerves. 'Twasn't an easy birth. But now all is well."

"Oh, Mam, when can I see the bairn?"

"Well, perhaps Maggie and John will come with the peerie one on a Sunday, when Maggie is strong again and the child has grown a bit. We are both needed here, you know." She smiled at her daughter. "Thank you, darling, for watching over the croft while I was away."

"I'm tired, but I shall sleep off my weariness and rise again in the morning," she said with determination.

"You are a dear, Chrissy."

"Only, Mam, we haven't much to eat. The taaties in the barn are running low, and we won't be having any fish, of course, now with Robert gone. We'll have to roo the sheep and then spin and knit to have the means to buy ourselves some basics, like salt and tea. And eggs and cheese would be nice."

"Yes, I know. Soon Robert will be home, and let's hope he has earned some money that will be ours to purchase what we need in Lerwick."

"But won't we owe the laird?"

"Yes, I am afraid we will." Ann ran her fingers through her hair. "We may have to sell a ram."

"Better now when the sheep are fat from grazing. Come winter, they will get scrawny and not sell for much."

"That won't leave us many sheep."

"Seven is all." Christina shook her head. "Should I go to Lerwick and get a job at the dock? They must be gutting, and I fancy I'd make more doing that than knitting."

"But then I would be crofting here all alone. There is no possible way I can do all the chores myself."

"You did when you were first married, and Father was at sea."

"But then I was young like you! And we didn't have animals at first, just a small garden. We made our living by your father's fishing. He was a skilled skipper and fisherman, you know."

"Yes, and I remember you always said he promised you wouldn't be wealthy, but you would never go hungry."

"Well, your father was wrong about that. We have endured many lean years. And now that he and James—and John—are gone, we are down to only Robert for fishing. And now he is gone to the haaf."

Agnes said, "'Tis too much work to be crofters and to have to pay the laird in fish. A woman cannot do it all alone. I am grateful that you took me in. How could I have fended for myself alone?"

"If it weren't for the trucking system, we Shetland women would be fine. We are strong and can plant and hoe and carry the peats. We just cannot fish at the same time!" She paused and rose from her chair. "I do hope Robert gets home soon," Ann concluded as she poured the tea water to steep and got out the last of the bannocks for their evening tea.

When Ann was finally warm and fed, she undressed and got into bed. With a sigh, she shut her eyes to pray silently . . .

> O God. I am tired and worried, as always, about not having enough. Forgive me for being so selfish. I should think of what we have, not what we lack. I thank for Chrissy and all she does to help me. And I am so happy about peerie Mary Ann. Thank you, God, for bringing the lassie into our family! God bless Maggie and help her rest while she can, as she cares for the bairn. God bless her John and incline him to work hard to help Maggie with the chores so that she can recover. God bless Annie and Robert, and bring them home to us soon, and with food and money to help the family. And God bless Agnes too for she is getting old and weak. Ease her suffering, O God. And keep our Chrissy well and strong too.

Let me sleep now, O God, and make me ever grateful for your blessings. Amen.

Ann watched the horizon from the field as she brought in the sheep. Dark clouds gathered off the coast, and she wondered how Robert fared. Perhaps a gale would send the fishermen home from the haaf. The rain lashed against the rocks along the voe, and Ann concluded she would begin her Sabbath before dusk for a change. Then she looked down the path to the south and spotted Annie walking toward her through the fog and shower. As she drew near, Ann smiled, for Annie carried a basket for the Sabbath with her mother and sister.

"Annie, dear! 'Tis you!" called Ann. "You've come early!"

Annie hastened her steps to the crofthouse to escape the downpour. Once inside, they embraced and warmed themselves by the peat fire before preparing tea. Annie unpacked her basket with jam, oatcakes, cheese, and cream. It was almost better than Christmas!

"The housekeeper let me come for all day tomorrow—and with these sweets."

"'Tis lovely, Annie. Thank you."

"'Tis Mrs. Bruce to thank. She knows we haven't much."

"Tell us, Annie, how has it been for you these weeks at the hall?"

"Do they work you night and day?" asked Christina.

"I do most of the cooking now. I am treated politely but, naturally, as a servant, which means, of course, I eat with the other servants in the kitchen, but I don't mind."

"Oh, to have cream and white scones with jam every day!" Christina was hungry.

"Well, shall we put these treats on the table for our tea and pretend we are wealthy Scots?" Ann suggested.

Annie explained, "I'll always be proud to be a Shetlander, like you, Mam."

"'Tis a blessing that you are not envious. We are grateful, though, that the laird's missus has a generous heart."

The next day the women spent the morning at chapel. When they re-turned to the croft, they found a sack of fish at the door. Ann exclaimed, "Can it be Robert has come home at last?"

Robert, who had been asleep by the fire, woke to the women's voices. He roused his tired body and threw his arms around his mother, his older sister Annie, and his younger sister Christina. Even Agnes received a warm hug, and everyone crowded into the but end to hear about Robert's two months fishing in the deep waters up north.

"We stayed at Fethaland, at the station there, and went out for two or three days at a time. The fishing was good; we caught lots of cod, ling, and herring. The sixareen was heavy on each return."

Ann asked, "Did you get enough to eat?"

"Yes, Mam. But it was cold. We warmed our hands and feet at the peat fire in the lodge, but I was always cold. 'Tis good to be home and warm again."

Robert stopped the telling long enough to remind them that he must salt the fish he had brought home to preserve it while fresh. He started to get up, but Ann motioned for him to stay and rest. Ann got up and scaled and gutted one large ling. She cut off the fins and chopped the long fish into chunks and dropped them in the soup pot for their Sabbath dinner. Meanwhile, Christina and Annie split open, boned, cleaned, and salted the rest of the whitefish. They laid them by the hearth to cure, and then washed their freezing hands in water warmed at the hearth.

Later that afternoon, while the soup was simmering, Maggie, John, and Mary Ann arrived from Quendale. Ann was beside herself with bliss to have the whole family together.

At the table she prayed before she ladled out the broth . . .

> Gracious God, we thank you for this reunion. Today peerie Mary Ann meets her Uncle Robert, and we celebrate with good foods from Annie's work at the hall and Robert's toil at sea. Fa-ther and the others will look down on us and smile. God bless this food that it strengthen us for come what may. Amen.

That night after they had talked and laughed together, Robert straight-ened in his chair and cleared his throat. Ann watched as the family qui-eted and turned their attention to him. "I want to tell you my thoughts. You know, on the sea there is plenty time for contemplating. And we also share dreams with the other seamen." He paused and looked around the circle. "Several of the young men are planning to leave Shetland for America." He stopped again. "I want to go too." The wind ceased rattling the windows, and silence dropped from the rafters onto the family.

Ann waited, stunned, so Annie was the first to speak: "To America?"

Christina's eyes filled with tears. "When?"

Robert looked into his sisters' eyes and then directly at his mother's face. "I plan to earn steerage by spring. *The Zetland Times* lists the sailings from Aberdeen and Glasgow."

"To where? To New York?"

"Yes, the ships go several times a season. They are by steam now, you know. There'll be one more trip out again to the haaf while 'tis light, and then I shall pay the laird the tithe, and after that I'll fish for myself here in the Ness through the winter. I'll bring home my catch for us to eat and hopefully enough fish to sell and save what money I can for the crossing. I'll have to be away most days and nights, but I think I can manage it."

No one breathed but Mary Ann, who cooed from her mother's lap. Ann spoke in a quiet voice, tentatively, "What will you do in America?"

Robert nodded, for no doubt he anticipated this question. "I will go to where there are other Scots, perhaps even Shetlanders, and I will find work."

Annie asked, "What kind of work will you do, Robert?"

They all stared into Robert's face.

"I'll do whatever work I find. Perhaps I'll find a job in a city. You know, I never really wanted to be a fisherman."

"But a farmer, a crofter? That's what you've grown up to be," said Annie.

Ann looked at her oldest. "Wait, let him tell us."

Robert began after a pause, "We all loved our father, and he was truly a great skipper and a skillful fisherman. And James was too, and even a whaler. And we've all been crofters. But I am one who likes history and reading about the world. I want to know lands beyond Shetland. I want to try my luck at another life."

Christina could not imagine losing her brother. "John left, and now you! What will we do without you?"

Ann looked at her youngest and spoke softly, "We are strong women. We will do our best, God willing."

"And I will send money home once I have work. And if all goes well, I will come back and fetch you to join me."

"Oh, my! Now that's a tall tale, Robert. We shan't talk about my leaving Shetland. I'm already far too old for that."

It was hard to know quite what to say. Ann imagined Annie's jealousy of Robert leaving. Annie too wanted more from life, something different, romance like in the books she read, and Ann could understand, for in Lerwick, she herself had studied German and dreamed of traveling to mainland Europe. She had hoped to attend university, even. What a fantasy! Marrying a crofter changed all that. She hoped Maggie was satisfied living her married life in Shetland. The bairn was already such a pleasure, and the family seemed content in Quendale by the mill. But Robert would never know his niece once he left for such a faraway place. And Ann's family would shrink again.

John and Maggie bid farewell when the rain stopped and darkness overcame the gloaming. They tucked Mary Ann into the shawl that John slung carefully over his shoulder, and she fell right to sleep. After eating so well and talking with the family into the evening, Christina, Annie, and Agnes dragged their tired bodies off to bed. Ann remained with her son by the peat embers. She tried to conjure up what Robert's new life might be like. She didn't even know, did they have peat in America? And would he get fish to eat in a city? Would there be a church to attend with a kind minister? Ann pushed her fears aside and smiled at Robert. "I love you, Robert, darling." Robert smiled shyly and yawned. "You are a brave lad. You'll do well."

"Thank you, Mam. I've been hesitant to bring this up. You must know, it feels wrong to leave you and the family. And you know that I shall miss you."

"And we you." Tears pooled in her eyes. "But your father would be proud." Robert couldn't think of more to say. Ann stood and added a peat to the fire. "Now we must both get some rest." She gave Robert a pat on the shoulder. "You'll sleep here by the fire?"

"Aye, thank you, Mam."

"Good night, son."

Robert looked away, blinking.

18

Partings

ANN SAT IN CHAPEL with the family, all except Robert who had gone fishing the night before so as not to be seen leaving for work on the Sabbath. The preacher framed his sermon on the prodigal son from the Gospel according to Luke, and Ann's thoughts drifted to her lost son, John. Would he "come to himself" and arrive home before Robert left for America? Of course, she would welcome him with open arms. And though they certainly had no fatted calf at the croft to slaughter, she would do her best to make a meal and treat him as the honored son, for he "was dead and is alive again," she said to herself. She hesitated as she continued the Scripture in her head, and she came to the words: he "was lost."—But would he ever be found?[1]

After the hymn, the preacher stood up to pray. But first he announced, "*The Zetland Times* reported a terrible disaster at sea this week. On April first, the steamship the *Atlantic* was wrecked in Nova Scotia on her way to New York. I fear there may have been Shetlanders on that ship. Five hundred souls were lost." The congregation gasped. "The captain hit a gale and hadn't the coal to finish the journey to New York. He changed his course and steered toward Halifax, Nova Scotia, instead; but the ship never made it. In the night she hit rocks, and though many clambered to

---

1. Luke 15:24a.

the deck, the water washed them overboard, and the steerage passengers yet below were trapped and drowned. The ship was with the White Star Line out of Liverpool. May God be with anyone who was aboard." Ann exhaled the breath she'd been holding and took Annie's hand beside her. They looked at each other and then at Christina, imagining what could happen to Robert when he would sail.

The minister prayed, "'Out of the depths I cry to thee, Lord God! Oh, hear my prayer! . . . My hope is in the Lord, my works I count but dust, I build not there, but on his word, and in his goodness trust.'[2] In this week of tragedy, we ask for thy comfort. May those who drowned in faraway waters rest in peace, and may their widows and children find comfort in thy abiding love. We pray for all the men from our villages who are now at sea. Make us worthy of their homecoming. Keep us as thy faithful disciples.

"This week we ask that thou wouldst teach us piety as we remember our Lord who prayed to thee in the garden, his trial, and then the road to Calvary and his crucifixion. Bring us to our knees in prayer at the cross. Humble our hearts, Lord, and make us quick to forgive others. Steer us from drink. Refrain our hearts from lust and indolence. And when the time comes, bring us blameless to thy heavenly gates. In the name of Jesus, our Lord and Savior, we pray. Amen."

The service ended with a Wesleyan hymn and the minister's announcement that the next Sunday would be Easter, the celebration of the resurrection. Ann smiled to her daughters as the hymn started, and they felt their spirits inflamed in the zeal only congregational singing could ignite:

> Praise the Lord who reigns above and keeps his courts below,
> praise the holy God of love and all his greatness show;
> praise him for his noble deeds, praise him for his matchless power,
> him from whom all good proceeds let earth and heaven adore.[3]

The Sabbath morning among fellow believers always heartened Ann, especially in times of hardship or troubling news. After the service, families probed one another as to whether relations having recently left Shetland for America could have been on that ship.

---

2. Luther, "Out of the Depths," with slight modification.

3. Charles Wesley, "Praise the Lord Who Reigns Above," #96 in *United Methodist Hymnal*.

Between fishermen dying at sea and young men emigrating to America and Australia, fewer and fewer able-bodied males remained in Shetland. Ann glanced at her oldest, Annie, on her right. Scant hope that she would find a husband. Naturally, at thirty-one, she could still bear children, but what lad would court her? Then her youngest, Christina, on her left let drop her shawl onto the stone floor. Ann bent down to pick it up and glimpsed her daughter's down-turned eyes with long lashes and rose rising in her cheeks. Chrissy, already eighteen, was the same age she was when she married her Robbie. Where had the years gone? Hopefully, a nice young lad would notice Chrissy. Ann would be glad to keep Annie at home to manage the croft, or without her she supposed she would have to go live at the Widows' Homes in Lerwick. That would be dreadful. She wondered, perhaps there were indeed Shetlanders on the *Atlantic*. Now their wives would be waiting to hear. Ann silently prayed that the Widows' Homes or the Methodist missionaries would come to their aid, should they lose not only their husbands but also their crofts and liveli-hood. Most of the men who departed promised to send funds and later fetch their wives and children. Robert had said he would come back for her and his sisters. But would she dare to leave her homeland? That would mean yet another ocean crossing. She visualized the ship sinking and the seawater flooding over the drowning passengers and crew.

In the Bible study following worship, Ann asked the other women to pray for her Robert, that he would come home without harm from over-night fishing, and that when he boarded a ship in the coming weeks, it would take him safely to the New World. In the class meeting, the leader read the story of Jesus entering Jerusalem on a colt. It was a homecoming with crowds of people crying to Jesus to save them.[4] That is what the leader said the word hosanna meant. How could it possibly have been a joyful day, for Jesus had known he soon would die? Ann thought about the Hebrew people who were anxious to see Jesus but crying out in their hunger and distress. Did they really think he could save them? She had dared to hope that her son's arrival home would bring security and well-being to the family. But the news of the *Atlantic* had left her fearful and on edge, as the people in the crowds might well have been that day long ago in Jerusalem.

On the walk home from chapel, Chrissy asked why the minister had preached on the prodigal son and not on Jesus entering Jerusalem, for it

4. Mark 11:1–10.

was Palm Sunday, the week before Easter. Annie answered before Ann could break away from her thoughts. "He knows we have comings and goings here in the islands, and we must accept them and offer understanding and forgiveness to one another."

"Yes, Annie, and perhaps Reverend Roberts did not choose to speak of the events of that last week of our Savior's life, for they bring such sadness. We needn't hear more sorrow in these times, what with ships sinking and neighbors losing their men and their crofts."

Christina replied, "Well, at least next week should be a canty message." She paused. "And Robert will be home, will he not?"

"We pray so," Ann answered in a quiet voice, as she closed her eyes for a moment and then locked arms with her daughters and walked along.

The days were lengthening as they expected, for summer approached. Tasks were plenty, but it was the Sabbath, so the women took turns reading aloud into the evening, while the others knitted around the hearth. Just as the last light from the windows began to dim, Robert appeared at the door. He had with him fish to salt for the coming weeks. Ann stood to greet him warmly. "Robert, dear! You're back!"

"'Tis good to be home, believe me. The sea was rough and rainy, but the catch was good. I hope it satisfies the laird. The six of us stayed awake all night and hauled in the heavy nets. We won't tell Reverend Roberts, but we fished all day today too. 'Tis the only way to bring home something for my family to eat and save a bit of the earnings as well."

"God forgives you, Robert. We've just heard a sermon this morning on forgiveness, between people, that is. Surely God forgives us too."

"'Tis a good thing to believe in a loving God," Robert said as he collapsed into the resting chair.

Annie smiled and added, "The laird's family are Calvinists, don't you know? They are all for pointing out your sins."

"Well, Annie, you can stay a Methodist," suggested Robert. "We don't have to be so strict. I always thought Reverend Wesley mostly spoke about loving God and your neighbor. Like Jesus said, these are the greatest commandments."

Annie nodded to Robert in agreement.

"So, who will salt the fish, while Robert gets cleaned up for bed?" Ann asked.

"Come along, Chrissie. You and I. Then I'll get to bed also and leave at dawn for the hall once again." Annie stretched and put on an apron to cover her dress.

"I wish you could stay, Annie, especially now that Robert is home." But Christina knew Annie needed to be at the hall to prepare the family's breakfast on Monday morning.

"Well, I try to make the best of it, and you should too." Annie replied and tossed Christina an apron.

When the girls went outside to salt the fish, Robert spoke gently to Ann. "I have a ship in mind, Mam, one that will take me from Glasgow to New York. If I pay the steerage by the first of May, I'll get a reduced rate. I'll just have to get myself to Lerwick to reserve a ticket, and then take a boat to Aberdeen and a train south to Glasgow."

"Oh, Robert! Such a journey! A train, and then a steamship! 'Tis hard to think of such!"

"Well, you are not to worry, Mam. I have spoken with many fishermen who know men who have done just this. My steamer will sail to Boston, but I'll go all the way to New York." Ann stared at her son with wide eyes. "'Tis where all who emigrate from our shores go, those that seek a better life."

"Oh, Robert, darling. Will it be better? I shall miss you, and I cannot deny, I shall worry about you."

"Mam, I just want you to be proud of me. I'm doing this for all of us."

"Aye, lad, I know." She wiped her eyes with her handkerchief. "You'd better go on to bed now."

Ann prayed that night . . .

> Dear God, 'tis truly going to happen. Robert is leaving for America. You must hold him every day and every night in your care. Please, God. And forgive me for being selfish and wanting him to stay. He is a grown man, and he is brave, and he wants to do this. Help me accept these comings and goings. In your holy name I pray. Amen.

❧ ❧

Robert left again and was gone fishing for a fortnight. The long days dragged. Ann fretted, wondering when he would be home and whether he still planned to sail for America. It was time for tea. She sat at the table while Christina dished up the soup. Agnes slept in the resting chair, as

she often did at the end of the day. With sore arthritic hands, even knitting was frequently too much for her. They heard a knock on the door.

"Who is it?" Ann called out.

"'Tis the minister, Mrs. Leslie."

Ann got up and opened the door, letting in a gust of wind. "Please,
come in, Reverend Roberts."

"Good evening, Mrs. Leslie. I don't intend to bother you at tea."

"Not at all, Reverend Roberts. Please join us."

"Well, I thank you kindly. I have been doing my rounds, visiting the
sick in the Ness, and I have a letter to give to you."

"A letter? From our Robert?"

"Yes, I believe so. It came to me by way of Reverend Anderson at the
Lerwick chapel." He reached into his satchel and handed Ann a folded
piece of paper with handwriting on one side.

Ann began to read silently. She looked up and smiled broadly. "Yes,
'tis indeed from Robert!"

Christina prepared a place for the minister at the table and motioned for him to be seated. "Mother, read it aloud, please."

"Well, all right. We shall then wait to say our blessing. Do you mind,
Reverend Roberts?"

"No, of course not. Do read."

Ann began:

Dear Mother,

I apologize for not reaching you sooner with news of my whereabouts. I know you worry. But rest assured, I am well. Here is
the thing: I have been invited to stay at the manse of the Adam
Clarke Memorial Chapel. 'Tis very generous of Rev'd Anderson
here. I tried to locate your family, but your parents' house is now
a poorhouse, and no one could tell me what became of Mary or
your brothers.

There is much work at the Lerwick piers in the herring
boom. Danish ships fill the harbor and every day look for fishermen to go out. You wouldn't believe it unless you saw it: boats
of all sizes fill the water as far as you can see from shore, and the
oceanfront is crowded with women standing and gutting the fish
as the boats come in—hundreds of women, many even brought
here from Ireland. The work is grueling, and the women must
be strong to endure the bone cuts and cold on their hands, and
of course, the ever-present rain and wind. The conditions for the

fishermen are naturally the same, but our pay is very good. And 'tis mine to keep, for this fleet pays no fees to the lairds. Hence, I have been working night and day, and when I get a day to rest, I attend prayer meetings here.

The chapel is beauty to behold. It was renovated last year for the jubilee of Methodism in Shetland. And they even have heat by hot air. On Sunday, hundreds attend, and the hymn singing is first-rate. Father would have loved it.

I plan to remain here and save my earnings, both for my steerage and for our tithe to the laird. I hope he will let you stay on at the crofthouse, even though I will not be there to fish for him. I pray Annie may still be employed at the hall.

I shall come to say goodbye before I leave. I set sail from Glasgow on the thirty-first of May. I'll see you at the Boe the evening of the twenty-eighth and leave for Aberdeen in the early morning from Sumburgh. I have paid my deposit, so I have made the commitment.

Until then, I send my affection.
Your son,
Robert

Ann's eyes filled with tears as she folded the letter and set it on the table. "Reverend Roberts, will you say the blessing?"

"Of course. Let us pray:

"Holy God, we come to thee grateful for this news that Robert is safe and well cared for in Christian love. May he prosper while in Lerwick in health and in his earnings, and may he be a blessing to the congregation there. Comfort the Leslie family and ease their hardship, dear God. We pray this night for all Shetlanders who plan a cross-Atlantic voyage. Guide the ships and fill the travelers with courage. And now we ask thy blessing on our repast. We thank thee for thy providence and for the family's generosity of sharing. May the food strengthen us in thy spirit to serve thee in the coming days. In the name of Jesus, we pray. Amen."

Christina ladled the broth and passed the oatcakes, while Ann poured hot water over the tea leaves to steep. "Thank you, Reverend Roberts, for bringing us this news and for your ministry to us as we anticipate Robert's departure. 'Tisn't easy for us, you know well. We already have so little, and then we shall have no man left to fish or help us tend the croft. 'Twill be just Christina and I here." She turned to Agnes, "And Agnes helps as she can."

"I shall speak to the laird in hope that he will spare you from vacating the croft in Robert's absence. 'Tis no fault of your own that Mr. Leslie and your other son were lost at sea. I can't promise any special favors from Mr. Bruce, though. I'm afraid he generally sides with the kirk. Or better said, the Established Church sides with him. We have our differences."

"Thank you, Reverend Roberts. We appreciate your sympathy and any assistance you can offer. We do what we can for our neighbors." She looked at Agnes, who nodded and kept her eyes on her soup plate. "And I am always willing to take in a child for lessons, as is Christina, for she teaches now also."

"I commend you, Mrs. Leslie, for educating your children in their letters and Bible. Likely, thanks to your training, Robert has been taken in at the Lerwick manse. A minister's wife can always use a bright, young lad to help counsel a stray or pray with a congregant who drops by. And thank you for your Christian charity toward Sister Agnes."

They finished their meager meal and the minister offered to lead devotions. Ann got the family Bible and passed it to him. "Please."

He read from the Epistle to the Romans:

> For we are saved by hope: but hope that is seen is not hope: for what a man seeth, why doth he yet hope for? But if we hope for that we see not, then do we with patience wait for it.
>
> Likewise the Spirit also helpeth our infirmities: for we know not what we should pray for as we ought: but the Spirit itself maketh intercession for us with groanings which cannot be uttered. And he that searcheth the hearts knoweth what is the mind of the Spirit, because he maketh intercession for the saints according to the will of God. And we know that all things work together for good to them that love God, to them who are the called according to his purpose. For whom he did foreknow, he also did predestinate to be conformed to the image of his Son, that he might be the firstborn among many brethren. Moreover whom he did predestinate, them he also called: and whom he called, them he also justified: and whom he justified, them he also glorified.[5]

"Christina, will you pray?" Reverend Roberts asked.

"Yes, Reverend Roberts." She blushed in embarrassment and paused to collect her thoughts. Ann and Agnes bowed their heads. "Let us pray together . . .

5. Romans 8:24–30.

"Dear God, we thank you for this reading from your holy word. May our family be encouraged by it, as were the people of Rome when they received this letter from the apostle Paul. Even when we do not see hope, dear God, may we feel it. Give us patience to wait for Robert's return. And even though we cannot know his future, help us to trust in you. Teach us that 'all things work together for good.' Amen."

"Thank you, Christina. Well done." The minister stood to get his coat and hat. Ann and Christina rose and followed him to the door.

"Reverend Roberts, thank you for coming and for delivering Robert's letter. It has raised our hope." Ann offered her hand to bid the minister adieu.

The minister shook hands before pulling on his gloves. "I thank you for tea, Mrs. Leslie. And may God bless you and keep you in good health." He wrapped his scarf tightly around his neck and headed down the track into the wind.

After cleaning up from their meal, Christina read from *The Zetland Times*, an edition she had purchased when last in Lerwick to sell her knitwear. "Here it says that David Livingstone died. You remember, the Scottish explorer and Christian missionary to Africa?"

"Of course. How did he die?" Ann asked.

"'Twas malaria. He had caught it several times living in Africa, and this time it did him in, it says."

"Wasn't he the one who opposed the slave trade?"

"Yes, that's right. He was quite a man."

"A Scot to be proud of, I would say," Ann added. "I think our Robert has a bit of Mr. Livingstone's taste for adventure in him."

"Let's hope there are no strange diseases aboard Robert's ship out of Glasgow." Christina read on. "It says here that David Livingstone studied medicine in Glasgow. That's where many of the ships depart, or else Liverpool."

"Well, Robert won't be a hero to go down in history like Mr. Livingstone, but if he settles well in America, he shall be our hero." Ann put the teacups by the basin. "Tomorrow is another day, lassies. I'll be wanting to get our news to Maggie. I don't know if she'll bring the bairn to see us this week. We'll hope she comes to bid Robert farewell."

There was no other way to get a message to Quendale but to walk, so Ann departed early the next morning. A westerly wind gusted in her face as she set out along the footpath. Ponies grazed in the grasses, oblivious of her hurry. Ann wanted to reach her daughter's house before she busied herself preparing the miller's noontime meal. Maggie would have barley to bake brönnies and perhaps oat for oatcakes too. Whereas the Leslies could count on fish, Maggie's husband and family were farmers, and their uncle was the miller, so corn was their staple. Ann had brought along a salted fish and garden taaties. At the last minute she had remembered the booties she had knit for Mary Ann. She smiled as she inhaled the fresh air, pleased to savor precious time for her own thoughts and the anticipation of seeing her granddaughter.

The Scripture passage Reverend Roberts had chosen to read at tea the night before had suited perfectly. As she recounted its implication, Ann concluded the future could not be seen, just as in a thick Shetland mist. So why trouble herself. Only hope, that was the message. Ann paused to remember all the times she had worried, yet she had nevertheless endured. Did "all things work together for good," after all? No, she could not accept such a naïve promise. Robert's and James's deaths were not good outcomes, nor was John's disappearance. Of course, more living would yet prove whether good could materialize out of these sorrows. Perhaps John would return and help raise Hannah, though Rachel hadn't asked for that. And would God create something good out of the shipwreck so long ago? Ann shook her head. No, there was nothing good about that tragedy. And yet, perhaps Robert's aspiration to depart for the New World was a product of that terrible misfortune. Could it be that God turned Robert's loss of father and brother into a gain of inner strength? Ann concluded she could never believe that God willed calamity on her family, but that perhaps God had somehow transformed each heartbreak into courage. It reminded her of putting new thatch on the roof, something new on top of the old. She remembered how she had cried after Jamie died as a wee bairn. And yet, eventually, touches of happiness crept back into her days again, like the tiny heather blossoms that broke away from the gray heath. Was it God's response to tragedy that repaired situations in life? She wasn't sure. And the same with Tina and Mary. The wind whipped her cheeks. What good came of their deaths, one after the other? Ann's forehead creased with the painful memory of burying her girls side by side in the pouring rain. Had their deaths taught her to care more for her remaining children? She shook her head. No, she had loved each child from the start equally well. She was convinced her capacity to love was never determined by having loved one child more or less. Every moment, every year, she had new people to love and new trials to surmount. On good days, the blessings outnumbered the misfortunes. God's grace had simply brought touches of healing over time, like new thatch or sprigs of blooming heather. But Ann knew she would never wish the death of a child on anyone. What was lost was never found. Still, she could be grateful she had had time with each, and that was precious.

Ann arrived at Maggie's to find Mary Ann crawling on the stone floor.

"Look, love, Granny is here!" Maggie exclaimed to her.

Ann put down her goods and lifted her granddaughter into her arms. A moment of pure joy! "Oh, what a bonnie lassie she is! And already crawling about!"

"And getting into the wool and the dog's food, Mam. How did you stop us from putting everything into our mouths?"

"I cannot say. 'Twas a long time ago, Maggie, darling." She sat down with the bairn in her lap, but Mary Ann wiggled to get down right away.

"See, she never stops moving. I hardly get a thing done!"

"Well, you're giving her what she needs: love and security. And she appears to be thriving!" Ann looked at Mary Ann and then at Maggie. "She has your golden baby curls, Maggie!"

"Aye, she's a Leslie lass." She touched her own curls that had escaped the bun at the nape of her neck. "'Tis a lovely surprise to have you come, Mam."

"Well, I have news. Reverend Roberts brought us a letter from Robert sent by way of the minister from the Lerwick chapel."

"And?" Maggie continued to pat the brönnies into a pan for the noon meal as she conversed.

"He's due home on the twenty-eighth of this month. Then he leaves the next day for Aberdeen, and then Glasgow by train. Can you imagine?"

"So, he's really going."

"Aye. He's put down a deposit for steerage and sets sail for New York on the thirty-first of May."

"Oh, this must be so hard for you and the girls."

Ann's eyes teared up. "Well, surely we are sad about it. I won't deny it. But 'tis what he wants. So that makes it right."

Maggie put gruel before Ann at the table and lifted Mary Ann again into her Granny's lap. "Will you feed her as I finish the meal for Uncle Alec?"

"Oh, with pleasure. Come, Mary Ann, precious. Have some lunch." She spooned the warm mush to the little one's mouth, and Mary Ann giggled. "Will you come to see Robert off? We could have a last meal together as a family."

"Yes, of course." She put the brönnies to bake and stirred the mutton stew. "His leaving saddens me too. To think that I shan't be able to see him perhaps ever again."

"We mustn't think so far ahead. You know he speaks of coming back for us, that is, for me and Annie and Chrissy." She looked at Maggie and suddenly realized that if she and the girls were to emigrate too, they would never see Maggie again. Nor Mary Ann!

"John and I will stay here, no question. He's tied to the land. The Leslies were always tied to the sea, with Father as a fisherman, and the lads too."

"And the sea is wide! New York is seven to ten days away, and that is by steam."

"Yes, indeed. So much is changing."

Ann watched her married daughter move easily around her kitchen. She seemed pleased with her bairn and her home. In fact, her face glowed.

After Mary Ann had finished eating, Ann washed the bairn's face and hands and gave her to her mam to nurse before her nap.

"I haven't much milk these days. But Mary Ann still likes to suckle."

"Well, you've given her a healthy start. Now at eight months, she should be able to eat everything we eat."

"Aye, she loves her daa's white scones the best, the ones made from wheat flour. We have plenty when the crop is in." She smiled at her mother. "I thank you for the fish and taaties. They'll keep, so we'll have them after the lamb is gone."

Ann smelled the stew and thought how long it had been since she had eaten meat.

John's uncle came into the house and greeted Ann. "So, Mrs. Leslie, you've come to see how the wee one has grown, have you?"

Ann rose to shake his hand. "And to see you, Mr. Eunson."

"But I haven't grown—unless from your daughter's fine cooking!"

Maggie remembered, "That's right, you met at the wedding, of course." She rose to take Mary Ann to her box bed in the next room.

"Weddings and birthings, they make the best of times."

Ann thought again about Robert leaving. "Aye, better than partings."

Alec lifted his eyebrows. "Well, Mrs. Leslie, you have had some losses, certainly, but who is parting?"

"'Tis our young Robert. He's emigrating to America."

"Is he, now! He has more courage than I, that I must say. You couldn't get me on one of those ships. Our life is meager some years when the harvest is poor, but I always know where I am when I'm standing on the earth."

Maggie returned to the kitchen and chuckled. She knew her husband and his family. Ann guessed that a miller would never want to sail. And Maggie's John would rather stay close to the farm where he grew up than travel to any distant port.

"Our Robert has always been attracted to far-off places. He used to read about the Indians in the great forests of America, and he learned the names of all the states—I think there are thirty-seven, Robert said."

"How old is Robert, then?"

"He's twenty-four. 'Tis old enough to know his mind and carry out a plan."

"True enough."

"Sit down, Mam and Uncle Alec. Ah, here is John! Good timing! Shall we eat?"

Alec said the blessing and Maggie ladled the stew and passed the brönnies. There was fresh butter too. The time passed happily, but Ann knew she must return to her own chores and let Maggie do hers. So, after finishing their meal, she peeked at her granddaughter asleep in her bed and then embraced Maggie. "Stay well, darling. Drink plenty of milk, since you have it. And thank you for the lovely meal." Very soon she would see them again at the Boe.

"Bye, Mam. We'll bring a cake for Robert's last night in Shetland. The chickens are laying, and we'll still have plenty of sugar, too."

❦ ❦

Ann and Christina got up early the day Robert was expected home. They prepared clean linens for his bed and mended the few good clothes he had left at the crofthouse. Chrissy had purchased soap in Lerwick, and she wrapped a bar in cloth and washed one of the family's best towels for Robert to take with him. He would need to stay clean on the ship, with so many people in one tight place. Ann tended the sheep and made a large pot of potato soup flavored with leeks and garden herbs. Robert might bring a fish, so that would go well with the oatcakes and kirn-milk she had saved. Maggie's cake would top off the meal.

Annie arrived midday with fresh scones and jam from the hall. The housekeeper had given her the day off, and Mrs. Bruce had provided a book as a gift for Robert to take with him to read on the ship. The book was called *Leaves of Grass*, a collection of poetry by the American Walt Whitman. Annie hoped she would have time to read some of its poems before giving it to Robert to pack. She helped her mother by bringing in the laundry from the line and chatted with Chrissy about the evening to come.

They assumed Robert would come by boat and walk up the path from Virkie. Ann let the sheep out onto the moor and suggested the women walk down to the voe and watch for Robert. Annie brought the Whitman book along and opened it to "Songs of Parting" as they sat by the shore:

> As the time draws nigh, glooming, a cloud,
> A dread beyond of I know not what darkens me.
> I shall go forth,
> I shall traverse the States awhile, but I cannot tell whither or how long,
> Perhaps soon some day or night while I am singing my voice will suddenly cease.[6]

Annie stopped there and asked, "What do you suppose it means?"

"He says he's singing." Ann suggested. "It's a bit like the psalms in the Bible; they are songs, and yet we read them." She paused to reflect. "Is Whitman perhaps a modern American psalm writer, speaking of his land and his time?"

"I think he means he will soon die," Annie said.

Christina asked, "Why are we reading something about death?"

"'Tis about life and its uncertainty. After all, no one can tell what will happen." Ann squinted her eyes. She thought about how John had disappeared. "Robert may traverse the whole continent of America, for all we know. And only God knows where he will settle." She added, "I may die before I ever see him again; you know, I am already sixty-two."

"Is there any hope in that book?" asked Christina.

---

6. Whitman, "Songs of Parting: As Time Draws Nigh," in *Leaves of Grass*, 600.

"Surely, let's see." Annie continued reading from "Years of the Modern":

> I see not America only, not only Liberty's nation but other nations preparing,
> I see tremendous entrances and exits, new combinations, the solidarity of races,
> I see that force advancing with irresistible power on the world's stage. . . .
> I see the frontiers and boundaries of the old aristocracies broken,
> I see the landmarks of European kings removed,
> I see this day the People beginning their landmarks, (all others give way;)
> Never were such sharp questions ask'd as this day,
> Never was average man, his soul, more energetic, more like a God.[7]

The verses piqued Christina's interest. "My, is America such a place of revolution? I can only hope that someday Shetlanders will be able to speak out against the lairds. Do you suppose that would then cause Britain to overthrow the monarchy?"

"This is a poet who has great aspirations for the future, I dare say." Ann said. "These changes may happen, but not in my lifetime, and not in Shetland." She pondered the changes she had experienced. One of the "exits" she had to accept was John's sudden disappearance. It had already been ten years. She needed to put her hope for a reunion to rest. The wind shifted. Ann turned to face the path from the south. She shaded her eyes from the sun. Was it Robert coming along with his fisherman's cap and knapsack? "Look, 'tis Robert!"

They sprang up quickly and ran to meet him.

Chrissy reached her brother first. "You're home!"

By the time they returned to the crofthouse, Maggie and her family had arrived. The reunion was more heartwarming than anyone could have predicted. Ann felt her eyes tearing up and asked herself whether hers were tears of joy or sorrow. Tonight it should be joy. She remembered the verse: "Take therefore no thought for the morrow: for the morrow shall take thought for the things of itself."[8]

After their festive meal, with dishes put away and animals fed, they all sat together by the fire. Little Mary Ann sat on Robert's lap, pulling at his whiskers. Robert laughed and told of his time in Lerwick, and in

---

7. Whitman, "Songs of Parting: Years of the Modern," in *Leaves of Grass*, 600–601.

8. Matthew 6:34a.

a more serious tone, he spoke of his travel plans, beginning with leaving in the early morning for Aberdeen. When they pressed him for where he would go from New York, he simply said he would follow his intuition.

John added, "That would be God's lead, would it not?"

"Aye," Robert answered, "I suppose."

John continued. "We have news, too." He looked at Maggie, who smiled shyly. "Mary Ann will have a peerie brother or sister."

"Ah! Good news and more reason to celebrate!" Robert declared.

"When is the bairn due to arrive?" asked Annie.

Maggie responded with a smile, "At Christmas!"

Ann disappeared quietly into the ben end and returned holding up the family fiddle.

"Robert, dear, this is your father's fiddle, and you must take it with you to America."

"No, Mother, it belongs here."

"Not at all. It belongs with the lad who will play it. You still remember the Shetland tunes your father played, the ones he learned from his father."

"Aye, I think I do. The Lerwick folks let me borrow a fiddle and play at the poorhouse for the children there."

Maggie urged him, "Robert, play us a tune now!"

He passed Mary Ann off to John and opened the case. More tears came to Ann's eyes. "Just like your father, and his."

After he had played Mary Ann to sleep with a lilting waltz, he put down the bow. "I'll need to protect the fiddle." He put it carefully into its weatherworn case.

"I have just the thing." Ann popped up again and returned with her husband's old knapsack. "It's time we put this to use again. 'Tis still good for a man called Robert." Ann opened the pack by its drawstring and reached inside. The leather was stiff but strong. Inside at the bottom of the satchel, her fingers closed on something hard. "Look! Here is the one-pound coin, the one left after the drowning."

"Has it been there all this time?" asked Chrissy.

"I reckon so! We never thought to spend it, I guess. Perhaps we thought it to be bad luck."

"But now, 'tis surely going to give Robert good luck!" cried Annie.

Robert put the fiddle into the pack, with only the neck of the case sticking out a few inches. Then he collected his possessions and fit them in around the fiddle: the soap and towel from Chrissy, the book from

Annie, his mended clothes from Ann, and a small New Testament from Maggie and John. He looked at his family assembled in the only home he had ever known. "I wish I had something to give you upon parting." He thought for a moment. "Oh, well, of course, I have your tithe for the laird." He opened his backpack, the one he had brought from Lerwick, and gave his mother an envelope with a wad of pound notes.

Ann rose to embrace her son. "Thank you, Robert. Your father would be so proud."

The Eunsons said their good-byes and left for Quendale, and the Leslies settled down for bed.

The night was short; the sky only briefly darkened, and all but Agnes rose early to see Robert off. They ate quickly: eggs that Maggie had brought, along with scones with jam and tea.

Together they formed a solemn procession down the path to the sea. Robert led, carrying his father's knapsack with the family fiddle sticking through the drawstring on his back. Annie and Chrissy, sisters side by side, alternated lugging Robert's other backpack over their shoulders, and Ann held in her arms a sack of food for the journey with kirn-milk and oatcakes, boiled eggs, and cold tea. It was the same path that had led the family from their father's wreckage sixteen years before, the same path her Robbie had followed over their twenty-eight years of marriage from their croft to the sea and home again.

Mist obscured Ann's view of the coast and the boat that awaited her son. She blinked away the spray and her silent tears.

Glossary of Shetland Words

bairn—Child.

band—Methodist group for same-gender adults.

bannocks—Flat bread made from bere, an ancient form of barley, usually cut in wedges.

barn—Room attached to crofthouse where grain is dried, milled, and stored.

ben end—Bedroom and company room in a crofthouse.

bere—Barley.

Boe—Short for Exnaboe (hamlet in South Mainland).

box bed—Wooden separations that enclose a bed. Sometimes several children sleep in one.

broch—Ancient cylindrical tower of the Bronze Age. There are hundreds standing in Scotland still today.

brönnies—Barley scones.

burn—Creek.

but end—Kitchen and family room in a crofthouse.

byre—Room for animals and peat.

canty—Joyful, happy.

class meeting—Methodist small group for faith development.

clinker—Overlapping plank style for a wooden boat.

closs—Alley.

consumption—Tuberculosis, also called phthisis or wasting away.

corn—General term for grain.

croft—Small farm owned by the laird.

crofter—Tenant farmer.

crofthouse—Stone cottage with two rooms (but and ben), with the byre and barn usually attached.

croo—Sheep yard.

Daa—Norse word for father used commonly by Shetlanders, *a* pronounced as in daddy.

fourareen—Four-oar boat rowed by four men.

gloaming—Twilight, after the sun sets.

grice—A young pig.

haaf—Deep sea.

hall—The laird's house.

head—Sumburgh Head, south tip of Mainland.

hill ground—Moorland heath, ground covered in heather.

jumper—Sweater.

kirk—Church; also, the Established Church, later called the Church of Scotland.

kirn-milk—Curds.

kishie—Basket made of straw and twine carried on the back for moving peat.

kollie—Fish oil.

laird—Landlord, generally from Scotland proper.

lea-rig—Grassy land left unplowed between fields for tenants to share for grazing.

limpets—Barnacles.

loch—Lake.

Mainland—The name of the principal island of the Shetland Isles.

Mam—Common name of affection for mother, *a* pronounced as in mama.

Minnie—Nickname for a grandmother.

mortal pox—Smallpox.

Ness—Short for Dunrossness (parish of South Mainland).

peerie—Little.

peerie mootie—Very little.

piltocks—Poor people's fish.

resting chair—The most comfortable, "company" chair.

roo—To pull off sheep's wool. (Shetland sheep do not need to be shorn.)

shot room—Part of the yoal where the catch is kept.

sixareen—Six-oar boat rowed by six men.

taatie crop—Potato crop.

taaties—Potatoes.

tea—Supper; also, the leaves and drink.

track—Rough trail or path.

trucking—System of the lairds owning land and the crofters paying rent with fish, knitwear, and products of the land.

voe—Seawater inlet.

whelks—Large sea snails.

winkles—Small sea snails.

worsted—High-quality, flat, medium-weight wool yarn, and fabric made from worsted.

yoal—Small boat for three men.

A study guide by the author is available for groups reading *Shetland Mist* at www.heatherlesliehammer.com.

Bibliography

Abrams, Lynn. *Myth and Materiality in a Woman's World: Shetland 1800–2000.* Manchester, UK: Manchester University Press, 2005.

The Annotated Book of Common Prayer. London: Rivingtons, 1876.

The Book of Common Prayer, and Administration of the Sacraments and Other Rites and Ceremonies of the Church, According to the Use of the United Church of England and Ireland; Together with the Psalter or Psalms of David, Pointed as They Are to Be Sung or Said in Churches. Cambridge: Watts, 1800. https://ia800906.us.archive.org/12/items/a5568018oounknuoft/a5568018oounknuoft.pdf.

Bowes, Harold R., ed. *Two Calves in the House: Being the Shetland Journal of the Reverend John Lewis, 1823–1825.* Lerwick, UK: Shetland Amenity Trust, 2005.

Browning, Robert. *Selected Poems.* Edited by Daniel Karlin. Penguin Classics. London: Penguin, 1989.

Burns, Robert. *Robert Burns: The Complete Poetical Works, 1759–1796.* Edited by James A. Mackay. Catrine, UK: Alloway, 2009.

Goethe, Johann Wolfgang von. *Gedichte, West-östlicher Divan.* Edited by Paul Stapf. Vol. 1 of *Goethes Werke.* Hamburg: Wegner, 1948.

Hammer, Heather Leslie. "God of Quiet Waters Flowing." Unpublished hymn text set to "Bundeshymne der Republik Österreich" (Austrian National Anthem), attributed to Wolfgang Amadeus Mozart and Johann Holzer.

Irvine, James W. *The Dunrossness Story.* Lerwick, UK: Shetland, 1987.

Luther, Martin. "Out of the Depths I Cry to Thee, Lord God!" Hymnary, 1524. From translation by Catherine Winkworth in *Lyra Germanica: The Christian Year,* 1861. https://hymnary.org/text/out_of_the_depths_i_cry_to_thee_lord_god/fulltexts.

Shakespeare, William. *As You Like It.* In *The Complete Works of Shakespeare,* edited by W. J. Craig, 249–78. New York: Oxford University Press, n.d.

"Shetland Lullaby." Shetlink, Apr. 18, 2009. Posted by fairislefaerie. https://www.shetlink.com/index.php?/forums/topic/3760-shetland-lullaby/.

Tomlyn, Alfred W., ed. *Scottish Songs.* Bruceton Mills, WV: Scotpress, 1988.

The United Methodist Hymnal. Nashville: United Methodist, 1989.

Wesley, Charles. "Eternal Beam of Light Divine." Hymnary, 1739. https://hymnary.org/text/eternal_beam_of_light_divine.

Whitman, Walt. *Leaves of Grass.* New York: Modern Library, 1993.

Made in the USA
Las Vegas, NV
22 April 2023